The Stranger at Home

Frank Spreader

Published by Frank Spreader, 2024.

This is a work of fiction. Similarities to real people, places, or events are entirely coincidental.

THE STRANGER AT HOME

First edition. October 23, 2024.

Copyright © 2024 Frank Spreader.

ISBN: 979-8227868121

Written by Frank Spreader.

Table of Contents

1 1
2 8
3 14
4 21
5 36
Tragic Discovery: Woman Found Dead in Vehicle at Bronx Heritage Suites 41
6 42
7 50
8 56
9 69
10 78
Tragedy Strikes Bronx Heritage Suites: Businessman Found Dead Alongside Security Guard and Housekeeper 87
11 89
12 105
13 109
14 132
15 143
16 145
17 151
18 160
19 167
20 171
21 178
22 184
23 189
24 196
25 198
26 204
27 223

28 225
   Brutal Murder Uncovered in Domestic Hostage Situation....248
   Unraveling the Threads of the Brutal Murder of Ajee Arizin Linked to Serial Killings in BHS and Jimmi the Butcher...............250
      Epilogue..252

To those who have ever questioned the familiar.

For the moments when home feels like a stranger,

and for the courage to face the shadows within.

1

Sprite stepped out of the carpool, and the image hit her like a punch to the gut: a shipwreck—splintered wood, tangled rigging, a skeleton lost to the sea. Her apartment, she thought with a shiver, must look exactly like that—chaos, broken dreams washed up on the shores of her life, abandoned to rot in the unforgiving tide.

Sprite had never seen a shipwreck in person, but there was no other word for what awaited her. She tried to picture the Titanic sinking into the abyss, but even that majestic wreck felt like luxury compared to her crumbling apartment. She could see it now: dry leaves scattered across the road like dead confetti, ceramic floors slick and sticky, stained with the world's filth. A mountain of laundry threatened to erupt, dishes piled into a greasy tower of neglect, and the plants in the window—wilted, forgotten ghosts of life. The only thing still clinging on was Doctor, the starling her husband Ajee—jobless and drifting—had claimed as his only project.

"Take care, Sprite! Bye!" Thyme called, leaning out the open window with a wave, her voice trailing off like a wisp of smoke in the fading light.

Sprite turned and managed a weak wave, too drained to offer more than a tired flicker of a smile. She watched the minibus groan away, ferrying her colleagues off to their own distant lives. At least her apartment was close, sparing her the torture of another minute crammed inside that metal box. As the vehicle disappeared around the bend, she trudged on, passing under the grand archway—*Welcome to Bronx Heritage Suites*—its cheerful greeting looming like a bad joke. The security post stood just ahead, along with the steel barrier, guarding this bland corner of suburban purgatory.

Sprite threw a weary glance at the man stationed by the post. He was burly, thick mustache twitching under the weight of a frown, dressed in the standard-issue white and dark blue of security. A whistle dangled from his pocket, and in his hand, he clutched a metal detector that looked just as grim and unyielding as he did. His eyes narrowed, a flicker of suspicion darkening them as he spotted someone slipping into the residential area.

"Hey, Waverley," Sprite said, giving him a nod that tried for friendly but landed somewhere between tired and resigned.

Waverley's face softened, a warm smile breaking through, and the suspicion melted away like ice under the sun.

"Hey, Sprite. Thought you were someone else for a second," Waverley said, the edge gone from his voice. "Just getting off work?"

"Yeah, just wrapped up some overtime," Sprite said, hesitating for a beat. She wasn't in the mood for small talk, but walking off without a word felt rude. She ran into Waverley almost every day, and keeping things friendly was a delicate balance she didn't want to upset.

"Yeah, that's gotta wear you down," Waverley said, nodding with a touch of sympathy, though his eyes still held a flicker of something more guarded.

Sprite could faintly hear his colleagues inside the post, their voices buzzing about the results of yesterday's basketball game. "Yeah," she said, forcing a smile and letting go of whatever she had planned to say. She knew it was just a rhetorical question, a friendly gesture to break the ice, and she wasn't in the mood to dive deeper.

"By the way, is my order ready yet?" Waverley asked, impatience creeping into his voice like an unwelcome shadow.

Shipwreck. The image in her mind morphed into something even more chaotic—a swirling maelstrom of splintered wood and tangled ropes—when she thought of the pile of fabric lying untouched next to her sewing machine. The relentless grind of her cleaning service job drained her, and the part-time seamstress gig felt like an anchor, pulling her deeper into the abyss.

"Next week. I haven't had a chance to get to it yet," she said, shrugging as if the weight of her unfinished work barely registered.

"That's fine. Just don't forget, okay? I'll settle up later," he said, his tone light, but the undercurrent of urgency lingered like a storm on the horizon.

"Yeah, once it's done," Sprite said, forcing a smile that felt more like a mask. "But I really gotta head out now."

"Sure, take care," Waverley said, then hesitated, as if weighing his words. "By the way, they still haven't found the culprit."

Sprite nodded, picking up the unspoken warning in Waverley's words. Lately, the area had been plagued by a surge of muggings and robberies, a dark tide rolling in to reclaim what it once owned, leaving a sense of dread in its wake.

As a security officer, Waverley must have felt the weight of these events pressing down on him like an invisible shroud. It was probably why he seemed more watchful, his eyes flicking over every passerby at the residential entrance with a nervous scrutiny, as if each face might hold a hidden threat.

Sprite kept walking, her mind drifting like leaves caught in a restless breeze. It struck her suddenly that she'd forgotten to ask Waverley about the security job he'd mentioned, a detail that gnawed at her as she moved further away.

But she didn't turn back. If Waverley hadn't brought it up again, there probably weren't any openings, she figured. As she walked, the chaotic vision of her apartment as a shipwreck flickered in her mind, only to be replaced by the serene, orderly landscape of the residential area. The sidewalks were pristine, devoid of litter, while street lamps stood like sentinels every few yards, accompanied by trash cans and park benches, all untouched by graffiti. Strolling through this neighborhood always felt like a brief escape, a small slice of peace amid the storm of her daily life. For a moment, an unusual calm washed over her, and she imagined what it might be like to truly belong in this world, where life mirrored the immaculate streets she walked each day.

Just before she entered the more heavily guarded section of the neighborhood, Sprite passed the park and sports facilities. She veered to the left side of the sidewalk, slipping into a narrow gap between towering walls—barely wide enough for two people to squeeze by. As she moved through the dim alley, it felt as if she were stepping into another dimension. But this wasn't some fantastical realm like Narnia or Hogwarts; it was the gritty, unvarnished reality of her world.

At the alley's end, she jumped over a deep gutter that reeked of stale urine, thankfully dry but still repulsive. A large bin overflowed with trash at the street corner, and sewer rats skittered away, startled by her hurried footsteps as she quickened her pace.

After weaving through two alleys and leaping over puddles once again, she finally reached her destination. There it stood: a small, rented apartment with a rusty entrance and walls flaking like old memories, a forlorn testament to better days long gone.

"My home, my shipwreck," Sprite murmured, taking a deep breath and exhaling slowly. Lately, she'd developed a routine of pausing like this before stepping inside. She gave the iron door a hard push—it groaned and squeaked like a wounded animal—before pulling it shut behind her.

The closer she got to her home, the heavier the weight of dread settled at the base of her neck—a persistent burden that seemed to grow with each step, wrapping around her like a vice.

She knocked on the door three times. "Hello?" The word escaped her lips like a timid whisper, and after one feeble attempt, she shrugged and let the silence swallow her.

Her husband was probably already asleep. What else would he be doing at this hour? The thought lingered, dark and heavy, as she envisioned him lost in the oblivion of slumber while she stood outside, waiting in the chill of the night.

If it weren't for the basketball game blaring on TV, he'd likely be snoring away in bed by now. Since getting laid off, Ajee had shunned the neighborhood watch and community meetings, avoiding even the simplest chats with the neighbors. "Too embarrassed," he said, as if the words were a shield he hid behind.

All he did was stay home, marking time as he waited for his wife to feed him. His days drifted by in a fog of crosswords and care for his pet bird—a feeble effort to stave off the encroaching emptiness that loomed ever closer.

He had always been rigid and stubborn, but he used to be a hard worker. The Ajee of today was a mere shadow of that man, a parasite clinging to the fringes of his former self. Guilt suddenly washed over Sprite for allowing such dark thoughts to creep into her mind about her husband's misfortune, like an unwelcome specter haunting her conscience.

She tried to push those thoughts back, burying them beneath the heavy weight that already hung at the nape of her neck. She slid the key into the door, but when she turned it, she discovered it wasn't locked. Slowly, she pushed the door open, the creaking hinges releasing a sound that felt more like a groan, slicing through the silence. As she stepped inside, a new sound caught her ear—something different, something off.

She heard music, soft and barely perceptible, drifting through the air. No one ever played music in her apartment.

Even when she craved music, Sprite always used earphones, isolating herself in a world of sound that kept the outside at bay.

Ajee never listened to music or the radio while he worked; he preferred silence, a refuge from the chaos. The only one who blasted music was her neighbor, Alhric—the hip-hop fanatic who turned his apartment into a pulsating rhythm of beats and bass.

But she was certain the music was coming from inside her apartment, and it definitely wasn't hip-hop. It sounded more like jazz, or perhaps classical, or maybe even world music—whatever it was, she wasn't familiar with that kind of sound. It was an unexpected intrusion, weaving through the familiar silence like an uninvited guest.

Suddenly, she recalled hearing music like that in some of the movies she'd watched. Without bothering to shed the cardigan that draped over her work uniform, Sprite quietly made her way toward the source of the sound. The melody beckoned her, drawing her toward the kitchen like a siren's call, each note pulling her deeper into the mystery of her home.

Amid her growing unease, she noticed that, unlike usual, the floor wasn't sticky or grimy. The couch and table in the living room were perfectly arranged, the TV was off, and not a trace of dust clung to the walls. These might have seemed like trivial details, but to someone who knew every inch of this apartment, they felt eerily out of place. Someone else had been here.

Sprite slowed her pace, narrowing her eyes as she began to creep forward. Should she turn around and bolt, go find help? The thought flickered in her mind but quickly dimmed. It was just music, after all. What kind of thief would play a tune during a break-in? Peeking around the corner into the kitchen, she was met with the unmistakable aroma of meat sizzling. It felt as if she had stepped into a clean, sterile restaurant kitchen, a stark contrast to her own, usually cluttered with old boxes and reeking of garbage. There, standing in front of the stove, was a tall, broad-shouldered man, his back turned to her.

She noticed the apron strings tied around his neck, the fabric hanging like a noose down his back, a sinister touch to the mundane scene.

He seemed to be cooking something, the enticing scent mingling with her unease. "You're home, huh? Didn't get caught up in traffic, did ya?" the man said, his voice casual, almost too casual, as he didn't even bother to turn around.

His voice flowed like warm honey, smooth and effortlessly charming, a stark contrast to Ajee's flat, monotone droning that lacked any of the grace of casual conversation. It was the kind of voice that drew you in, making you lean closer, while Ajee's words felt like a weight, a dull thud against the walls of her mind.

Sprite's tongue felt heavy in her mouth, her thoughts slipping through her fingers like grains of sand. When the man turned, his smile radiating warmth and charm, she found herself blurting out the most absurd question she could imagine: "Who are you?" It hung in the air between them, a surreal interruption to the ordinary chaos of her life.

2

Sprite couldn't shake the memory of Ajee's last stunt, a final act of lazy defiance that danced like a ghost in the corners of her mind. Every time the thought of cooking or brewing coffee flickered to life, a shudder ran down her spine, as if Ajee's memory had wrapped itself around her like a cold, clammy hand, reminding her of the chaos that once reigned in their kitchen.

He'd sit by the window, cigarette smoke curling around him like a ghostly shroud, occasionally whistling at his pet bird, a little creature that never stopped chirping. Then, without so much as a glance at his wife, he'd mumble under his breath, "Doc, the preacher said that a wife who does what she's told gets into heaven. But what about a wife too lazy to even make coffee? Where's she supposed to end up, Doc?" Ajee said this as if he were sharing a secret with the starling, his words laced with a bitterness that hung heavy in the air.

Doctor let out a raucous chirp that rang out like a mocking laugh, as if the bird found amusement in its master's words. If it had an ounce of intelligence, it might've understood that those words weren't really meant for it; they were a twisted echo, bouncing back toward Sprite, sprawled on the mat, lost in a soap opera that had long since blurred the lines between fiction and reality.

When that happened, Sprite would let out a resigned sigh and shuffle off to the kitchen, compelled to brew the coffee her husband demanded. Soft grumbles would slip from her lips, a low murmur of frustration. How merciless he was, dragging heaven and hell into a debate just for a cup of coffee—as if whipping up instant coffee was some monumental task worthy of divine intervention.

He had no clue how wiped out she was from scrubbing through a mountain of laundry and tackling sewing orders. What a hypocrite, twisting religion to suit his own agenda. As she stirred the coffee, Sprite's resentments spilled out of her mouth, her movements becoming almost frenzied. Coffee grounds splattered onto the rim of the cup, and a few drops escaped, prompting even more sarcastic remarks from Ajee, his voice a sharp reminder of the weight she carried.

Sprite couldn't have cared less. To her, that chaotic stirring was a quiet act of rebellion, a small, defiant gesture cloaked in the mundanity of her routine. In those moments, she found a flicker of power, a way to push back against the chaos that threatened to swallow her whole.

Typically, Ajee would sip his coffee, propping one foot on a chair or emptying the ashtray, his movements almost ritualistic. To Sprite, he seemed incredibly old-fashioned. At just thirty-three and childless, he carried himself like a man decades older, as if life had weighed him down with the burdens of time. It was said he had adopted his father's mannerisms—a man now estranged from his mother, who had raised Ajee with a stern hand. That harsh upbringing had chiseled him into a rigid, drab figure, a shadow of the vibrant man he might have been.

Even though Ajee swore up and down that he loathed his father, he was slowly morphing into the very man he claimed to despise. Praise rarely left his lips, and a simple *thank you* was a rare commodity, leaving Sprite to wonder if the man she married was slipping away, replaced by a reflection of the father he detested.

To him, Sprite was merely ticking off her wifely duties, just as he was dutifully bringing home a paycheck. It was a transactional existence, each of them fulfilling their roles in a play neither wanted to be part of, bound by obligation rather than love.

Of course, he could only maintain this mindset as long as he kept pulling in a paycheck. But then came that fateful evening, the one that would shake the foundation of their carefully constructed lives, leaving everything hanging by a thread.

On this unusually dark evening, Ajee trudged home, the grim news he'd been hiding for days hanging over him like a storm cloud. He didn't ask for coffee, didn't demand a massage. Instead, he shed his work uniform and slumped onto the porch in a worn tank top. There was no whistling to Doctor this time. Instead, he just stared at the bird, fixing it with a look, as if somehow, through sheer will, they could share a silent understanding of the weight pressing down on him.

Doctor chirped, but its master didn't respond. The silence between them thickened, hanging in the air like a fog neither could shake. Minutes dragged by until Sprite finally appeared, holding a cup of coffee. It was a rare gesture—this coffee, made without demand or request—an offering in the quiet, a bridge between them that neither seemed willing to cross.

With a voice rough and ragged, Ajee finally confessed: he and a slew of other employees had been let go. He didn't know the real reason behind it. Officially, the company claimed it was drowning, trimming down to stay afloat. But the whispers told a different story—retaliation for the labor protests last May. Severance pay had been promised, though in vague installments no one could pin down, like a ghost of a check that might never arrive.

Ajee couldn't muster an answer; his mind was spinning too wildly to latch onto any clear thought. Leaving Sprite behind, her eyes glazed as she stared at the untouched cup of black coffee, he stumbled off to bed. The moment his head hit the pillow, sleep swallowed him whole. But an hour later, he woke with a violent jolt, his body betraying him. His skin was on fire, sweat pouring down his face in rivulets, and his breaths came in jagged gasps, as if the air had turned to lead in his lungs.

He tried to call for Sprite, but his voice crawled out as a weak, trembling whisper, barely slicing through the thick, suffocating air. It was as if the words themselves had lost the strength to leave his throat, dissolving into the stillness of the room.

Sprite, lost in the rhythm of her sewing in the living room, didn't hear him. It wasn't until half an hour later, when she went to the bedroom to fetch some thread, that she found Ajee—slumped on the bed, his body limp, barely clinging to consciousness. The sight of him, pale and drenched in sweat, sent a cold shock through her, as if the air had been sucked out of the room.

Sprite sprang into action, moving with a swift, almost mechanical efficiency. She fetched a drink and fever-reducing medicine, pressing them into Ajee's trembling hands. Her fingers worked with a practiced urgency, applying cool compresses to his burning skin, her movements sharp and precise, as if the situation had flicked some hidden switch inside her. There was no time for panic, only action.

No matter how grim things had become, Ajee was still her husband, the man she had promised to stand by, even when the darkness threatened to swallow them whole. That bond, frayed but unbroken, flickered like a stubborn candle in a storm.

Sprite had never chosen him. Before her family had matched them, she didn't know Ajee from Adam. Even after five years of marriage, his past, his quirks, and the ailments he'd battled still felt like a hazy blur, a collection of fragments that never quite came into focus. Each detail remained elusive, as if their shared life was a puzzle missing key pieces, leaving her grasping at shadows of a man she was still trying to truly understand.

Ajee had bouts of high fever that struck out of the blue, as unpredictable as a summer storm. There was a story that when he was a kid, he took a nasty fall from a maple tree, and ever since, his body had been a fragile vessel, more susceptible to illness. That single moment had carved a path through his life, leaving him vulnerable, a man marked by the shadows of his childhood.

In that moment, though, she couldn't shake the nagging suspicion that her husband was simply reeling from the shock of losing his job. Watching him so frail and vulnerable tugged at her heartstrings, igniting a sharp sting of guilt that pierced through her. It was a bitter reminder of the fragility of their lives, and the weight of his struggles pressed heavily on her conscience.

Sprite came to a harsh realization: she had nurtured a steady resentment toward her husband, often regretting their marriage in silence. She'd never summoned the nerve to voice her discontent outright; the thought of starting a fight over a cup of coffee or a cluttered apartment felt too risky, too likely to tear their fragile union apart. The only outlet she had left was her soft, persistent grumbling, a quiet rebellion against the mounting frustrations that threatened to suffocate her.

She recalled a Facebook article she'd read, claiming that the shape of crystals in water could be swayed by the words spoken to it. Kind or positive words supposedly created beautiful, orderly crystals, while harsh or negative ones led to a chaotic mess. It all sounded like nonsense, of course. But if that theory held even a shred of truth, then the coffee Ajee had been drinking was likely swimming with nothing but nightmarish crystals, tainted by all the unspoken bitterness lingering in the air between them.

Sprite began to wonder if her constant grumbling while making coffee had somehow made Ajee more prone to illness and misfortune. Maybe those negative vibes had seeped into him, filling his body with malevolent crystals that messed with his brain, transforming him into someone who, oddly enough, seemed to be... better. It was a twisted thought, as if her own resentment had unwittingly reshaped him, forging a version of Ajee that felt strangely more authentic, more real, despite the illness that haunted him.

3

"Hey, you haven't eaten yet, have you?" Ajee asked, his voice soft but with an edge of knowing. He slid a chair across the old floor, the legs scraping with a low groan. He gestured toward it, a smile playing at the corners of his mouth. "Sit, Sprite. You look like you could use a break."

Sprite froze, stiff as a deer in headlights. Every muscle clenched, her jaw wired shut, thoughts jammed like gears grinding in her head. She stared at Ajee, but he felt like a stranger, a glitch in her reality. Was this really her husband—the man she'd lived beside for so long? What the hell was wrong with him? A cruel prank? A twisted trick of the mind? Then Ajee cleared his throat, a sharp sound that yanked her back from the brink. Her mind snapped into place. Had she eaten? Yes. But that wasn't the question she wanted to answer.

She'd just been treated to a birthday feast of paella, the kind of meal you're supposed to savor, each bite a warm indulgence. But now, with Ajee's question hanging in the air, her throat felt like it had locked up, tight as a vise, refusing to let out a single word. Ajee's face was a mask—hopeful, expectant—like he was waiting on something that could either lift him up or shatter his day into pieces.

She just shook her head, a small, wordless surrender, and sank into the chair. It was already there, perfectly placed, almost as if it had been waiting for her all along. Like it knew she'd give in eventually.

Ajee's fingers dug into Sprite's shoulders, firm but careful, the kind of pressure that knew just where to push. Each stroke was a quiet promise of relief, so gentle yet insistent that Sprite's eyes fluttered shut before she even realized. The tension leaked out of her like air from a punctured tire, slow and inevitable.

"You look wiped," Ajee said, his voice low and easy. "Don't worry about a thing. I'm cooking something up for you. Just sit tight for a minute, alright?" His words had a weight to them, like he knew more than he was letting on.

Sprite's face was a picture of disbelief, her mind struggling to reconcile the scene in front of her. The Ajee she knew would never—could never—do something like this. Cooking dinner? For her? That was as alien as him flying to the moon. The kitchen had always been forbidden ground, a place he barely acknowledged, let alone stepped foot in. And as far as she knew, his culinary talents didn't stretch beyond boiling water and making instant ramen. Even then, it was hit or miss. Yet here he was, acting like a chef, and it made her skin prickle with unease.

He wouldn't have lifted a finger unless he could bark orders from his recliner, like moving a muscle was a punishment worse than death. But now, Ajee dashed back to the kitchen with an urgency that set Sprite's nerves on edge, like he'd just remembered something was burning. He hummed a tune, even whistled as he passed Doctor's cage, but the bird just huddled in the corner, indifferent to the act. Something twisted in Sprite's gut, a primal warning flashing in her mind: this wasn't Ajee. Not really. His movements were off—his steps too fluid, too sure. There was a strange mix of enthusiasm and grace, with an edge of dominance he'd never had before. It was like watching a stranger wear his skin. The thought crept in, chilling her to the bone. Did Ajee have a twin she never knew about? The idea of being in her home with someone who only *looked* like her husband made her breath hitch. If this wasn't Ajee, then who the hell was it? And where was the real Ajee?

Sprite fidgeted, restless, shifting in her chair as if her body couldn't settle into the space. She drew in deep, shaky breaths, trying to anchor herself, but the apartment felt different now—eerie, almost wrong. The furniture was too perfect, the soft hum of romantic music creeping through the air, and the rich scent of something meaty wafting from the kitchen. For a moment, everything teetered on the edge of uneasy calm—until Doctor's cage erupted with a sharp, bone-chilling screech. The sound tore through the room, too real, too raw. Doctor usually mimicked harmless things—cat meows, human laughter—but tonight, it was different. The bird screamed with a terror that sent shivers crawling down Sprite's spine. Then, in the thick silence that followed, the lights flickered and went out, plunging the room into darkness.

Doctor's cries fell silent, and in that suffocating stillness, Sprite's breath hitched. From the kitchen, a single flame sparked to life, small but menacing, casting long, flickering shadows that stretched and twisted across the walls like specters creeping toward her. It moved slowly, deliberately, inching closer, as if it had a will of its own. Something about that flame wasn't right. It felt... alive.

"Candlelight dinner, just for you," Ajee murmured, his voice barely more than a whisper, low and intimate. There was something unsettling in the way he said it, like the words were meant to be comforting but carried a weight that made Sprite's skin crawl.

In the flickering candlelight, his face transformed, taking on a ghostly pallor that gave him an otherworldly glow. He looked less like a man and more like a spectral apparition, hovering just beyond the edge of reality, caught between the shadows and the dim light.

He placed the candle on the table, then struck a match, its flame leaping to life as it joined the first. The room brightened just a fraction, but the shadows only deepened, thick and oppressive, clinging to the corners like dark memories refusing to fade.

"For what's the occasion, babe?" Sprite asked, summoning the courage to break the silence. Her voice trembled slightly, a thread of uncertainty weaving through her words as she tried to mask the unease coiling in her gut.

"To shoo away the flies," Ajee replied with a chuckle, the sound unsettlingly light in the heavy air. But there was an edge to his laughter, a hint that something deeper lay beneath the surface, lurking just out of sight.

A fly that had been buzzing erratically around the room suddenly fell silent, as if it had vanished into thin air—spooked by the flickering candlelight or perhaps by the shadowy figure who had conjured it into existence. Its absence hung in the air, thick with unease, like a warning that something wasn't right.

"Just messing around. It's to make my amazing wife happy," Ajee said with a grin, the kind that didn't quite reach his eyes. Then he turned and strode back to the kitchen, leaving the flickering candles behind, moving through the shadows as if he possessed some kind of night vision, slipping away into the dark with an unsettling ease.

The room sank back into an oppressive silence, darkness pressing against the walls like an invisible weight. Aside from the two flickering candles on the table, the only other light seeped from the kitchen—faint and feeble, as if it too were fighting to shine. It felt as if Ajee hadn't just turned off the lights in the dining room; he had plunged the entire apartment into shadow. In that dim, wavering glow, Sprite's mind raced with unsettling possibilities. The first thought to slink into her consciousness was the disturbing notion that this might all be some elaborate joke, a cruel trick played by a man she hardly recognized anymore.

Ajee wasn't the type to indulge in pranks, especially not ones so meticulously orchestrated. Unless, of course, something had pushed him over the edge. Perhaps the weight of their recent financial struggles had driven him to the brink, compelling him to dive into some reality show or twisted stunt just to escape the suffocating pressure. It had been ages since she'd watched television, but before burying herself in work, she'd been hooked on those mindless shows, where people traded their dignity for a fleeting moment of fame. The thought made her uneasy, like a bad taste she couldn't wash away.

Deep down, she knew they were all just scripted nonsense, a parade of manufactured drama and shallow conflicts. Yet, despite that knowledge, she couldn't help but get pulled in, mesmerized by the absurdity of it all. It was like watching a train wreck unfold, the kind of spectacle that kept her glued to the screen, even as a part of her screamed to look away.

If this was some kind of show, Ajee could be starring in something like *Ideal Husband*, *Makeover Husband*, or maybe even *My Husband Is Possessed*. Another, darker possibility gnawed at her: what if Ajee had genuinely changed? The thought was almost laughable. How could a man as rigid and stubborn as he was suddenly transform overnight? No amount of preaching from the most revered pastors or motivational speakers could pull that off. A far more plausible theory was that her husband had lost his grip on reality. With his job gone, his authority eroded, and his self-confidence shattered, it was no wonder his sanity seemed to be slipping through the cracks. His bizarre behavior had been creeping into their lives ever since he'd been laid off and struck down with a high fever, like a slow, insidious shadow enveloping him.

At first, Sprite had brushed Ajee's fever off as nothing more than a common illness, a fleeting bug that would pass with time. But as the days dragged on and his condition lingered, an unsettling sense of foreboding began to take root in her gut, a whisper that something was far more sinister at play.

He was the type to fall ill under stress—his temperature would spike, his body would tremble, and he'd retreat into a restless sleep, mumbling away in a fever dream until he bounced back. Even as his behavior seemed to soften, who could say what torment was brewing beneath the surface of his mind? That explanation had been enough to pacify her—until Ajee emerged from the shadows a moment later, casting a chilling doubt over everything she thought she knew. The shift in the air was palpable, as if the very walls had turned to listen, waiting for the truth to spill from his lips.

He appeared out of nowhere, surfacing from a thick, murky haze as if he'd been submerged in darkness. His sudden arrival wasn't entirely unexpected, yet it bore a chilling, unsettling edge, like the first hint of a storm lurking on the horizon. The air around him seemed to thrum with tension, as if the very shadows recoiled at his presence.

He carried the plates, heavy with steak, potatoes, and water, and set them down on the table with an unsettling deliberation. As he leaned over, the candlelight flickered across his face, casting eerie shadows that danced like dark secrets waiting to be revealed. The soft glow seemed to pull at the edges of his features, transforming him into a stranger lurking in the half-light.

At that moment, Doctor the starling let out a harsh, raucous screech from its cage, the sound slicing through the stillness like a jagged knife. In the thick, oppressive atmosphere, Sprite's mind slipped into darker territory, spiraling into unsettling possibilities that clung to her thoughts like fog creeping into the night. The bird's cry echoed, amplifying the tension in the room and reminding her that not everything was as it seemed.

She recalled the old tales from her town about demons that could masquerade as one's spouse, slipping into the roles of loved ones with a sinister ease. There were eerie stories of women seduced by incubi and men unwittingly marrying succubi, their hidden natures lurking just beneath the surface. Those chilling legends swirled in her mind, their combined dread coiling around her stomach like a serpent, twisting tighter with each thought. The unease settled in her bones, a creeping suspicion that perhaps the stories weren't just tales after all.

"I hope you dig it," Ajee said, placing two pairs of forks and knives on the table with a casualness that felt just a shade too rehearsed. His voice carried an undercurrent of expectation, as if he were trying to mask something lurking just beneath the surface, a hint of tension hanging in the air. The clatter of the utensils echoed softly, an odd sound in the thickening silence.

4

Every time Sprite caught the glint of candlelight dancing in Ajee's eyes, an odd, almost sinister warmth crept over her. It began as a mere whisper of heat deep in her chest, like the flicker of a flame teasing the edge of her skin. But then it spread, growing fiercer and more insistent, searing her from the inside out, as if a hidden fire had awakened within her, beckoning her closer to whatever dark secret lay behind those mesmerizing eyes.

For a fleeting moment, she felt a comforting warmth she hadn't known she'd been craving. But as she stared longer, that warmth twisted into something insidious, the flame transforming, growing fiercer and more demanding, searing her with a relentless heat that seeped into her bones and whispered of danger lurking just beneath the surface.

"Why the silence, huh?" Ajee asked, a grin spreading across her face as she raised an eyebrow, the kind of smile that hinted at mischief and a dark curiosity lurking just beneath the surface.

"It's nothing," Sprite said, brushing off the thought with a dismissive shrug, though the words felt hollow in her chest, echoing a truth she wasn't ready to confront.

"Sorry, I'm no gourmet chef," Ajee said, waving his hand toward the two sizzling steaks on the hotplate, the scent of charred meat hanging thick in the air. "This is the best I've got," he added with a shrug, his casual tone masking a flicker of self-doubt lurking in the corners of his smile.

Flanking each plate were a fork and knife, poised like silent sentinels bracing for battle, their polished surfaces gleaming ominously under the light, ready to cut through more than just the meat.

Sprite found herself frozen in place, her mind buzzing with a hundred unanswered questions that swirled like a storm. How had her husband picked up these cooking skills? Where had he unearthed all this gear? Each query tangled in her thoughts, a knot of confusion and disbelief that threatened to choke her.

But instead of voicing any of these thoughts, she sat there, her gaze fixed blankly on the steaks before her, as if they held the secrets she was too afraid to unravel. Each sizzling cut seemed to mock her silence, whispering answers she both craved and dreaded.

Fortunately, Ajee didn't flinch at Sprite's icy reception. His face remained a mask of unchanging calm, his eyes piercing and alert, a smile hovering unsettlingly on his lips. To Sprite, that smile was more than disquieting; it was a chilling reminder of the very people she dreaded—those who wore a fixed grin, as if joy was their permanent state. It spoke of a terrifying certainty, a sense that fear was alien to them, leaving everyone else utterly at their mercy.

Sprite knew better than to provoke such individuals; their fury would be far more terrifying than the rage of those who never smiled at all. She could almost feel the heat of their wrath simmering beneath the surface, a volcanic anger that would erupt with little warning, leaving nothing but ash in its wake.

Ajee wore that smile now—the kind that made Sprite feel like she was walking a tightrope over a pit of vipers. It was the sort of grin that filled her with a creeping dread, making her wary of every word she might utter, each one a potential misstep that could shatter the fragile peace of the evening and unleash a deadly chaos she wasn't prepared to face.

She grasped the knife and fork in front of her, her fingers trembling as they gripped the unfamiliar utensils. She could handle meatloaf and chili without a hitch, but steak was another beast entirely. She'd watched people on TV carve into their steaks with practiced ease, yet the sight of it hadn't prepared her for the awkward dance she was about to undertake, a clumsy struggle that felt like a high-stakes performance where one misstep could turn dinner into a disaster.

"You're doing it wrong," Ajee chimed in, his voice cutting through the tension as he caught her eye, a glint of amusement lurking behind his calm demeanor.

Sprite's grip faltered, and for a heartbeat, it felt as if the knife and fork might tumble from her hands, a momentary lapse that sent a jolt of panic coursing through her.

"The knife goes in your right hand, babe, and the fork in your left. Otherwise, you're going to have one hell of a time cutting that," Ajee said, his tone light but edged with an unspoken authority as he gently took her hand, guiding it with a steadying touch.

His grip was eerily delicate, as if he were applying no pressure at all—like their touch was siphoning Sprite's very essence, a silent exchange of energy that pulsed between their skin, leaving her both unsettled and strangely drawn to him.

With the careful patience of a parent guiding a child, Ajee adjusted the knife and fork in Sprite's hands, his touch firm yet unsettlingly tender, as if he were not just teaching her how to eat, but also weaving an invisible thread of control between them.

"Like this?" Sprite finally asked, breaking her silence as she carefully attempted to slice into the meat. She pressed down with the fork in her left hand, anchoring it to the plate, her focus sharp as she fought against the tension that threatened to unravel her composure.

It was a struggle; every movement demanded more effort than it should have, each slice a battle against the meat's stubborn resistance, and the weight of unspoken tension hung heavily in the air.

If she hadn't been so worried about disappointing Ajee, she might have simply grabbed the meat with her bare hands. But that thought evaporated the instant her fingers brushed against the scorching plate, the heat jolting her back to reality with a sharp reminder of the stakes at hand.

"Sorry if it's not as tender as it should be," Ajee said, his voice light as he picked up his own fork and knife. He sliced through the steak with effortless precision, handling the knife as if it were an extension of his own hand, the ease of his movements a stark contrast to her clumsy struggle.

Sprite finally managed to get the meat into her mouth, where it rolled around between her molars. To her surprise, it was tender, far from the tough struggle she'd faced while trying to cut it. A few strands of meat wedged themselves between her front teeth and the gap where her upper molar once was, a reminder of her clumsy battle with the steak.

She tried to pry the meat loose with the tip of her tongue, but no matter how she maneuvered, the stubborn strands remained stubbornly wedged between her teeth. The urge to dig them out with her fingernails or grab a toothpick gnawed at her, an itch she couldn't scratch, but Ajee seemed blissfully unaware of this small yet crucial detail, his attention elsewhere as if the discomfort didn't exist at all.

"How did your day at the office go?" Ajee asked, his voice casual as he sliced effortlessly into his steak, the blade gliding through the meat like it was butter.

Sprite was caught off guard. The question felt strange, almost foreign, as if he were referencing a life she didn't recognize. No one ever called her workplace an office; that term seemed to belong to corporate drones, and she was anything but.

Sure, she worked in an office building, but she spent most of her time in the restrooms and hallways, far from the actual office space. That territory was reserved for the well-dressed, sweet-smelling folks she cleaned up after every day, their polished lives a stark contrast to her own.

"Good," Sprite replied, nodding slightly, though the word felt hollow in her throat, like a veneer over the thoughts swirling beneath the surface.

"Your boss, Mr. Gegge, was pissed off again?" he asked, a hint of amusement playing at the corners of his mouth, as if he found her misfortunes oddly entertaining.

The piece of meat nearly lodged itself in Sprite's throat as she struggled to process Ajee's question, her mind choking on the unexpected query like a fish caught in a net, thrashing for air.

She fought to swallow the meat without breaking into a coughing fit, her breaths coming in sharp, uneven gasps. How did Ajee know about Mr. Gegge? The thought gnawed at her, unsettling and persistent, a worm burrowing deeper into her mind with each passing moment.

She distinctly remembered never mentioning her boss to Ajee, let alone his name. So how did he know she frequently got reamed out for incompetence? The question loomed over her like a dark cloud, heavy and ominous, casting a shadow over her thoughts.

"No, he doesn't..." Sprite said, her voice trailing off as she struggled to remember if she'd ever discussed her work life with Ajee. The uncertainty hung in the air, thick and suffocating, making her feel as if she were grasping at shadows.

Never. The word echoed in her mind, stark and definitive, like a sentence carved in stone, unyielding and immutable, leaving no room for doubt or escape.

Ajee had never asked, never shown an ounce of curiosity, and Sprite had never felt the urge to share. Had he spoken to one of her coworkers? Thyme, perhaps? The thought seemed improbable, like a shadowy whisper in the dark, slipping away just as she reached for it.

Sprite recalled that the only entity privy to her work grievances, aside from herself and her coworkers, was her diary, tucked away behind the kitchen cupboard. Had Ajee stumbled upon it and read her deepest thoughts? Should she be furious? It wasn't Mr. Gegge or her work troubles that gnawed at her; it was the scathing complaints about Ajee she'd penned in that diary—how she loathed his quirks, how she fantasized about a better man, her ideal, a long-held dream that felt more like a betrayal now. The realization sent a chill down her spine, her hands trembling so violently that the fork and knife clattered against the hot plate. Was Ajee's sudden shift in behavior a result of discovering her darkest secrets? Could he be so wounded that he'd set out to manipulate, trap, and ultimately humiliate or divorce her? It made a cruel sort of sense. What man wouldn't feel devastated to learn his wife longed for an imaginary figure instead of him?

Yet Sprite clung to her defenses. She had never cheated, never so much as flirted with another man, even though some of her coworkers had silently admired her as the most attractive member of the cleaning staff. She had been a loyal wife, despite the discontent simmering within her. Surely, every husband or wife harbored such dissatisfaction. Even Ajee might be dreaming of a more obedient, more diligent, and more graceful partner—a haunting thought that tugged at her, chillingly persistent, like a shadow refusing to fade.

Unfortunately, she wasn't like Ajee. She couldn't lay all her grievances bare, confronting him with every ounce of discontent. Instead, the dissatisfaction festered within her, a relentless ache that gnawed at her insides, feeding on her silence and growing stronger with each passing day.

She never wanted to hurt anyone but herself. The only safe outlet for her frustration was her diary, a refuge where her secrets lay buried. If Ajee had read it without her permission, that was on him, not her—a betrayal of trust that twisted like a knife in her gut.

She knew she should have been more cautious, more protective of her private thoughts. She could have jotted them down in her phone, secured with a password—something she always had on hand. But that never felt right, like trying to capture a fleeting shadow in a jar.

She was still attached to the habit she'd picked up in junior high—scribbling in a thick-covered diary, decorating the pages with markers and colored pencils. No one had taught her to keep a diary; her parents, always busy, preferred the precision of accounting ledgers and debt records. Sprite's habit was shaped by the movies she watched as a teenager, where girls lay on their beds, hugging teddy bears, beginning their entries with "Dear diary, today I..." The only difference was that Sprite didn't have a big teddy bear to comfort her, and she spent most of her time writing on a mat while helping her parents at the market, the words flowing out of her like a lifeline amid the chaos.

Besides, Ajee had a knack for going through her phone. Sometimes he'd be upfront about it, other times he'd pretend he just needed to borrow it for some phone credit or to send a quick text, his casual demeanor masking the intrusion like a wolf donning sheep's clothing.

Sprite couldn't lock her phone with a password—it would only stir up unnecessary suspicion from Ajee. She reached for the glass of water beside her plate, taking a sip to soothe her dry throat. If Ajee had really read her diary and uncovered all her secret grievances, she'd just have to accept it. There was no going back now. Denying it would be futile, and fighting it would only drag her deeper into the dark.

Oddly enough, beneath the fear, she felt a strange sense of relief, as if she'd finally released all her bottled-up feelings without having to wrestle with the words. It was a disconcerting liberation, the weight lifting just enough to let her breathe, even in the shadow of her own secrets.

Maybe Ajee would blow up, maybe they'd have a big fight, but that felt better than keeping everything bottled up. Perhaps, after the argument, he would finally see his own faults, and they could patch things up, promising to communicate better in their marriage. At least, that was the flickering hope she clung to, fragile but persistent, like a candle fighting against the dark.

But in reality, Ajee didn't explode. He remained unnervingly calm, that unsettling smile still plastered across his face—the kind that whispered, "I know everything. It's fine. Don't be scared. But don't push your luck." It was a façade that sent shivers down her spine, a calm before the storm that left her teetering on the edge of uncertainty.

For a few tense seconds, they sat in silence, the only sound the sharp clinking of forks and knives against plates—a metallic rhythm that seemed to echo their unspoken fears. The air grew thick with unacknowledged tension, each clink amplifying the growing chasm between them, as if the cutlery were a choir of tension, singing their silent discontent.

After finishing his meal, Ajee wiped his mouth and sat back, watching Sprite wrestle with her last bite. "Hang on a sec," he said, rising from his seat. As he headed toward the kitchen, a wave of confusion washed over Sprite, leaving her to grapple with her unease. When he returned, he held a sleek black bottle, its gold label glinting in the dim light like a warning sign, drawing her attention and curiosity in equal measure.

The label featured elegant calligraphy in a language she didn't recognize, the swirling script almost mesmerizing, as if it were a secret incantation waiting to be unraveled.

With the remnants of her school English classes echoing in her mind, Sprite was certain it wasn't English. It could've been French, Dutch, or even Latin, but the language eluded her grasp. All she knew was that the enigmatic bottle exuded an air of opulence, as if it held secrets far richer than anything she could comprehend.

In addition to the bottle, Ajee brought two stemmed glasses—glimmering and elegant—that Sprite couldn't recall ever having seen before.

She suspected the glasses might be leftover wedding gifts, relics of tableware that had never really suited their tastes. Yet in Ajee's hands, they appeared utterly ordinary, stripped of any special significance, like mundane props in a play they'd never agreed to perform.

"Ah, I completely forgot about this," Ajee said, setting the bottle down on the table. "I was just drinking plain water."

"What's that?" Sprite asked, her curiosity sharpening like a blade.

Ajee laughed, as if Sprite's question was merely a formality. "The only drink worthy of tonight," he replied, producing a bottle opener from his pocket—a relic that had clearly seen better days. With the casual grace of someone who'd done this a thousand times before, he cracked open the bottle, the sharp pop echoing in the tense silence.

The sharp pop pierced the air, followed by the satisfying gurgle of liquid pouring into the glasses. In no time, one glass was half-filled—or half-empty—with a rich, deep red liquid that glimmered like dark rubies in the dim light.

At first, Sprite mistook it for last year's leftover Christmas grape juice, but then reality set in, jolting her with clarity. The hip-hop track *Redrum* blared in her mind, drowning out the instrumental music wafting from the kitchen. This was the first time she'd ever seen it up close, and the sight sent a chill creeping down her spine.

She had watched her neighbors get plastered on cheap beer during card games and seen teenagers near her apartment snagging cans from the corner store, but this was a whole different vibe. Romantic—that was the only word that sprang to mind, a term she had long discarded after graduation and the harsh realities of life. Now, it resurfaced, whispering seductively in her thoughts. So captivated was Sprite that she momentarily forgot the drink was meant to be enjoyed, not merely admired. The weight of that reality made her uneasy. Eating steak with her left hand felt one way, but drinking alcohol was another—an unspoken taboo, a fear that she might lose the carefully crafted identity she had built for herself.

She felt that if the liquid even brushed her lips, it might erase her identity as Sprite Karson, as if the very essence of who she was could be swallowed away. Maybe she'd lose consciousness, maybe she'd morph into someone else entirely. But who? Someone like Ajee? The thought curled around her mind, unsettling and insidious. Had he been drunk or high all this time? The implication hung in the air, a shadow lurking just out of sight, threatening to consume her.

She envisioned herself transforming like Ajee, emerging braver, more independent, stronger—sexier. In that fleeting moment, an unexpected desire to get drunk washed over her, a wild impulse that threatened to shatter the walls she had carefully built around herself. The thought flickered like a flame, dangerously alluring, promising an escape from the suffocating weight of her reality.

"To the beautiful Sprite," Ajee proclaimed, raising his glass, "and to our happiness." His voice was steady, the words rolling off his tongue like a practiced incantation. The glass glinted in the light, a promise hanging in the air, and for a heartbeat, Sprite felt her heart quicken, caught between the warmth of his toast and the chill of uncertainty.

Sprite realized Ajee was proposing a toast, a gesture she had yearned for since childhood. The simple joy of clinking glasses had always struck her as enchanting, a small yet delightful ritual she had eagerly anticipated. It was a fleeting moment of magic, a flicker of intimacy in a world that often felt cold and distant, igniting a spark of hope within her that maybe, just maybe, this was the beginning of something more.

She craved that crisp clink, longing to embody the charm of those people she admired from afar. Compelled by instinct, Sprite lifted her glass, convincing herself it was merely to spare Ajee's feelings. And then came the satisfying chime she had yearned for, a sound that resonated within her like a forgotten promise.

Ajee downed the liquid without a second thought, a smooth motion that spoke of confidence. But Sprite's hand trembled, the glass growing heavier with every passing second, her wrist feeling alarmingly delicate, as if it might shatter under the weight of her uncertainty.

For a fleeting moment, Sprite considered setting the glass down untouched, but Ajee's intense gaze ensnared her, holding her captive in its grip. She felt entranced, as if caught in a spell. Maybe this was the trick of magicians—applying mental pressure to make their volunteers do the absurd, like waddling like ducks or climbing like monkeys, all while they smiled for an audience that wasn't even there.

Alright, this was it—she had to take that sip. Curiosity gnawed at her, as it always did when something unknown lingered just out of reach. She needed to know what it tasted like, what Ajee saw in it, what made it so special. This was her moment, her chance to finally find out.

Without a second thought, she whispered a silent grace and took a sip. The taste jolted her—a flavor so startlingly foreign it felt like an electric shock, awakening something deep within her.

Truth be told, she would have preferred a whole glass of Italian ice over this drink. Yet, the sight of Ajee's approving smile sparked a flicker of validation deep inside her. An unexpected impulse surged within, and with a deep breath, Sprite tossed back the entire glass in one swift motion, leaving not a single drop behind.

Ajee chuckled, his gaze fixed on her with a mix of amusement and something deeper. "Thanks," he said, his voice carrying an undertone of sincerity. "Thanks for giving me this chance."

Chance. The word hung in the air, thick with meaning, brimming with unspoken possibilities and consequences that seemed to loom larger with each heartbeat.

Sprite mulled over what kind of chance he meant, yet the sincerity in his voice sent a flush of warmth spreading through her chest, igniting a flicker of hope she hadn't expected.

"Alright, for the last one," Ajee said, his voice smooth and inviting. "Close your eyes for me."

"Why?" Sprite asked, her curiosity bubbling to the surface, a mix of apprehension and intrigue in her voice.

"A surprise," he replied, a grin spreading across his face like a cat who'd just spotted a canary.

A surprise hardly felt like a good enough reason to comply. The last time someone had asked her to close her eyes was back in high school.

Just a few seconds after she finally gave in to her boyfriend's request, she experienced her first kiss—a moment that clung to her like a lingering shadow, creeping back into her thoughts even a decade later. It haunted her most when Ajee, her rightful husband, kissed her on their wedding night and asked if it was truly her first.

Back then, she could only nod and lie, and tonight felt like a replay of that same deception. Sprite shut her eyes, her heart pounding with a frantic rhythm. What was the worst that could happen?

When she opened her eyes, she half-expected to be greeted by blinding lights, cameras stationed in every corner, and a host with a microphone declaring, "Congratulations! You're on TV!"

Maybe that wouldn't be so terrible after all. The sudden scrape of a chair against the floor jolted her, signaling that Ajee had risen. Her heart raced even faster, each beat drumming up a mix of excitement and anxiety.

Then she heard footsteps—was Ajee really wearing leather-soled shoes indoors? She'd never noticed his feet before, but now the sound of each step was unmistakable, deliberate. One footfall after another echoed in her ears. Sprite's breathing grew ragged, each inhale coming harder than the last, her pulse quickening with a mix of anticipation and dread.

She couldn't quite understand why she was so insistent on keeping her eyes shut. After all, she could have sneaked a peek if she wanted to. Perhaps it was the fear of what she might see that kept her frozen in place. Then, without warning, a hand gently brushed her cheek. It was cool to the touch, impossibly soft. The fingertips skimmed her skin, sending a shiver through her, before vanishing for a moment. When the hand reappeared, it no longer rested on her face but glided to her neck, leaving her breathless.

Sprite jolted, panic surging through her like a tightening vise around her neck. Every instinct screamed at her to fight back, to flee if this wasn't truly Ajee. Her breath came in shallow gasps, squeezed out by an unseen force, adrenaline coursing through her veins, urging her to break free from the suffocating grip of fear.

But as Sprite opened her eyes, clutching the cool wrists, reality twisted into something entirely unexpected. The hand wasn't constricting her throat; it was gently fastening a necklace around her neck.

"You peeked before I gave the go-ahead," Ajee said, his voice tinged with amusement rather than annoyance.

Sprite stared down in silence, her mouth pressed into a tight line. Her gaze fell on the necklace resting against her collarbone, catching the candlelight with its golden gleam. The delicate chain was woven from tiny, shimmering links, and at the end dangled a small white pendant, a speck of moonlight ensnared in gold.

She couldn't quite place the stone, but it shimmered, shifting from white to a golden hue that perfectly matched the necklace. Then, a kiss brushed against her forehead—warm, soft, and unexpectedly tender. In that moment, tears began to flow, streaking down her cheeks and dripping onto the delicate chain, a bittersweet testament to emotions she could no longer contain.

She recognized the gold necklace immediately—it was hers, a cherished family heirloom passed down from her grandmother and mother, both long gone. The weight of its history pressed against her heart, a bittersweet reminder of love and loss intertwined.

A few weeks after the wedding, Ajee took a sudden turn for the worse. A high fever struck him down, plunging him into unconsciousness and landing him in the hospital. His salary and savings barely made a dent in the mounting medical bills, each day adding to a burden that felt more suffocating than the last.

In that desperate moment, Sprite found herself forced to part with the necklace, despite her mother's stern warning never to sell it. She buried the secret deep within, clinging to the fragile hope that someday she'd be able to buy it back. But no matter how hard she tried, the cash she scraped together never seemed to be enough, and soon she learned the necklace was worth far more than the pittance she had been offered.

A crushing sense of betrayal washed over her as the necklace slipped away, vanishing into the store and drifting through unknown hands, leaving no trace behind. "Honey, where'd you get—"

Before she could finish her question, Ajee raised a finger, silencing her. "Hold on," he said, his voice steady. "I wanted to thank you for everything you've ever given me. Tonight's our anniversary, and you forgot." He gently stroked her hair, his touch tender yet charged with unspoken emotions.

Sprite stood frozen, shock paralyzing her as she scrambled to align the dates in her mind. The realization hit her with a cold clarity—Ajee was right. They had never celebrated their wedding anniversary; the only dates that mattered to her were paydays and the relentless march of bills. Her gratitude evaporated, swallowed by the unexpected warmth of Ajee's embrace, a kind of comfort she had never experienced in their marriage. It enveloped her like a cocoon, filled with a strange, deep warmth. That night, something profound shifted between them, a fragile yet unmistakable change in the air.

Even though Sprite could barely recognize the Ajee before her until the very end, she knew deep down that this tender, romantic man was the one she had always envisioned marrying. As he gently carried her into the bedroom, she made the choice to surrender to the moment. For her, this night felt like the culmination of all her patience and loyalty throughout their marriage—a long-awaited reward, a flicker of the love she had once dreamed of.

5

As Sprite slipped into the deep folds of sleep, the dream came on slow, sneaking in like a shadow, soft and patient, whispering just beyond the edge of darkness.

In the dream, she found herself in a vast, opulent room, the kind that oozed wealth but felt heavy, like the air was thick with a secret. A crowd of people sat before her, all eyes fixed on her, their smiles stretched tight—too perfect, too rehearsed, like they'd been painted on. They were dressed sharp, like they were heading to a party—or maybe a funeral. Their faces said joy, but the glint of tears in the corners of some eyes told a different story. To her right and left, a line of people stood flanking her, each one wearing the same unnerving, too-happy grin.

She glanced at her hands, then down at her body, and the realization hit like a cold slap: she was dressed in something absurd. A dark, flowing robe wrapped around her, streaked with blue and yellow, twisting her into a bizarre figure—like a wizard ripped from the pages of some ancient, forgotten nightmare.

Sprite reached up and felt the stiff square cap on her head, the tassel swaying like a pendulum, ticking away time she didn't have. Her eyes darted to the people flanking her, all wearing the same strange headgear. Then, from the shadows at the room's edge, a burly, bald man emerged, his footsteps heavy, each one a thud that echoed with purpose, thickening the air with something darker than fear.

He carried himself with authority, even though his ridiculous outfit was just as laughable as the rest. Slowly, deliberately, he moved down the line, greeting each person with a smile that teetered on smug, adjusting their tassels with a precision that felt ritualistic. When he reached Sprite, the room blurred, like reality itself was slipping away. Her heart pounded like a war drum, and her body shook—not with fear, but with a strange, overpowering joy that threatened to tear her apart. He clasped her hand, his grip firm and steady, anchoring her in place, her trembling wrist finally silenced.

His handshake stayed steady, a wordless gesture of equality, an unspoken pact of mutual respect. It wasn't the grip of a teacher to a student, an elder to the young, or a man to a woman—it was something simpler, an exchange on level ground. As he toyed with the tassel on Sprite's cap, his face edged closer, the space between them shrinking, a growing intensity crackling in the air, making her pulse race.

Sprite jolted, a sudden shiver crawling up her spine, like something unseen had just grazed her skin—a cold, ghostly touch she hadn't expected.

He hadn't done that with the others—only her. Then he leaned in, closer than before, his voice dropping to a strange, echoing whisper. "This ain't a dream," he murmured. "It's all real now." And just like that, he was back where he started, standing there like nothing had happened at all, like the moment had slipped through time's fingers.

The shift came in an instant, like a heartbeat skipped, as if time itself had been sliced open, leaving a jagged, empty void where a moment should've been.

Without a word, he moved to the person on Sprite's left, greeting them with the same mechanical precision. Sprite's mind spun, caught in a fog, but then her gaze found a single point ahead—something solid in the dizzying blur—grasping for stability as everything else swirled out of reach.

In the sea of faces watching from the crowd, Sprite caught sight of two people glowing with wide, genuine smiles. Her parents. In this dream, her mother radiated life, a vibrancy so real it felt almost tangible. Her father stood beside her, clad in a sharp black suit and a dark blue tie, every inch the dashing figure she remembered—a vision of gallantry and grace, a comforting anchor in a storm of uncertainty.

He gave Sprite a small nod, a silent affirmation that said, "Yeah, I'm proud of you, kid." It was a simple gesture, but it carried the weight of a thousand unspoken words.

Meanwhile, her mother dabbed at the tears pooling in the corners of her eyes with a delicate handkerchief, each movement a careful dance to avoid smudging her flawless makeup. It was the first time Sprite had seen her mother so impeccably dressed. Her hair was twisted neatly into a bun, and her body was wrapped in an orange dress that made her look as if she'd shed a decade or more, radiating a youthful vitality that felt almost surreal.

Though she fought to maintain her composure, Sprite sensed her mother teetering on the edge of tears, emotions threatening to spill over. It wasn't disappointment driving her to the brink, but something deeper—a pride so intense it felt almost too big to contain. The details of what happened next blurred like shards of a shattered mirror. What remained vivid was the image of her arms wrapped around both parents, a rush of warmth flooding her chest, enveloping her in a comforting embrace. It was as if she'd been transported back to her childhood. The love from her parents, a feeling she'd nearly forgotten, washed over her with a ferocious intensity, like a memory resurrected from the depths of her soul.

"Thanks, Mom. Thanks, Dad. Thanks for standing by me," she said, her voice trembling as she struggled against the swell of tears.

Then, turning her head to the right, she caught sight of a handsome guy beaming at her, his warm smile cutting through the emotional haze.

The man was impeccably groomed, his hair slicked back with a precise application of pomade, every strand meticulously in place. His mustache and beard were trimmed to perfection, framing his face, which was smooth and unblemished, giving him an almost polished, sculpted appearance.

He wore a black suit over a maroon shirt, sans tie, and cradled a bouquet of roses so vibrant they seemed to pulse with their own inner light, a brilliant splash of color against the darkness of his attire.

Sprite shot a quick glance at her parents, and they responded with a reassuring nod. Her father's gaze drifted to the man, and a smile spread across his face, as if recognizing an unspoken understanding that lingered in the air between them.

Sprite rushed toward the man, her steps a frantic half-run, and wrapped her arms around him in a tight embrace, as if clinging to something solid amid the chaos swirling around her.

He carried a rich, intoxicating scent that lingered in the air, and his embrace enveloped her in a warm, comforting heat. As she turned to face him, a shiver of recognition slithered up Sprite's spine, a whisper of familiarity stirring from somewhere deep within her memory.

He was Ajee. Ajee Arizin. But not just any Ajee; he was *the* Ajee she had longed for, the one who eclipsed all others, a figure etched into her heart with a longing that felt both familiar and electric.

He kneeled before her, gently lifting a small black box. Inside, cradled against the velvet lining, lay a ring of gold so brilliant it seemed to outshine every other piece she had ever seen, regardless of how many lights flickered around it.

"Will you marry me?" Ajee asked, his voice the sweetest sound she had ever heard from a man, each word dripping with sincerity and promise.

Sprite glanced at her parents, a silent plea for their approval hanging in the air. Their smiles offered a quiet reassurance—a tacit blessing that enveloped the moment like a warm, comforting embrace, soothing her nerves and filling the space with unspoken love.

Without hesitation, Sprite answered Ajee's question with a firm nod. She extended her ring finger, and Ajee slid the engagement ring onto it with a tender, practiced touch. They embraced again, the room buzzing with cheers and applause. Friends surged forward, their voices rising in a chorus of congratulations, marveling not only at her graduation with honors but also at how she had captured the heart of a dashing, wealthy man.

Sprite received the flood of compliments with a gracious smile, attributing it all to a blessing from above and insisting she had merely done her best. The next vivid memory that surfaced was of her and her friends gathered together, poised for a group photo, the moment crystallizing into a blur of camaraderie and celebration, laughter echoing like music in the air.

Sprite stood in the front row, at the center of it all, feeling as though they weren't just taking a group photo but that everyone was there to capture a moment with her. A sharply dressed photographer directed them with practiced ease, guiding them through a series of poses that shifted from stiff and formal to playful and spontaneous. The dream culminated in a scene straight out of a cheesy private university commercial: they tossed their caps into the air and leaped together, a burst of joyful exuberance frozen in a single, perfect moment.

Tragic Discovery: Woman Found Dead in Vehicle at Bronx Heritage Suites

Mott Haven, NY — A tragic incident unfolded Thursday morning when a 40-year-old woman was found dead inside a sedan parked near the entrance of the Bronx Heritage Suites. The grim discovery was made around 7:00 AM EDT by a local resident out for a morning jog.

The witness, who observed the vehicle in an unusual state, noted, "The window looked cracked, so I got curious." Upon closer inspection, the witness saw the victim slumped in the car's seat, her neck covered in blood. Alarmed, the witness promptly alerted security personnel and contacted the police.

According to the NYPD, the victim has been identified as Mrs. T, a resident of the Bronx Heritage Suites and a CEO at a private company. Authorities believe she was murdered around midnight while returning home from work. Colleagues reported that Mrs. T preferred to drive alone and seldom used a chauffeur.

Initial investigations indicate that the incident may have involved robbery, although the police have yet to identify a suspect. The community is left in shock as investigators continue to probe this tragic case, seeking answers to a crime that has shaken the neighborhood.

Further updates are expected as the police continue their investigation into this unfortunate incident.

6

The rain whispered against the window, a soft, persistent murmur that teased at Sprite's ears like a secret half-told in the dead of night. It was the kind of sound that slinked through the darkness, curling around her thoughts, coaxing out memories she'd rather keep buried.

As the cold air crept beneath her blanket, she stirred, consciousness pulling her back like a reluctant prisoner being dragged from a dark cell. Her eyes fluttered open, heavy with the weight of lingering sleep, while every inch of her body pleaded to sink back into the comforting abyss of slumber. The reasons for her reluctance lurked just beyond the edge of her thoughts, shadowy figures she couldn't quite grasp, whispering promises of peace if only she would let go.

First, she craved the unfinished dream that still held her in its grasp, like a story left dangling in the dark, begging for resolution. Second, the soft patter of drizzle against the window wrapped around her like a cherished lullaby, a sound she'd adored for as long as she could remember, perfect for surrendering to sleep's deep, inviting embrace.

She was the sort who preferred the rainy season to the blistering heat of summer, relishing the cool embrace of night over the sun's merciless blaze. As she tugged the blanket, which had inched down to her waist, back up to her chin, an odd realization struck her:

she'd fallen asleep in nothing but her underwear—a black bra and plain white panties. It felt like a secret she hadn't meant to keep, a vulnerability exposed in the dim light of her room.

Normally, she'd be tucked into one of her favorite, worn-out nightgowns or a loose T-shirt she'd picked up in Fresno. And she never, ever used a blanket. When had that changed? Her eyes snapped open wide, and still drifting in and out of wakefulness, she scrutinized the fabric draped over her. It wasn't a blanket at all, but a scrap of cloth that had been gathering dust in her wardrobe for ages—a relic of another time, now strangely intimate against her skin.

She recalled how her husband had always cringed at the sight of cloth being used as a blanket, as if it were some kind of sacrilege, a crime against comfort. It was one of those quirks that had made her smile, even in the midst of their arguments, a strange tension that now felt like a ghost hovering just beyond her reach.

"Looks like a dead body," he'd mutter with a shudder, his distaste palpable in the way he pronounced each word, as if the very thought sickened him. It was a phrase she'd grown used to, a mix of humor and horror that painted a vivid picture, one that lingered long after he'd said it.

She couldn't quite grasp why she'd drifted off in such a state, a sense of vulnerability lingering like an unwelcome guest. A heavy sigh escaped her lips, a release of tension that felt both necessary and futile, echoing in the stillness of the room.

For a fleeting moment, she envisioned waking up in a lavish room, cocooned in a plush blanket on a grand, springy bed, a breakfast tray perched on a dainty table beside her. Not the usual pasta or congee, but bagels and real English tea, the kind that made the world feel just right. But that was all a fantasy, a mirage shimmering in the dim light of morning, dissipating as reality crept back in, cold and unyielding.

She was still emerging from the haze of sleep in her cramped, musty room, where the walls hadn't seen a coat of paint in years. The bed was a relic, its creaking corner a constant reminder that it might one day give way beneath her weight. It was sturdy, though, built from old wood that had seen far better days. There was no breakfast tray or bedside lamp—just a wardrobe that looked as ancient as the bed. Its door was adorned with a mirror, framed by stubborn remnants of stickers—her high school's emblem, the logo of a basketball club, and a few faded quotes of wisdom. That wardrobe belonged to Ajee, a ghost of her past still haunting the corners of her life.

He had hauled it in with a truck when they first moved into this place. Ajee? Where had her husband vanished to? The space beside her felt emptily vast, a stark reminder of her solitude, as if the air itself was heavy with the absence of his presence, a silence that echoed like a haunting refrain.

Sometimes, Ajee would wake before her, slipping out for a bit of light exercise in the park before the shadows of his depression crept in like a thief in the night. Other times, he'd simply sit and stare vacantly at the sky, lost in the void that had swallowed him whole, his mind adrift in an ocean of despair.

She glanced at the wall clock, a gaudy gift from some instant coffee brand, its bright colors clashing with the drab room, hanging next to the wardrobe. Four in the morning. Way too early for this kind of reckoning, the hour draped in a heavy blanket of darkness that felt almost sinister.

She was no stranger to waking at this ungodly hour, even on holidays, but today she felt groggy, as if sleep clung to her like a second skin. Maybe it was the soothing, lullaby-like drizzle outside, whispering promises of rest she was reluctant to abandon. Then, like a half-remembered whisper, her dream from last night surfaced—a strange, unsettling dream that clung to her thoughts like fog, its edges blurred but its essence vivid and haunting.

Ajee had transformed, a complete reversal of his former self. He'd become tender and romantic, orchestrating a candlelit dinner with an air of quiet elegance that felt almost surreal. He'd shown her how to savor steak and sip wine with a grace she had never known, and, as if to seal it all, he'd gifted her that necklace she'd been longing for—an anniversary present that seemed to shimmer with his newfound affection, a dazzling reminder of the man he had become and the love that now wrapped around them like a warm embrace.

Sprite let out a soft, knowing chuckle. "I really need to lay off those soap operas," she muttered to herself, the words laced with self-mockery, as if acknowledging that life had started to feel like one big, melodramatic episode, complete with all its absurd twists and turns.

People had been right all along—bingeing on soap operas and TV dramas could send your imagination spiraling into overdrive, transforming everyday life into a series of overblown plots and absurd scenarios that felt all too real.

She sat up in bed, carefully adjusting the fabric to keep it in place, the movement deliberate and almost ritualistic. Even though she was alone, her own reflection in the mirror on the wardrobe door made her feel oddly self-conscious, as if the glass were an audience critiquing her every move, every hesitation.

She secured the fabric and reached for the hair tie that always rested on her left wrist. As she pulled her hair back, a realization dawned on her—something she should have noticed sooner if she hadn't been so groggy. A necklace hung around her neck, identical to the one from her dream, its presence both comforting and unsettling, as if the boundaries between reality and fantasy had blurred overnight.

Sprite edged closer to the mirror, her eyes locked on the necklace, as if it might whisper its secrets if she stared hard enough. Disbelief lingered in the corners of her mind, but she couldn't ignore the truth staring back at her, undeniable and heavy, like a shadow that refused to fade.

She unclasped the necklace and examined it inch by inch, tracing the delicate chain with trembling fingers. It was unmistakably real, cold against her skin and heavy with meaning. The only conclusion that made sense was that what she'd experienced last night hadn't been a mere dream—it was a message, or perhaps a warning, woven into the fabric of her reality.

Clutching the necklace, she turned back to the bed, where shadows from her imagination danced in her mind. Last night, she and her husband had shared an intimate moment on that very bed—but it wasn't the man she knew, and it wasn't the same kind of intimacy they'd shared throughout their marriage. Her body stirred at the memory, a warm sensation spreading through her as the shadows replayed the scene from the night before. The body held its own memory, more vivid and persistent than the mind's; it was an unsettling feeling she'd thought was just part of the dream, now creeping back in with a familiar dread. If the necklace was real, then Ajee's transformation was real, too. But where was her husband now?

She had to unravel her suspicion as quickly as possible. Only by confirming it could she begin to process the whirlwind of emotions swirling within her, a chaotic mixture of longing and fear that threatened to consume her whole.

Without a second thought for proper clothing, she slipped out of the room. The gentle patter of the drizzle faded as she stepped into the living room, where darkness enveloped everything. The windows loomed dark and unwelcoming, while Doctor lay curled up and snoring softly in its cage. The only hint of life was the dull red glow of the TV antenna booster, casting a faint, eerie light in the corner, as if the room itself were holding its breath, waiting for something to break the silence.

"Ajee," Sprite called out, her voice raspy and raw from sleep, like gravel scraping against glass. "Ajee." The name hung in the air, heavy with longing and uncertainty, echoing back to her like a distant memory.

The name drifted through the murky shadows of the room, a ghostly plea for a presence that had vanished. The silence that followed was thick and heavy, pressing in on her like a shroud, offering no reply, just the echo of her own voice fading into the void.

Sprite moved past the vacant, spotless dining table, its surface untouched and unblemished, as if time had paused around it. There were no traces of a meal, no hint that anyone had recently gathered there, but then a memory struck her, sharp and sudden, like a flash of lightning illuminating the darkness.

She spun around and returned to the dining table, her fingertips grazing the surface. It felt immaculate, smooth from edge to edge. But as her fingers glided toward the center, they encountered a faint, soft residue—thin yet stubbornly clinging to the otherwise pristine tabletop, like a secret refusing to be washed away.

She traced her fingertip over the spot, the slick sensation confirming her suspicion. "This is definitely wax," she muttered to herself, no room for doubt. As she continued her search, the pieces began to fall into place: the necklace was real, and the wax on the table was an undeniable clue, whispering of secrets that lingered just beyond her grasp.

So, it was starting to feel all too real—Ajee's transformation was not just a fleeting illusion but a tangible truth, solid and undeniable, lurking in the shadows of her mind.

As she mulled over this unsettling possibility, she made her way toward the stairs. The apartment entrance stood ajar, just a handspan wide, allowing the cold air to seep through the gap, a chilling whisper that sent a shiver down her spine.

Sprite instinctively wrapped her arms around herself, shivering as the cold gnawed at her bare shoulders. With a slow, deliberate motion, she pushed open the door. There sat Ajee on a bench, cigarette smoke curling from his lips in ghostly tendrils, shrouding him in an eerie haze. He remained silent, his eyes fixed somewhere distant. Her heart raced, pounding with a frantic rhythm. Was this the Ajee she knew, or was something else lurking beneath the surface of the man before her?

"Ajee?" she called, the name slipping from her lips like a fragile thread, woven with equal parts hope and dread.

Sprite's voice wavered, suspended in the air like a fragile question caught between hope and dread, teetering on the brink of revelation.

Ajee gave her a fleeting glance, his expression one of calm indifference, as if he'd been waiting for her all along, a stone statue in the night, unmoved and inscrutable.

Though the sidewalk was shrouded in shadows, Sprite could still make out the deep lines of exhaustion etched into Ajee's face, like a map of unspoken struggles and weary nights, each wrinkle a testament to the burdens he bore.

He stubbed out his cigarette in the ashtray with a resigned sigh. "What's up, Sprite?" he asked, his voice heavy and worn, stripped of warmth. He used her name, plain and unadorned, devoid of the endearments that once flowed easily—no *dear* or *honey* to soften the distance between them.

That simple fact—Ajee's casual, unceremonious tone—convinced her that the man sitting and smoking before her was the same old Ajee. Could the other Ajee have been nothing more than a figment of her dream, a trick of her imagination? Yet the thought felt like a dark joke; how could that possibly be?

"Do you remember what happened last night?" she asked, her voice tinged with a mix of curiosity and trepidation, like stepping onto thin ice, uncertain if it would hold.

A surge of relief emboldened her to ask. The Ajee before her might still be the same frustrating, at times ineffectual husband she'd always known, but he was unmistakably the Ajee she recognized—not the enigmatic figure from her dream. For a few moments, the only sound was the steady patter of rain on the street, drenching the leaves of the wave of love plants, as if nature itself held its breath in anticipation.

"Last night, I crashed," Ajee replied flatly, his voice empty of inflection. "I had this dream."

"What was your dream about?" Sprite asked, her voice laced with a blend of curiosity and unease, like a tightrope walker teetering between fear and intrigue.

Ajee sighed again, this time laced with a hint of frustration. It was the same frustration he'd been grappling with before Sprite had even arrived, a burden that clung to him like a shadow.

As expected, Ajee offered no answer. He stubbed out his cigarette in the ashtray and strode briskly back into the apartment. "What are you doing out here, all wrapped up in that rag?" he snapped, brushing past Sprite, who stood frozen at the door, unable to summon the strength to move.

7

The sun dragged itself over the horizon, like a tired old man forcing himself out of bed, spilling a sluggish golden light across a world that was still half-asleep.

Ajee stood in the bathroom, the hiss of the shower blending with the soft, muted splashes of the toilet. Since the layoff, he'd transformed these simple, everyday routines into a drawn-out performance, stretching the minutes, trying to carve some kind of order from the chaos his life had become.

In the kitchen, Sprite fought with the old metal cupboard wedged against the wall, its bulk a stubborn, immovable beast. Every shove sent a chorus of clinking utensils rattling inside, the thing groaning like it resented being touched. It wasn't a big move she was after—just enough to nudge it closer, make it useful. But that cupboard wasn't giving up easy.

All she had to do was nudge the cupboard a little closer to the stove, hardly any effort at all. But when the gap between the cupboard and the wall finally cracked open, she spotted the dark, narrow crevice between the wooden boards behind it. And there, in that hidden sliver of space, lay her diary, forgotten but waiting like a secret that refused to stay buried.

Sprite had made it a ritual, slipping her diary in and out of its hiding place whenever Ajee was out of sight—like now, with him lost in the steady beat of the shower. Keeping a diary, and keeping it hidden, wasn't easy when your life was so tangled up with someone else's. But she managed, weaving secrets into the small spaces left between them.

Sometimes, she'd tuck the diary into her work bag, sneaking in moments between tasks or while waiting for a ride to carve out a small sanctuary. In those stolen minutes—sitting at a cramped bus stop or catching a quiet break—she'd scribble her thoughts. It felt safer, jotting down her secrets among the indifferent hum of colleagues, than trying to do it under the ever-watchful eyes of her husband. But the diary had been gathering dust lately. As her workload mounted, writing and reading started to feel like luxuries, like something reserved for people with too much time on their hands—people who didn't have lives weighed down by everything else.

She was starting to understand why her parents had always looked at her hobby with a raised eyebrow, like they couldn't quite figure it out.

"That's the kind of thing rich kids do for kicks," they'd sneer, their words dripping with disdain, like the very idea of it was too far removed from real life to even consider.

The book she pulled from its hiding spot behind the cupboard was coated in a fine layer of neglect, as if it, too, had given up—accepting the hard truth that her free time was slipping away, piece by piece.

She wiped away the thick layer of dust clinging to the maroon cover, her fingers leaving clean streaks in the grime. Deep down, a flicker of relief stirred. The dust was a comforting sign—it meant the book had stayed untouched, a silent guardian of her secrets. Ajee hadn't found it, hadn't flipped through its pages. For now, her hidden world remained safely sealed away, just out of reach.

She flipped through a few pages, her eyes skimming over the familiar scrawl. The entries chronicled her struggles, her desperate attempts to self-motivate like a clinger to hope. There were rants about her tyrannical boss and whispers about Thyme, rumored to be tangled up with someone from the office. The last entry was a snapshot of Iron, her old high school flame, whose name had unexpectedly resurfaced on Facebook. Suddenly, a long-buried memory surged to the forefront—a romantic dinner that had only seemed romantic through the rose-tinted lens of a suburban teenager. The realization hit her like a cold splash of water: she, someone like her, had once dined in a fancy restaurant. It felt absurd now, a fleeting moment from a past that seemed as distant and implausible as a fairy tale.

Iron was the epitome of the cool kid from a privileged family, showing up to school on a green Yamaha R6, license be damned. He sported the latest Timex Ironman watch and spiked his hair with gel—pomade was already a relic of the past. When Valentine's Day rolled around, and the usual anti-Valentine's crusades were in full swing, Iron did something unexpected: he handed Sprite an invitation to dinner at the swankiest restaurant in town. For Sprite, dating Iron felt like a stroke of miraculous luck. There was no way she could turn down his offer; it was a chance she could only dream of.

With a mix of excitement and secrecy, Sprite accepted the invitation, hiding it from her parents. They sat across from each other in a restaurant where couples were scattered like whispers in the dim light. Despite the bustling crowd, the atmosphere was cozy and romantic—soft lights cast long shadows, candles flickered on every table, and a pianist wove delicate melodies from the corner. Considering the teenage clientele, the setting was toned down; no wine, just fruit juice, yet it still felt like a world apart from the mundane reality of everyday life.

After all, she was just a run-of-the-mill teenager from a conservative family, a world away from the glittering freedom of city kids. Yet, despite her ordinary life, this was the most lavish date she'd ever experienced—a slice of luxury that felt almost otherworldly in its splendor.

Iron was her fantasy made flesh—handsome, wealthy, and dripping with romance. He seemed to embody everything she'd ever dreamed of. Yet, beneath that flawless façade, one glaring thing was missing: honesty.

A week after the most enchanting date of her life, Sprite uncovered the bitter truth: Iron had seen her as nothing more than a bet, a trophy to be won and paraded among his friends.

He ditched her for another girl—one who was prettier, sexier, and carried a glimmer of popularity that completely outshone her own.

Sprite endured a long, drawn-out heartbreak during those days. After graduation, she learned that Iron had knocked up his new girlfriend, twisting the knife even deeper into her already bruised heart.

Iron was thrust into an early marriage, settling into the grind of humble fatherhood. The last she'd heard, he was running a small eatery. With his privileged upbringing, one might have expected his life to sail smoothly, but that was a serious miscalculation. His parents had seen to that, casting him adrift as punishment for the shame he'd brought upon their family.

Amid her quarter-life crisis, when everything felt like it was unraveling, Sprite crossed paths with Ajee.

Ajee was an older ex-schoolmate, four years her senior. Unlike Iron, who thrived on playing games, Ajee was all about seriousness—a stark contrast that intrigued her.

In her eyes, Sprite saw a man who was hardworking and steadfast, someone ready to shield his family with fierce devotion.

Ajee skipped college and dove straight into factory work right after high school, embracing the grind of a contract employee. It was this unyielding work ethic and determination that earned him Sprite's deep respect as her senior.

But she never envisioned Ajee as her husband. So when he unexpectedly proposed, Sprite flatly turned him down. To her father, her refusal seemed utterly irrational—a puzzle he couldn't quite piece together.

He couldn't bear the thought of his daughter drifting through life unprotected, left to face the world alone. Too old and frail to shield her himself, he longed for another man to step in and offer the care and support he could no longer provide.

Reluctantly, Sprite eventually yielded to her father's relentless persuasion. She accepted Ajee and let go of her dream of becoming a designer. At first, their marriage settled into a comfortable routine. Life was simple, and Sprite, content with the everyday, didn't ask for much.

As her husband toiled away to support her and his younger siblings in a distant city, Sprite stayed home, honing the sewing skills her late mother had passed down. In the quiet of her daily routine, a tiny spark of hope flickered in her heart—a faint, perhaps naïve belief that she might still chase her dreams. It was a small, delicate hope, yet one she clung to with a quiet sense of appreciation.

About a year into her marriage, Sprite began to see Ajee for who he truly was. It became painfully clear that this wasn't the life she had envisioned; her dreams and ambitions had withered into unfulfilled hopes that felt beyond her reach.

In her frustration, Sprite turned to social media for a brief escape, but instead of finding solace, her anxiety only deepened—a harsh reminder of her discontent. By a twist of algorithmic fate, she stumbled upon Iron's Facebook page, complete with an open photo gallery. Though she no longer harbored any feelings for her past lover, her curiosity was impossible to stifle.

As she flipped through the photos, she was struck by the stark contrast between Iron's apparent happiness and her own discontent. The images told a story of success and joy, revealing how his once modest eatery had blossomed into a thriving franchise across major cities.

Iron had clawed his way back to financial stability, though Sprite couldn't shake the suspicion that his wealthy parents had lent a hand at the start. Now, he and his wife—the one he'd gotten pregnant before marriage—had two kids, a boy and a girl. The photos painted a picture of domestic bliss, erasing any trace of the affair and scandal that had once marked their beginning. They were living a fairy tale, while Sprite remained trapped in her own hardships—childless and alone.

Sprite couldn't help but question the fairness of it all. In her private moments, she envisioned what her life might be like if she were in Iron's shoes. Surely, her existence would be far more enjoyable if fate had dealt her a different hand. Just then, the bathroom door creaked open, the wood groaning and scraping against the floor, announcing that Ajee had wrapped up his shower.

Sprite hurriedly shoved the book back into its hiding spot, but not before tearing out a page about Iron—just to cover her bases.

8

The sewing machine's relentless clatter filled the room, its staccato rhythm hammering against the walls like an uninvited guest. It mingled with the crackling voice of the local radio, an odd companion spitting out a ceaseless religious Q&A punctuated by bursts of fervent hymns from some well-meaning local group. Each note collided with the machine's noise, creating a bizarre symphony of devotion and drudgery that hung heavy in the air, as if the very walls were holding their breath, waiting for something—anything—to break the monotony.

Sprite kept her eyes glued to the stack of orders from Waverley, her concentration as sharp as a needle. She knew if she didn't wrap this up soon, she'd be in deep trouble when she crossed paths with Waverley later—either on the way to or from work. That's why she'd left the TV off; its flickering images were a siren call to procrastination, a trap she couldn't afford to fall into. The radio, with its steady hum, felt like a safer bet, warding off the gnawing boredom without tempting her to stray from her task. It played a background tune of reassurance, a reminder that the outside world would still be there when she finished her work, and that Waverley was a force to be reckoned with.

On the windowsill, Ajee tossed crickets into Doctor's cage—a motley mix of bugs he'd snared himself and a few he'd splurged on with Sprite's hard-earned cash. The bird, now oddly serene, sat in stark contrast to the frantic chirping and screeching that had punctuated the candlelit dinner the night before, a cacophony that felt like a ghost of chaos lingering in the air. Doctor pecked at his meal with an almost meditative calm, as if he'd taken it upon himself to erase the memory of the previous night's frenzy, reminding Ajee that even in the aftermath of madness, there could be moments of quiet grace.

Sprite recalled how Ajee's collection of birds had once seemed almost endless, a riot of feathers and sound. There had been hill mynahs, doves, and even a barn owl—each one a piece of a peculiar avian puzzle that had filled his life with restless flutters and haunting calls. Their cacophony had woven a tapestry of wildness that surrounded him, a reminder that life, much like the birds, could be unpredictable and free, fluttering just out of reach but always leaving a mark. Each call echoed in her mind, a ghostly reminder of a time when the air was alive with their untamed spirits, a world now muted and still.

Sprite had always had a soft spot for birds like cockatiels and rosy-faced lovebirds, their cheerful songs a balm for her spirit. But Ajee had never shared her fondness for such bright creatures; he preferred the wild and untamed. In the end, it hardly mattered—when the money dried up, all the birds had been sold off, their cheerful chirping silenced for good. Only Doctor, the starling, remained, a solitary reminder of what had once been. He perched there, a dark silhouette against the fading light, embodying the ghost of a joyful past that lingered in the corners of her memory, a reminder of laughter and fluttering wings that had long since vanished.

Doctor was unlike any of Ajee's other birds—he was more like a talisman. The story went that Doctor had appeared out of nowhere during Ajee's feverish misery, landing near his bedroom window and chirping day after day, as if summoned by some unseen force. The bird's persistent song became Ajee's constant companion through his restless recovery, a small, feathery anchor in a turbulent sea of discomfort. With each note, Doctor infused Ajee's dark days with a flicker of hope, a reminder that even amid pain, life had a way of creeping in and clinging stubbornly to the edges of despair.

When Ajee finally managed to catch the wild creature, he named it Doctor, convinced that its song had been his unseen healer, a balm for his fevered soul. "Waverley's order?" he called out as he passed by, heading to the bathroom to wash up. The question hung in the air, a casual inquiry that belied the urgency of the task at hand. Ajee's mind was still half-lost in thoughts of the bird, its melody echoing in his ears, while the mundane realities of work beckoned him back to the present.

"Yeah, it's the wedding dress for Waverley's daughter. I just got back to working on it after two weeks," Sprite called out, her voice slicing through the apartment like a knife. She hoped her husband could hear her from inside the bathroom, though the running water drowned out her words. The weight of the dress, still fresh in her hands, felt heavier than ever—a mix of anticipation and dread swirling in her gut as she returned to the delicate stitches, a task that loomed larger with each passing moment.

"Why doesn't he just rent a wedding dress?" Ajee asked again, a hint of frustration creeping into his voice, like a shadow settling in. His brow furrowed as he paced the small space, the question hanging in the air like a stubborn cloud, refusing to dissipate. It wasn't just about the dress; it was about the endless demands that seemed to pile up around him, suffocating in their urgency.

"Come on, you know Waverley's daughter. Her body size is a bit tricky," Sprite said, exasperation lacing her words. She rolled her eyes, as if that alone could conjure up a dress that would fit. The memories of past fittings swirled in her mind, a collage of awkward moments and desperate adjustments, and she couldn't shake the feeling that this task was destined to be just as complicated.

"Oh, the one with no curves? Got it. Makes sense," Ajee replied, a wry smile creeping onto his lips. His tone dripped with a mix of sarcasm and resignation, as if he had just uncovered a well-worn truth about Waverley's daughter. The image lingered in his mind—an awkward silhouette that seemed to defy the very essence of a wedding dress, a puzzle that Sprite would have to solve with every stitch.

"It's not *no curves*—she's plus-size," Sprite corrected him, her voice steady but edged with irritation. The words hung in the air, a reminder that the topic was more delicate than Ajee seemed to grasp. She shot him a pointed look, the kind that told him she wasn't about to let his flippant remarks undermine the importance of the task at hand. In that moment, the weight of expectations settled heavily on her shoulders, a stark reminder that every detail mattered in the fragile world of wedding dreams.

"Yeah, whatever." Ajee stepped out of the bathroom, drying his hands on a faded towel, the fibers rough against his skin. He glanced at Sprite, a hint of distraction in his eyes. "Has Waverley said anything about a job opening?" The question hung in the air, casual yet loaded, as if he were searching for an escape route from the tension that crackled between them.

Sprite fell silent, the realization crashing over her like a cold wave. She'd completely forgotten to ask Waverley about it. The thought gnawed at her, an unwelcome ghost haunting the corners of her mind, refusing to let her focus on anything else. Each tick of the clock seemed to amplify her oversight, a relentless reminder that even in the chaos of her sewing, the world outside was moving on without her.

While placing the sewing order, Waverley had casually dropped a hint about an upcoming job opening at his workplace. His words hung in the air, light yet charged with the weight of unspoken possibilities, like a shadow that might stretch and deepen into something more. The promise of change lingered, creeping into Sprite's thoughts, unsettling yet enticing, a reminder that her life could take a turn she hadn't dared to envision.

Sprite had asked about it a week ago, and the answer had been a flat no. Now, the possibility of an opening felt as distant as ever, like a flickering light at the end of a long, dark tunnel, teasing her with the promise of something just out of reach. Yet, a small part of her clung to the hope that this week might bring a glimmer of change, a shift in the shadows that could transform her lingering doubts into something more tangible.

"Not yet," Sprite replied, her voice steady but laced with an undercurrent of frustration. It was a simple answer, but it felt heavier than it should, as if the weight of unfulfilled dreams hung in the air between them, thick and palpable. Each word was a reminder that time was slipping away, leaving her hopes suspended in uncertainty.

"Did Waverley mention that?" Ajee asked, his tone curious but edged with skepticism. The question lingered in the air, a fragile thread connecting their thoughts. He studied Sprite's face, searching for clues in her expression, hoping for more than just a simple answer.

"Yeah," Sprite said, nodding slowly, as if she were trying to convince herself just as much as him. Her hesitation hung in the air, heavy with unspoken doubts. Each nod felt like a fragile affirmation, masking the uncertainty swirling inside her, a flickering candle struggling to stay lit in the growing darkness.

"I think he was just making small talk. Who'd want to hire me? I don't meet the requirements—I never went to college, and I can't do much of anything," Ajee said, his voice heavy with resignation. He sighed, the sound deep and weary, as if he were carrying the weight of her doubts along with his own. The air between them thickened with unspoken fears, a silent acknowledgment that the walls of their lives felt all too confining, closing in with each passing day.

"But you can still do electronics repairs, right?" Sprite asked, a flicker of hope sparking in her voice. She remembered Ajee had attended professional development courses in the past. Even if he hadn't used those skills in a while, she figured he could always brush up on them. The thought of him offering TV or washing machine repairs lingered in her mind, a lifeline tossed into the murky waters of their uncertainty, if only he was willing to refresh his memory and take the plunge.

"Electronics repair? Who even does that anymore?" Ajee muttered, his voice laced with cynicism. "If something breaks, people just toss it and buy a new one on credit." He turned away, heading back toward the window, as if the sight of the outside world could offer him some relief from the suffocating weight of his own doubts.

Sprite turned her attention back to the sewing, her fingers brushing against the fabric of Waverley's dress. As she studied it, a sinking feeling settled in her gut; it felt woefully inadequate for the task ahead. Waverley's daughter had a body size that was decidedly unique, and that fact only amplified the dress's shortcomings, making it seem even more out of place. The fabric, once vibrant and full of promise, now felt like a cruel reminder of the challenge before her, as if it had absorbed her doubts and fears with every stitch.

Waverley had mentioned he'd tried to find a place to rent a wedding dress, but nothing seemed to fit her body. The search had turned into a frustrating parade of misfits, each dress a stark reminder of how out of sync her needs were with what was available. Each one felt like a slap in the face, a reflection of a world that didn't accommodate her uniqueness, leaving behind only a lingering sense of disappointment and despair.

Despite everything, Waverley was determined to make his daughter look flawless on her big day. His commitment ran so deep that he sold his cherished motorcycle, a sacrifice that echoed louder than words about his desire to see her dreams come true. It was a decision that painted a vivid picture of a father's love, the kind of love that could cut through the noise of life's chaos and focus on a single, shining moment, no matter the cost.

Deep down, Sprite was grateful for her metabolism, which seemed to keep her weight in check no matter how much she ate. Friends often told her she looked like a model, but she always felt too thin, yearning to add a little more shape. Recent months had only worsened her plight, with scant food and relentless work whittling her down further. This morning's breakfast—a meager serving of corned beef hash and a cup of tea—served as a stark reminder of her struggle, barely enough to fend off the hunger gnawing at her insides, a constant reminder of how quickly her vitality was slipping away.

After dawn, Sprite set out for Lullie's apartment to pick up some congee and pretzels, leaving Ajee behind in the silence of their home. The morning air was cool and thin, a fitting backdrop for her solitary errand. As she walked, she felt the weight of the stillness pressing in around her, leaving Ajee to his own thoughts—lost in the echoing quiet of their shared space, where unspoken worries lingered like shadows in the corners.

Lullie had long stopped being surprised by Sprite's choice of a simple breakfast, but the embarrassment still clung to her like a second skin. It pierced through especially sharply when she ran into Mr. Salene, their landlord, whose judgment seemed as inevitable as the dawn. His gaze lingered on the modest meal in her hands, and she could almost hear the unspoken critique hanging in the air, a reminder of the disparity between her choices and the expectations that loomed over her.

Mr. Salene reminded Sprite that next month marked the deadline for their annual rent payment, but he offered an extension if her finances were tight. His kindness was genuine, yet it only deepened Sprite's unease, making her feel as though she were teetering on the edge of a precipice she couldn't quite escape. The religious Q&A on the radio had wrapped up, giving way to the next program—a chaotic mix of interviews, songs, and the latest so-called breaking news. The radio host was now chatting with a young entrepreneur from the real estate world, probing into his secrets for balancing business success with family life. The abrupt transition from solemn religious talk to upbeat commercial chatter felt like a jarring shift in the soundtrack of Sprite's day, underscoring her sense of disconnection from the world around her.

Sprite had a vague notion of what real estate entailed—people like Mr. Salene who dealt in apartments, land, and rental properties. But the real estate entrepreneur being interviewed sounded nothing like him. His speech lacked the religious undertones that characterized Mr. Salene, who frequently peppered his conversations with *praise the Lord*. As the Q&A wrapped up, the host pivoted to breaking news: tales of waterlogged streets, football scores, and the latest robbery reports. It was a stark shift from the solemn religious talk that had dominated earlier, leaving Sprite feeling as if she were caught between two worlds, neither of which offered her any solace.

"Here's the latest update on the criminal case: Authorities have confirmed that the murder of Mrs. T, which occurred two days ago, was indeed a robbery gone wrong. As we reported earlier, the incident unfolded early in the morning on the roadside, roughly one hundred yards from the entrance to Bronx Heritage Suites. Mrs. T, a forty-year-old resident of the complex, was discovered dead in her car, a fatal wound to her neck inflicted by a sharp object. Investigators believe her wallet, phone, and necklace were among the items taken. At this time, the perpetrator remains at large, a specter lurking in the shadows, raising the specter of fear in the community."

Sprite shivered at the news. From the moment she'd first heard about the case, she'd suspected it was tied to theft or robbery, but hearing that one of the stolen items was a piece of jewelry sent a cold ripple of unease through her. It felt as if the shadow of the crime had reached out, touching something deeply unsettling within her, stirring a primal fear that coiled tight in her gut. The world outside suddenly felt more dangerous, a dark undercurrent rippling just beneath the surface of her everyday life.

She halted her sewing, a sudden chill gripping her. Reaching into the pocket of her sweatpants, she retrieved the mysterious necklace she had been keeping hidden. Carefully, she drew it out, shielding it from view beneath the sewing machine table. Fear coiled tight in her chest as she examined every inch of the necklace—each chain link and the pendant—her hands trembling as if the shadows of the crime might leap from the necklace itself. In that moment, it felt less like an innocent piece of jewelry and more like a sinister token, a thread connecting her to a dark, unfolding mystery she couldn't quite comprehend.

She promised herself that if she spotted even a single trace of blood on the necklace, she'd call the police immediately. But as she scrutinized it, she found no crimson stains, no telltale signs of the horror that had unfolded. The necklace remained disturbingly clean, its surface untouched by the blood that might have linked it to the crime. Instead, it glimmered innocently, a chilling contrast to the grim reality surrounding her, as if it were taunting her with its pristine façade, daring her to draw connections that simply weren't there.

I'm being way too paranoid, Sprite thought, but the unease clung to her like a second skin, wrapping her in a suffocating layer of doubt.

What she'd experienced last night defied all reason, but that didn't mean she should connect it to the recent murder case. The events felt too surreal, too out of the ordinary, yet her mind stubbornly circled back, searching for a link where there might be none. It was a dangerous game, threading shadows into her reality, but she couldn't shake the feeling that something deeper was at play, lurking just beneath the surface of her ordinary life.

She slipped the necklace back into her pocket and returned to her sewing, but the clatter of the machine barely masked the gnawing fear inside her. This necklace wasn't just a trinket; it was expensive, the kind of luxury only someone with deep pockets could afford. It felt heavy against her thigh, a reminder of the secrets it held and the danger it might invite, tightening the grip of anxiety in her chest as she tried to focus on the rhythmic hum of the machine.

Despite his strange behavior the night before, Ajee remained unemployed—a grim reminder of how little had changed in his life. The days blurred together, each one a dull echo of the last, with his hopes of finding work slipping further away like shadows at dusk.

Sprite had never seen him work or earn a dime since he'd been laid off. So how could he afford to buy meat, cook dinner, and present her with this necklace? The question gnawed at her, a dark undercurrent to the unease that churned within, like a persistent whisper warning her that something was terribly amiss.

Maybe he stole it. Maybe he robbed someone to get it. The thought slithered into her mind, unsettling and sinister, casting a pall over everything she'd seen and heard. It wrapped around her thoughts like a cold, creeping fog, obscuring the truth and turning her trust into doubt.

Sprite knew, despite Ajee's constant irritations, that he was fundamentally straightforward—a man whose honesty was as stark as it was unwavering. The thought of him doing something like that felt like a slap to her senses, a distortion of everything she believed to be true about him. It clashed with the essence of who he was, as if the mere suggestion was too grotesque to entertain, a dark shadow threatening to swallow the light of her trust.

But after last night with Ajee, doubt began to creep in, unsettling her. Sprite knew she wasn't a detective, a cop, or a journalist, but the fear gnawing at her was impossible to ignore. Suddenly, she shut off the sewing machine, stood up, and glanced around, her heart racing with a jittery, uneasy alertness. It was as if the walls themselves were closing in, whispering secrets she wasn't ready to confront.

Ajee lingered at the window, oblivious to her watchful eyes, while the apartment wrapped around her like a shroud. The silence pressed down on her, heavy and oppressive, as if the walls themselves were bearing witness to her mounting unease.

With a furtive motion, she glided into the kitchen and gently shifted the cupboard aside to reach her hidden stash. There lay her diary, cradled in its secret nook—untouched and safe, like a forgotten relic tucked away from prying eyes, holding the weight of unspoken truths within its pages.

She tucked the necklace into the same crevice, nestling it beside the diary. Just then, the starling erupted with a screech, its call slicing through the silence with an eerie intensity that sent a shiver down her spine.

Doctor was screeching again, the sound cutting through the quiet like a jagged blade. Sprite's heart thudded in her chest, each frantic beat a drumroll teetering on the edge of silence.

She shoved the cupboard back into place, her hands trembling as she checked and rechecked her hiding spot, making sure it was secure. The last time Doctor had screeched like this was the night before—when Ajee, in that moment, had seemed to morph into someone she barely recognized, a stranger lurking behind his familiar face.

She moved swiftly toward the window, her pulse quickening with each step. Just a few feet from the door, she saw Ajee with Doctor in his hands, pulling the bird from its cage. The screeching hadn't stopped—whether it was joy or terror, Sprite couldn't tell, but the sound chilled her all the same. Something in the way Ajee held the bird felt... off.

"Ajee," Sprite called, her voice quivering like the faint tremor before a storm. "What are you planning to do with Doctor?" Her words hung in the air, fragile, as if she already knew she didn't want to hear the answer, but couldn't stop herself from asking.

Ajee turned to face Sprite, and a slow, deliberate smile crept across his face. For a heartbeat, Sprite swore the world froze around her. That smile—it had warmth, even sweetness, but beneath it lurked something darker, something disturbingly commanding. It wasn't the smile of the man she'd married; it was the smile of someone in control, someone with secrets.

"You know, babe," Ajee said, his smile never faltering, "why did God give birds a pair of wings?" His tone was light, almost playful, but the question hung in the air like a shadow, and Sprite felt the chill of it creep into her bones. That smile—it stayed fixed, unsettlingly steady, as if there was something more behind the words than just idle curiosity.

"Yeah," Sprite replied, but the word felt thin, hollow. In her mind, the answer seemed so obvious—*so they can fly, right?*—but something about the way Ajee asked the question made her uneasy. It was as if there was more to it, something darker lurking just beneath the surface, waiting to take flight.

"Exactly, so they can fly," Ajee said, his voice soft, but there was an eerie edge to it, like he could read the unspoken words in her head. "Keeping a bird in a cage is like going against God's plan." Without waiting for a response, he opened his hands, releasing Doctor into the air. The bird took off in a frantic flurry of wings, a small, panicked blur against the dull morning light.

The bird fluttered briefly, its wings beating the air in a desperate burst of freedom, only to settle on the cold iron bench. There it sat, unnervingly still, as though it had been carved from stone. The world around it seemed to hold its breath, frozen in an eerie, unnatural pause.

Sprite could feel the bird's unblinking gaze locked on her, its beady eyes glittering with a strange, silent urgency. It was as if it were trying to tell her something, some dark secret fluttering just out of reach. But no matter how hard she strained, the meaning eluded her, slipping through her mind like a half-remembered nightmare.

Moments later, Doctor burst into flight again, its shrill, frantic chirps cutting through the stillness like a warning bell. In a blur of feathers, the bird disappeared behind the hackberry tree and the roof of the next building. And then, just like that, it was gone. The silence that followed felt suffocating, as if the whole world had narrowed down to just the two of them—Sprite, Ajee, and the empty cage between them, standing like a monument to something lost, its emptiness humming with a cold, hollow finality.

9

After Doctor left, Ajee slipped away, dissolving into the cracks of time like a shadow swallowed by dusk—gone, without a trace, never to be seen again.

From that day on, every time Sprite stirred awake, blinking sleep from her eyes, he was there—a man with a grin so warm it could melt the frost off a Maine winter morning. He'd lean in close, his lips brushing her forehead. "Good morning," he'd murmur, his voice smooth and soft, like the sweetest dream she never wanted to wake from.

On the table beside the bed sat a plate of bagels with cream cheese and lox, the scent of the tea beside it curling through the air like a warm, invisible blanket, wrapping around her. It was the kind of comfort that settled in her bones, a quiet, familiar presence she couldn't resist.

But every now and then, on certain days, she saw something different in him—a flicker of restlessness, like a man who could feel the shadows creeping closer, stretching longer, as if he knew they were coming for him.

He'd burst through the door, hair still dripping, the towel barely clinging to him, like some ghost from another world. That same ageless grin teased Sprite, always familiar, never changing. He'd stand in front of the wardrobe mirror, combing his damp hair, humming tunes Sprite could never quite place, like echoes from some lost, forgotten corner of time. Dinner was often his ritual, though the romance of candlelight had flickered out long ago.

Instead, he'd come home with greasy takeout—chicken over rice or slices of New York-style pizza. At first, Sprite's stomach recoiled at the change, rebelling against this bold, brash menu. Mornings were bagels slathered with cream cheese and lox, nights dominated by pizza from the city that never slept. She couldn't deny it—the food was mouthwatering, every bite a burst of flavor. But deep down, there was a truth gnawing at her, something stubborn and unshakable: if you hadn't tasted potatoes, you hadn't really eaten.

More often than not, she found herself doubling up on breakfast. At work, she'd slip away to a corner stand, grabbing grits with a side of oatmeal and crispy hash browns. It wasn't a betrayal, not really—just a quiet indulgence she kept from Ajee. Not out of deceit, but to spare his feelings, as if the truth might crumble something fragile between them.

She didn't want to tear at the delicate fabric of his affections with the truth of her secret cravings. Some truths, she knew, could cut deeper than lies.

Ajee might blow his top, convinced she was snubbing his efforts, or worse, that Sprite was nothing more than a cold, ungrateful soul. It wouldn't take much—just a spark to set off the kind of fire that leaves nothing but ash behind.

Sprite couldn't quite make sense of this new version of Ajee. It was like trying to grasp smoke—familiar, but slipping through her fingers every time she thought she had a hold of it.

He was an enigma, disappearing each day into shadows that had no names, yet always managing to beat her home. Tonight, he was there, waiting with bagels laid out and two steaming cups of Peet's Coffee. With a sly wink, he called it a little treat, a slice of normalcy in their unraveling world. As they snacked, he gestured toward the living room, inviting Sprite to sit and share the details of her day, as if everything were perfectly fine—even when she knew better.

"Not much, really. We had a big meeting at the office today, all the bosses in one room. A bunch of directors showed up. I made coffee for them, cleaned up after, then hung out with Thyme in the pantry. Luckily, no overtime, so I got to head home early," Sprite said, taking a sip of the coffee. Its bold, rich flavor lingered on her tongue, a comforting warmth that wrapped around her like a soft blanket.

"Oh yeah? So, what do you and Thyme, your best friend, usually talk about?" Ajee asked, sinking his teeth into a plain bagel, as if the answer could be found in its doughy depths.

"Mostly, I just listen to her vent. She goes on about who she's vibing with and who's trying to chase her," Sprite replied, a hint of amusement in her voice, like she was sharing a secret from a world just outside their door.

Their conversations were often dominated by Sprite's stories, her words spilling out like a river—flooding the space between them, carrying with them the weight of her world.

Every time she tried to dig into Ajee's day, he deflected, deftly steering the conversation away. When Sprite pushed a little harder, pressing for answers, he silenced her with a kiss—sweeping her off her feet and carrying her to the bedroom before she could utter another word.

Sprite usually never turned down her husband's advances; she felt it was her duty to satisfy him in bed—anytime, anywhere. But this time, it wasn't just obligation; she craved it too. They made love with an intensity that left her utterly drained, slipping into a deep, dreamless sleep. Yet in that slumber, Ajee vanished once again, like a shadow dissolving into the night, leaving only silence in his wake.

Sprite first sensed something was off when she woke at two in the morning—a time she usually reserved for her night prayers—and found Ajee's side of the bed cold and empty. She pushed herself out of bed, her head spinning from the sudden movement, waiting for the dizziness to pass. Once steady, she made her way to the bathroom. The door was closed, and the sound of water dripping from the faucet echoed in the stillness of the night, unnervingly loud in the thick silence, amplifying the tension in the air.

Sprite always kept the bathroom door closed, even when it was empty—she couldn't bear the sight of the exposed interior. She knocked, expecting some sort of response, but was met with silence. Slowly, she pushed the door open, surprised to find it unlocked. The bathroom was empty, as if no one had ever been there. Yet her curiosity gnawed at her, leaving a restless ache that refused to be satisfied.

Sprite hurried to the kitchen, a flicker of hope igniting in her chest—maybe Ajee was up to something, cooking in the dead of night, stirring up a secret just for her.

Maybe he was making hot dogs or brewing coffee—nothing was out of the question, considering his recent quirks. But when Sprite reached the kitchen, it was deserted, save for a stack of clean plates and glasses by the sink, left to dry like forgotten dreams. The apartment felt small, almost claustrophobic. If someone wasn't in the bedroom, kitchen, or bathroom, they were simply gone—swallowed by the night, leaving only silence behind.

Sprite walked to the front room, her heart pounding in her chest, before making her way to the front door. Her fingers gripped the cold iron handle, and her heart nearly stopped when she realized the door was locked—a chilling reminder that the world outside was still out there, beyond her reach.

Sprite peered through the keyhole, but it was empty—nothing dangled there. Normally, the key hung there every night, a familiar sentinel. Its absence sent a chill down her spine, a stark reminder that the door had been locked from the outside, trapping her in a cocoon of uncertainty.

Still in shock, she flicked on the living room light and scanned the table, the top of the TV, and every shadowy corner of the room. Not a single key was in sight. Panic clawed at her throat as she tried to force the door open, but it wouldn't budge. It was definitely locked from the outside, and with no other exits in the apartment, Sprite realized she was effectively trapped. Where could her husband have vanished to, leaving her in this suffocating silence?

She yanked on the door with every ounce of strength she had, but it remained stubbornly shut, a silent sentinel against her desperation. The door was heavy, crafted from rich, antique wood that felt far too luxurious for such an old apartment, as if it held secrets of its own, whispering them into the dark.

Maybe Ajee had locked her in out of anger, a cruel act born from some hidden resentment lurking just beneath the surface, twisting their lives into a chilling game she never wanted to play.

Maybe she'd done something to set him off, to poke at the simmering anger he kept buried deep inside, like a ticking time bomb waiting for the slightest spark.

Maybe he'd slipped away to indulge in secrets he didn't want her to uncover. Perhaps Ajee was sneaking off to some mistress's place, sharing stolen moments with another woman right after being with his wife, weaving a web of betrayal that tightened around them both.

Yes, Sprite had read it again—an article linked on a Facebook page—that warned of the telltale signs of a cheating man: a sudden shift in behavior. The guilt from the affair twisted him into an overly sweet and accommodating husband, as if trying to erase the stains of betrayal. But this forced, unnatural change felt excessive and eerie, striking a chilling resemblance to Ajee's recent behavior.

She struggled to piece together the fragments, her mind racing in a chaotic dance to make sense of the disjointed shards. Each thought felt like a puzzle piece that refused to fit, leaving her teetering on the edge of confusion.

By day, Ajee toiled away at work, but by night, he vanished into the shadows to meet his mistress. Was there a link between his new job and those secret rendezvous? Could it be that her husband had taken on the life of a gigolo, all to support her? The thought spun her head in a whirlwind of disbelief, each possibility more outrageous than the last.

Sprite fought against the dizziness, grasping for a sliver of hope as she struggled to think positively. Steadying her breathing, she tried to convince herself that maybe Ajee had no choice but to lock the door from the outside—perhaps it was a temporary measure, a momentary lapse in judgment, not a betrayal.

Perhaps he hadn't wanted to disturb her deep sleep, and leaving the door unlocked at two in the morning was simply out of the question—a thought that twisted like a vine around her mind, tightening with every passing second.

In her mind's eye, she envisioned Ajee leaning in to kiss her forehead while she slept, moving with the utmost care, as if afraid to shatter the spell of her deep, rumbling slumber.

Then, he would slip out of the apartment like a shadow, leaving her alone in the quiet. Where could he be headed? Off to work, perhaps? Or into the arms of someone else?

Considering the lavish meals and luxurious items he'd been bringing home lately to pamper her, he might be pulling extra shifts at night, working more than he'd ever let on—a dark secret wrapped in the guise of generosity.

She couldn't decide which theory seemed more plausible. Sprite pulled back the curtain and peered out the window onto the street. Everything appeared as it always did—the plant pots in their usual spots, the bench undisturbed, and the sidewalk devoid of footprints. The only movement came from the leaves fluttering in the night breeze, dancing like whispers of a secret, as if they had swept Ajee away with them.

She flicked on the television, desperate to shatter the oppressive silence. Since childhood, whenever loneliness loomed and fear crept in, she had turned on the TV or radio. There was something soothing about the hum of voices and the flicker of screens—a comforting illusion of company, as if invisible friends were sharing her space. The noise drowned out the faint, eerie sounds of the wind rustling outside and the persistent drip of water in the bathroom, wrapping her in a cocoon of distraction.

She flipped through the channels, landing on nothing but reruns of old movies and endless basketball games. *Basketball!* The thought struck her—maybe Ajee had slipped out to catch a game somewhere, lost in the crowd and the chaos, leaving her to wrestle with her growing unease.

In the past, he'd often gathered with neighbors in the apartment next door or wandered over to Sugma's coffee shop, which was open around the clock for just such occasions. But since losing his job, he'd been relegated to watching games alone at home, trapped in the silence of their apartment. Now, who knew—maybe his old habits had resurfaced. On the screen, two unfamiliar teams darted across the court. Perhaps it was the NBA, or maybe just another mirage in a fading world.

Sprite had tried to embrace basketball, convincing herself it was a way to bridge the gap between them. She felt no obligation to like the sport—after all, why should she?—but the hope lingered that sharing a common interest with Ajee might draw them closer. Besides, women who indulged in traditionally masculine interests were often regarded as more intriguing, more appealing, like rare collectibles in a world full of mundane trinkets.

Take Thyme, her coworker—she was a basketball aficionado and an action movie junkie, a whirlwind of energy wrapped in a slightly tomboyish exterior. This young woman had a legion of male friends and a social circle that sprawled out like a well-worn map, her laughter echoing in crowded bars and bustling cafés where Sprite felt out of place, like a shadow in a vibrant painting.

Yet, Sprite let the thought drift away like smoke on a breeze, fully aware that Ajee wouldn't take kindly to it. The last thing she wanted was to stir the pot and watch it boil over, especially when the tension between them felt like a tightrope walk on a windy day.

Ajee had little patience for tomboyish women; to him, they were a jarring disruption of the natural order. In his eyes, a woman's role was to embody gentleness, love, and nurturing—qualities he clung to like a lifeline in a world that often felt chaotic and unruly.

Sprite wasn't sure if Ajee still clung to those outdated beliefs, but the uncertainty gnawed at her. Amid the endless drone of the basketball commentator, she cast furtive glances out the window, straining to catch a glimpse of anyone—Ajee—passing by the iron-barred entrance. It wasn't that she was eager to leave; she had no intention of going anywhere, especially not at this hour, but the weight of confinement pressed heavily on her, wrapping around her like a shroud.

She just needed to convince herself that she wasn't a prisoner in her own home, held captive by the man who was supposed to protect her. But the figure she longed to see never materialized, leaving her to grapple with the chilling thought that perhaps she was alone in more ways than one.

She stole a glance at the wall clock—three in the morning already. The thought of taking a ritual bath and performing her night prayer flickered through her mind like a dying ember, but before she could summon the energy, her eyelids grew heavy, weighed down by an invisible force, pulling her into a darkness that felt both inviting and unnerving.

She could no longer distinguish where wakefulness ended and sleep began; the TV's noise melded into a soft murmur, like distant waves crashing on an unseen shore. Less than half an hour later, she lay sprawled on the floor, deep in slumber. Through the fog of her dreams, she faintly registered a door creaking open and footsteps drawing nearer. Then, a sensation, unsettling yet gentle, enveloped her as her body was lifted and carried away, drifting further from reality.

10

When her eyes fluttered open, they fell upon Ajee's reflection—distorted, ghostly, like a wraith trapped in the tarnished glass of the wardrobe mirror. It was as if the mirror had captured a fleeting moment, a whisper from the past she wasn't sure she wanted to remember, a secret lurking just beneath the surface, waiting to be uncovered.

He fidgeted with his tie, the knot pulled snug against his plain white shirt like a noose tightening around his neck. There was something deeply unsettling about seeing her husband dressed like this, as if that tie were a shackle, binding him to a version of himself that felt both foreign and ominous—a man lost in a costume he never chose, haunted by shadows of who he used to be.

In all her years, Sprite had never seen Ajee like this—dressed as if he'd stepped straight out of a fever dream. The only semblance of neatness in his wardrobe had been a wrinkled white shirt and black pants, and if you dared to stretch the definition of neat, those gaudy wedding clothes that felt more like a bad joke than anything resembling formalwear. This new look hung on him like a mask, hiding the man she thought she knew, and in that moment, he felt more like a stranger than ever.

Sprite felt an odd urge to tie Ajee's tie herself, a whimsical impulse stirred by the soap opera fantasies that danced in her mind. She imagined scenes from those melodramas—wives cinching ties on their husbands, whether steely-eyed CEOs or hapless door-to-door salesmen, just before they trudged off to their daily grind. What was it about ties? Was there some inscrutable mystery woven into their fabric? Did those soap opera wives also knot their husbands' shoelaces and button their collar ties, as if each twist and tug unraveled some great cosmic riddle, a secret that lay just out of reach?

Sprite recalled the last time she'd wrestled with a tie—it was back in her school days. After a few fumbling attempts with the old-fashioned kind, she had abandoned it for one of those instant ties with a clasp at the back. It was all about practicality, a clever way to sidestep the morning scramble and the ever-looming menace of tardiness that hung over every school day like a dark cloud. Now, her nose felt a bit clogged, her throat scratchy and raw, but despite the discomfort, she could still catch the lingering traces of Ajee's perfume and the unmistakable scent of his hair oil. It clung to the air like a ghost of something familiar, haunting her senses even as her body betrayed her, a bittersweet reminder of a world she desperately wanted to hold onto.

She had never quite grasped the allure of men's perfume, but this one was different. It didn't hit you like a sledgehammer; instead, it wrapped around you like a comforting shroud. Subtle and almost soothing, it stirred a quiet sense of ease that melted away the world's harsh edges, leaving behind a lingering warmth, like a soft embrace on a chilly evening.

"Hey, next time don't crash on the floor—you're gonna catch a cold," Ajee said, his eyes flicking toward her in the mirror's reflection, a mix of concern and exasperation dancing in their depths.

His tie was fastened with meticulous precision, as if it were a delicate artifact held together by some unseen force. It secured more than just fabric; it seemed to tether a sliver of his sanity, binding him to a version of himself he could barely recognize.

In the shadowy corners of her heart, she wondered when her husband ever slept. Did he even rest at all, or was he forever adrift in a restless, sleepless void, a shadow wandering through the night, haunted by unspoken fears?

Sprite shot up, fumbling around her pillow until she snatched her hair tie from the bed, pulling her hair back with urgency. She used to rely on Erie's salon for all her hair needs, but since Timothye, Erie's assistant, had left and her budget took a nosedive, she'd resorted to doing it herself. "So, where'd you disappear to last night?" Sprite asked, a hint of curiosity mixed with accusation in her voice.

It felt almost unnatural to call Ajee anything at all these days. Terms like *darling* or *babe* might have suited him better, but the thought of using them now filled her with unease. The silence that followed hung heavy in the air, an empty echo that swallowed her words and left her with the oppressive weight of unspoken things, as if the air itself conspired to keep them apart.

Ajee just whistled, as if her question hadn't pierced his ears at all, despite Sprite's certainty that she'd spoken loud and clear. It was a defiant, almost eerie silence, as if he'd consciously chosen not to hear her—or worse, as if he was deliberately tuning her out, letting the tension hang in the air like a thick fog that refused to lift.

"Ajee," Sprite called out again, hugging herself for warmth. A shiver crept over her, a cold wave that hinted she was on the verge of coming down with something, like a dark cloud settling over her, ready to unleash a storm.

The silence persisted, thick and unyielding, as if the very air conspired to swallow any response whole, wrapping around her like a heavy shroud that smothered the words before they could escape.

Ajee continued to whistle, the sound low and persistent, as he methodically worked the comb through his hair. The tune lingered in the air, an eerie counterpoint to the deliberate, almost mechanical motion of his grooming, each stroke of the comb echoing like a heartbeat in the tense silence surrounding them.

Feeling brushed aside, Sprite turned inward, her mind racing with doubts. Maybe her hunch was right—her husband was angry with her. But what had she done to deserve this cold shoulder? The question gnawed at her, a relentless itch she couldn't scratch, burrowing deeper into her thoughts like a persistent splinter, reminding her of a past she couldn't quite grasp.

She rifled through her memories of the past three days, searching for something—anything—that stood out. But everything felt disturbingly ordinary, each moment blending into the next with an unsettling normalcy, like a bland wallpaper that concealed the cracks lurking beneath the surface.

She was at a loss, her every move dictated by Ajee's constant caretaking. So thoroughly pampered that she felt utterly powerless, a familiar cause suddenly flickered in her mind—the same old reason that always sparked Ajee's cynicism. Without a second thought, she bolted from the room, her hurried steps so frantic that she nearly stumbled over the small threshold at the door. She had to move fast, urgency driving her forward like a whisper of dread on her heels.

If she didn't act quickly, Ajee would vanish into the shadows of his enigmatic new job once more, slipping away into the dark corners of his secrecy like a wraith fading into the night, leaving her alone to grapple with the growing sense of dread.

She hurried into the kitchen, filled the kettle with water, and set it to boil on the stove. As the water heated, she reached for the tin of ground coffee, scooping out two generous spoonfuls into a cup. It was Ajee's favorite—a simple ivory mug with delicate blue trees etched on one side, a small comfort amid her growing unease. A small smile crept onto her face, amused by the realization that she knew this little detail about her husband. Maybe their relationship wasn't as hollow as she'd feared after all. Before long, the coffee was ready, its rich, familiar aroma flooding the kitchen, wrapping around her like a warm embrace.

She sprinkled a teaspoon of granulated sugar into the cup, watching as the crystals dissolved into the dark brew, swirling like tiny stars vanishing into the abyss, adding a touch of sweetness to the mix that contrasted with the bitterness of her thoughts.

Ajee wasn't one for coffee that was too sweet, but he couldn't stand it too bitter, either. "Sweet coffee's for wimps, bitter coffee's for shamans," he'd always say, his voice laced with that signature mix of jest and seriousness that left her unsure whether to laugh or roll her eyes.

She set the cup of coffee on a small plate, preparing to bring it to Ajee. The last time she'd done this was when he had come home with the news of his layoff, the weight of that moment still lingering in her mind like a shadow that refused to fade.

Now, as she stood there, she couldn't shake the nagging thought of why she was doing this again, especially with Ajee's unsettling behavior lately. Was she afraid he might be seeing another woman—someone more attentive, someone who made his coffee with a little more care? The thought gnawed at her, a dark seed of doubt taking root in her mind, spreading its tendrils through her thoughts like an insidious vine choking out the light.

Before Sprite could leave the kitchen with the coffee, Ajee poked his head around the wall. "What're you up to?" he asked, a smile tugging at his lips as his eyes landed on the cup in her hand, a spark of curiosity dancing in his gaze that momentarily chased away the shadows hanging over them.

That smile made Sprite's heart melt. If only Ajee had worn that smile more often from the start of their marriage, perhaps her life would have been a bit brighter, a little less burdened by the weight of regret that clung to her like a second skin.

"This coffee's for you," Sprite said, her voice soft as she held out the cup, her hand trembling slightly as if the simple gesture carried the weight of unspoken words between them.

"Thanks," Ajee replied, walking over to Sprite, his steps measured yet casual, as if the moment held more significance than either of them dared to acknowledge.

They stood there, eye to eye, an uncomfortable silence stretching between them like a taut wire ready to snap. The moment felt painfully awkward for Sprite until Ajee finally reached out and took the cup from her hand. Their fingers brushed, and a strange tingle shot through her, leaving her bewildered. Why did it feel like they were newlyweds all over again, caught in that fleeting magic they once had but thought long gone?

Ajee lifted the edge of the cup to his lips, giving it a quick, practiced blow before taking a sip. It struck Sprite that this might be the only thing that hadn't changed about him—the ritual of savoring his coffee, a small, stubborn remnant of the man she once knew, like a flickering candle in a darkened room, defiantly holding onto its light.

Sprite wasn't a coffee aficionado like her husband. When she did indulge, she usually opted for white coffee or one with a splash of milk. Yet, there was something about Ajee's methodical, almost reverent way of sipping his coffee that always piqued her curiosity, making her wonder if it tasted as exceptional as he made it seem, as if each sip held the secrets of the universe, waiting to be uncovered.

After placing the coffee cup back on the table, Ajee turned to Sprite and smiled, his expression softening the edges of their tension. "Merci," he said, the word hanging in the air like a fragile truce.

Sprite hesitated, her mind racing as she pondered whether *je vous en prie* was the right French reply to *you're welcome*. In the end, she simply nodded and smiled before hurrying to the bathroom, where the faucet still ran and the tub was already overflowing. After shutting off the water, she emerged to find Ajee by the door, buttoning the cuffs of his long sleeves with a methodical precision that made her heart quicken. Next to him stood a rectangular work bag, its serious demeanor mirroring the tension that crackled in the air between them.

Once again, Sprite was struck by the unsettling realization that Ajee possessed such an item. The sight of it sent a shiver through her, as if each new discovery drew her deeper into a web of disquieting revelations, wrapping around her like an inescapable trap.

Noticing Sprite standing behind him, Ajee turned and grinned, a flash of warmth cutting through the tension. "I'm heading out, babe," he said, the casual endearment feeling both familiar and foreign, like a ghost of the intimacy they once shared.

"Yeah, be careful out there," Sprite replied, her voice trembling just beneath the surface as she fought to keep it steady, each word a fragile tether to the moment they shared, a reminder of the distance that loomed between them.

Ajee's hands tightened on Sprite's shoulders, his grip a mix of reassurance and an unsettling possessiveness, as if he were trying to anchor her in a moment that felt precariously close to slipping away.

He leaned in and pressed a kiss to her forehead, the touch lingering with an unspoken weight, as if he were trying to anchor them both in a moment that felt as fragile as glass, teetering on the edge of breaking under the pressure of everything left unsaid.

Sprite was stunned, the moment feeling surreal—like she had stepped into a TV show where everything was scripted and polished, each emotion exaggerated and larger than life, leaving her questioning the reality of what was unfolding around her.

The only thing missing was a school-aged kid in a crisp uniform, leaning in to plant a quick kiss on her cheek while chirping, "I'm off to school, Mom," a simple scene that would have felt like the icing on the absurd cake of her surreal existence.

And she would respond with something like, "Study hard, my child. Always be diligent, and you'll surely succeed." But she shoved that fantasy deep into the recesses of her mind, a hidden corner where dreams went to gather dust. Over their five years of marriage, she'd endured countless questions from neighbors and family about why she wasn't pregnant, each inquiry a tiny dagger twisting deeper into her heart.

Every conversation about having children felt like a slow descent into arguments, each exchange echoing with the same painful notes of frustration and despair. Eventually, they'd agreed to drop the topic altogether, a silent truce that hung between them like fog. For her, the question of whether they would have a child was a matter of fate—if the time was right, it would happen. Until then, it lingered in the air like a shadow, a dark uncertainty that taunted her from the edges of her thoughts.

Ajee stepped out of the apartment, casting one last smile over his shoulder, his wave almost too casual—as if trying to wipe away the earlier tension with a flick of his wrist. Sprite's hand moved instinctively in response, but her mind was elsewhere. Across the street, a neighbor sat on a bench, feeding her grandchild, her gaze fixed on them with a mix of curiosity and quiet suspicion, as if trying to unravel the enigma of their fleeting exchange.

Sprite suddenly realized she needed a plausible explanation for when the neighbors inevitably questioned Ajee's sudden change in behavior. It was Sunday—what kind of work actually gets done on a Sunday? Certainly not the sort of office work most people would recognize. Could Ajee have become a salesman, or had he somehow fallen into the clutches of a successful MLM hustler? The possibilities twisted in her mind, each one more unsettling than the last. As she made her way to the kitchen, her thoughts spiraled. It wasn't far-fetched; not long ago, a colleague had tried to pitch Ajee on an MLM scheme—promising passive income, flexible hours, mountains of bonuses, cruises, and exotic trips. Those promises had sounded almost too good to be true, and now she couldn't shake the gnawing feeling that he might have been ensnared by them.

Sprite had taken the plunge, sacrificing her own pocket money for the registration fee. But after just a month, the relentless pressure from her overly aggressive upline drove her to the brink. Each relentless pitch and high-pressure tactic chipped away at her resolve, until she felt drained and disillusioned, like a deflated balloon tossed aside after a party.

Maybe Ajee had indeed dived headfirst into an MLM, rapidly ascending the ranks to become a model member. But what kind of upline or motivator could have brainwashed the stubborn Ajee so completely that his attitude shifted overnight? Whoever this person was, they had to be nothing short of extraordinary—some kind of charismatic sorcerer, wielding words like spells, ensnaring even the most resistant minds.

As Sprite continued to mumble about these unsettling possibilities, she picked up the coffee cup, preparing to wash it out. That's when she noticed there was still more than half a cup left. It struck her—Ajee didn't like her coffee. The realization hit like a sharp, uncomfortable jab, a fresh detail on an ever-growing list of things she couldn't quite grasp.

As she washed the cup, Sprite clung to a shaky optimism, trying to convince herself that it wasn't half full but half empty. It was a feeble attempt to fend off the creeping sense of defeat, as if reframing the situation could somehow alter the stark reality lurking just beyond her grasp.

Tragedy Strikes Bronx Heritage Suites: Businessman Found Dead Alongside Security Guard and Housekeeper

Mott Haven, NY — In a shocking incident, businessman Chancy Dare, 50, known for his café and restaurant, was found dead in his home located in the Bronx Heritage Suites residential area. The victim was discovered lifeless on his sofa with the television still on, raising concerns over the circumstances surrounding his death.

Authorities reported that Chancy was likely murdered, with signs indicating he may have been strangled with a cord, as evidenced by marks on his body. This tragic case has taken an even darker turn, as it also claimed the lives of a security guard and a housekeeper, both of whom were found dead with multiple stab wounds.

The grim discoveries were made the following day by Chancy Dare's driver. At the time of the incident, the driver was away from the residence, attending to his family, which included accompanying his wife and child on an overnight trip.

Police suspect that the incident is related to robbery and are investigating connections to two other robbery cases that occurred at Bronx Heritage Suites. Investigators revealed that four CCTV cameras in the vicinity were found to be inoperable, while the remaining footage captured only a shadowy figure passing through on the night of the incident.

As the community grapples with this tragic loss, police are urging anyone with information related to the case to come forward. Further updates are expected as the investigation continues into this disturbing event that has shaken the neighborhood.

11

In the dim light of the kitchen, she saw it—a smudge, small but unmistakable. Blood red. The kind of color that screams danger and whispers secrets in the dark corners of your mind, where you don't want to go.

She'd seen that shade before, and it sure as hell wasn't from her own tube. That red, it had a history—late-night meetings, quiet lies, and the kind of betrayal that twists the knife. As she stared at that damn stain, a cold certainty wrapped around her like a noose. This wasn't just lipstick—it was a bold, blood-red announcement that another woman had been here, maybe even in the bed they once shared. The truth didn't whisper—it screamed.

If she had any guts, she'd burst into the room, questions flying like bullets, tearing into his lies until the truth bled out. She'd back him into a corner, make him squirm, expose everything. But if fear had its claws in her, she'd scrub that mark off, all the while tucking it away in the back of her mind, a dark secret festering. She'd become a shadow, haunting his every move, gathering the pieces of his deceit, unraveling just how deep this betrayal really went—until it swallowed them both whole.

This morning, Sprite spotted a red stain on her husband's shirt collar, so faint it could've been a trick of the light. It wasn't the obvious kind of mark that screamed infidelity—more like a ghost of crimson, maybe ketchup, maybe makeup. So small, so easy to ignore, she might have missed it if she wasn't already drowning in her own suspicions. That tiny smear wasn't just a stain; it was a whisper from the shadows, teasing something darker, something she wasn't sure she wanted to uncover.

Driven by a gnawing curiosity, she lifted the damp, white shirt to the window, letting the thin morning light cut across it. As the sun slid over the fabric, the stain sharpened—no longer a faint blur, but something darker, something worse. It wasn't lipstick, she knew that much. What she saw could've been blood, syrup, maybe tomato sauce—each option more unsettling than the last. But deep down, her gut clenched around the first, cold thought that hit her: it was blood. And blood, she knew, told a truth you couldn't wash away.

She couldn't shake the unease that had wormed its way into her thoughts, couldn't understand why her mind had latched onto such a grim possibility. Maybe it was the unsolved robbery and murder case, still hanging like a specter over the neighborhood. Or maybe it was the grim news on the radio, droning from the living room, its dark tidings sinking into her subconscious like poison. Whatever the reason, the thought of blood now felt tied to something far darker than a simple stain—something deeper, more dangerous, lurking just beneath the surface.

"Good morning, New York. In our top story, a man was found dead under gruesome circumstances at his Bronx Heritage Suites residence. Authorities are investigating this as a potential robbery, possibly linked to last week's chilling Mrs. T case. This string of violent incidents has drawn sharp criticism from the community, with growing outrage over lax security at Bronx Heritage Suites and the sluggish response from law enforcement. Once praised as a premier, state-of-the-art complex, Bronx Heritage Suites is now a place where fear is creeping into every hallway. Meanwhile, the developers remain..."

"Now, in our next story, social media is lighting up with disturbing reports of children and homeless individuals being kidnapped by an alleged organ trafficking ring operating in Mott Haven. As of now, authorities have not confirmed the source of these claims, and the police are urging the public to remain cautious. They warn against falling prey to potential hoaxes or the unsettling rumors spiraling online. Still, the whispers are spreading like wildfire, casting a shadow of fear over the neighborhood..."

Sprite dropped the shirt into the bucket, the water and detergent swirling together like some murky, unholy concoction. She attacked the stained area with grim determination, scrubbing and scrubbing as if trying to wipe away not just the mark but the very shadow it cast. When she finally yanked the shirt free, the stain remained, stubborn and defiant—like a dark secret refusing to be buried, mocking her efforts with its persistence.

She attacked the stain with a ferocity that felt almost possessed, scrubbing so hard that her frustrated groans filled the bathroom, her hands moving with a desperation that threatened to shred the shirt. At last, when the damned mark finally vanished, she collapsed onto the cold bathroom floor, drenched and indifferent to her soaked dress. As she struggled to steady her ragged breath, a knock echoed from the door. It was only then she realized the knocking had been relentless, the visitor now calling her name with a growing urgency that sent a chill down her spine.

"Hello?"

Sprite pushed herself up, her damp dress clinging to her like a second skin. She was about to head for the front door, but the haunting image of that shirt pulled her back. With a restless urgency, she spun around and returned to the bathroom, her hands fishing through the soapy water. She sifted through the clothes, fingers fumbling, until she finally unearthed the shirt—a wet, heavy thing that felt as if it carried the weight of her fears. Lifting it, she inspected it with grim resolve, and a wave of relief washed over her when she saw that the red stain was finally gone. Thank God for small mercies.

"Hold on a sec!" She dashed to the front door, her footsteps quick and jittery, as if the urgency of the moment electrified the air around her.

As she crossed the short stretch of hallway, her mind raced with unsettling possibilities. Who could be knocking at her door in the middle of the day while her husband was out? Was it a neighbor, or perhaps Mr. Salene come to collect the rent? Or, God forbid, could it be the police, here to dig into the murder case that had everyone on edge? Just the thought of that sent her heart into a frantic thrum, each beat echoing her rising anxiety, amplifying the tension in the air.

Sprite unlocked the door, her fingers trembling as they wrapped around the handle. She leaned in to peer through, but the view was obscured—a murky blur that revealed nothing. The uncertainty gnawed at her insides, as if the door itself were guarding some dark truth, waiting to be unveiled.

She swung the door open, and there he stood—Waverley.

He stood on the threshold, a solid figure with a thick mustache and a build that suggested he could handle more than just a door. Clad in a gray T-shirt and black trousers, his presence filled the space with an air of unspoken tension, as if he carried secrets heavy enough to crush the silence.

Without hesitation, she threw the door wide open, the motion sharp and decisive, as if she were casting aside the lingering doubts that clung to her like shadows.

Waverley stood there, his head lowered as if weighed down by an invisible burden, his posture cloaked in an aura of quiet resignation that hinted at untold struggles.

Even though his mustache tried to conceal it, Sprite could still make out the downturn of Waverley's lips—a subtle but unmistakable sign of his unhappiness. The frown was there, hidden yet persistent, like a shadow lurking just beneath the surface, waiting for the right moment to emerge.

When he finally lifted his head and met Sprite's gaze, he forced a smile that felt more like a grimace, the strain evident as he struggled to mask whatever darkness lurked behind his eyes.

"Waverley?"

"Afternoon, Sprite. Sorry to drop in like this," he said, his voice tinged with an awkwardness that only deepened the tension in the air.

"Oh, you're here for the order, right? No worries, it's all set," Sprite replied, the words slipping out with an ease that belied her racing thoughts. She remembered Waverley's request, neatly wrapped up the night before. A familiar thought crossed her mind—how he always checked in on his orders whenever they crossed paths, as if he were keeping tabs on more than just business.

The order was crucial, wrapped in a web of significance. Rumor had it that the altered dress had once belonged to his wife, a cherished wedding gown transformed for their daughter's reception. This wasn't just any dress; it was to be the centerpiece of a momentous occasion, a thread woven into the fabric of a family's pivotal night.

Waverley had mentioned the date of his daughter's wedding, but the details had slipped through Sprite's memory like grains of sand. It might be just a week away. That's why, despite battling sleep and the sharp sting of needles pricking her fingers, she had pushed through the night to finish the order. The looming deadline hung over her like a storm cloud, propelling her to work through the weariness and discomfort.

With quiet determination, Sprite turned and headed toward the clothes she had hung by the sewing machine. The fabric held its own secrets, draped there like silent witnesses to her late-night toil, each thread echoing the whispers of her struggles.

But Waverley stopped her with a wave of his hand. "No need to trouble yourself," he said, his voice steady. If he weren't a man of decorum, he might have reached out and grabbed Sprite's wrist to halt her from slipping back inside, the urgency of his unspoken thoughts nearly overwhelming.

Sprite turned back, a frown knitting her brow. "Why not? Haven't you been checking in on it since last week?" Her voice was edged with disbelief, as if the answer held a deeper significance she wasn't ready to confront.

Waverley took a deep breath, his chest rising as if he were bracing for impact. "Well, Sprite..."

Noting Waverley's gestures, which hinted at a long-winded explanation, Sprite motioned for him to step inside. The air between them thickened with unspoken words, a palpable tension settling like dust, and she knew this wasn't going to be a quick chat.

Yet, as he took in the emptiness of the apartment, Waverley opted to settle on the bench outside. He clung to the old-fashioned belief that a gentleman should never step inside a woman's home in her husband's absence, lest he stir up unwelcome suspicions. The stillness of the common hallway felt heavy with judgment, as if the very walls whispered caution, warning him to tread lightly.

Sprite grabbed a glass of water without a word, her mind racing ahead. She could have made tea or coffee, but she had no intention of letting Waverley linger at her front door any longer than necessary. Placing the glass down with a soft clink, she took a seat on the bench beside him, the tension between them settling like a thick fog, suffocating and electric.

"Where are the birds?" he asked, glancing up at the window, now occupied only by a few geckos. "Last time I was here, Ajee had some pet birds, didn't he?" His tone held a hint of nostalgia, as if the absence of their chirping made the air feel a little emptier.

"Oh, they've all been let go. Some were even sold," Sprite replied, her tone casual, as if she were discussing the weather rather than the disappearance of creatures that once filled the room with life.

"Oh, that's a shame," he said, the words slipping out before he could catch them, a hint of disappointment weaving into his voice like a thread of melancholy.

"So, why aren't you picking up the order?" Sprite asked, redirecting the conversation with a measured urgency, her eyes narrowing slightly as she sought answers behind his carefully crafted façade.

Waverley's expression darkened again, the sadness settling in like a stubborn shadow that clung to him, refusing to lift even in the light of day.

He dropped his gaze, and as he spoke, his thick mustache twitched, as if it bore the weight of unspoken burdens. The air around him thickened, heavy with the gravity of whatever he was about to reveal, as though the air itself held its breath.

"The wedding's going to be postponed," he said, the words slipping from his lips like a death knell, heavy with implications that hung in the air between them.

The silence draped over them like a thick, oppressive fog, lingering for a few uneasy seconds. It was the kind of quiet that felt heavy, pregnant with anticipation, as if it were bracing for some dark and foreboding truth to shatter the stillness.

Sprite was at a loss, grappling for the right words to counter the weight of his bad news. It felt as if the very air had been siphoned away, leaving her floundering for a response in the stifling silence that pressed down around them.

Waverley had been mulling over his only child's wedding for what felt like an eternity. He often spoke of his pride in his daughter, especially after she'd completed her degree. To him, orchestrating this wedding was the final chapter of a story he'd been writing for years—a task he was determined to see through, even if it meant draining every last cent from his savings.

"Postponed? I thought it was just around the corner. What happened?" Sprite asked, her voice laced with caution, as if she were stepping onto thin ice.

"Yeah, it was supposed to be soon, but my circumstances won't allow it. I won't be able to cover the remaining balance for you, Sprite. At least the catering and tent have already received their down payments."

"What's really happening here?"

"I lost my job. If you've been following the news, you know there's been a surge of crime in my area—robberies, murders, muggings, kidnappings. That's just the stuff they're willing to report; rumors are swirling like a storm. Residents and developers are pointing fingers at us. I've received multiple warnings. In the end, I'm out of options; they're overhauling housing security because it's been deemed a failure," Waverley said, his words spilling out in a frantic rush.

Sprite was taken aback by his explanation, her mind struggling to absorb the gravity of his words. There was something unsettlingly familiar in Waverley's expression, a flicker of recognition that gnawed at her memory like a long-forgotten dream just out of reach.

She had seen that look before, and it wasn't a good sign. "Waverley, did you get fired?" she asked, a chill creeping in as memories flooded back—like the day Ajee came home with the news that he had lost his job, the air thick with uncertainty and fear.

Could Waverley be grappling with a similar nightmare, poised to deliver the kind of soul-crushing news that could shatter his wife's world? What torment was he enduring as he prepared to tell his daughter that the wedding she'd been dreaming of for so long was now postponed indefinitely? The weight of those words must be suffocating, a dark cloud looming over every syllable he would have to force out.

Sprite could almost feel the weight of his daughter's crushing disappointment and Waverley's gnawing guilt, as if the very air around her crackled with their shared anguish. In that moment, her own sense of isolation began to fade, replaced by a haunting kinship with their suffering.

"You could say that," Waverley replied softly, swallowing hard, as if the saliva in his mouth turned bitter. "My daughter already knows. Thankfully, she understands the situation. She even suggested we postpone the wedding."

After he spoke, tears pooled at the corners of Waverley's eyes, glistening like trapped regrets desperate to break free.

Feigning a casual scratch at his nose, he wiped away the tears, his throat constricting as he fought to dislodge the lump forming there. The pretense was fragile, barely holding up against the raw emotion bubbling just beneath the surface.

Sprite found herself at a loss for words. She couldn't force Waverley to settle his bill, nor could she stomach the thought of all her hard work going to waste. A fleeting idea crossed her mind—maybe she should just hand over the clothes and let him pay when he could. It was a small gesture, but it felt like a lifeline amid the swirling uncertainty.

But she couldn't shake the feeling that it might not be the right call. Her past experiences with lending had been disastrous; four out of five items she'd ever loaned never found their way back to her, and she wasn't the type to chase down debts. Plus, handing over the clothes wouldn't guarantee that Waverley's daughter's wedding would actually happen. There were likely other financial troubles lurking beneath the surface, far beyond just the inability to pay for the order. The whole situation felt like a dark, tangled web, one she couldn't quite unravel.

"Don't worry, I'll pay you later," Waverley assured her, his voice steady but the hint of desperation lurking beneath. "I just ask that you hold onto my order for a little while longer."

Sprite nodded, her silent agreement weighing heavy in the air. The only price she paid was the growing sense of claustrophobia in her home, the dress hanging on the wall like an unwelcome guest, encroaching on the already shrinking space. The fabric whispered of promises unfulfilled, a haunting reminder of the shifting tides in her own life.

Once Waverley's expression settled into something resembling normalcy, Sprite hesitated before broaching the subject of the murder case making headlines. She tread carefully, mindful of its delicate nature—the very reason for his dismissal. The air between them thickened with unspoken tension, as if the shadows of those grim stories were lurking just out of sight, waiting for a moment to creep in.

"I can't shake the feeling that the culprit might be a ghost," Waverley said, his voice barely above a whisper, as if speaking too loudly might summon whatever specter he feared.

"A ghost? You can't be serious," Sprite replied, disbelief creeping into her tone. The idea felt absurd, yet something in Waverley's eyes hinted at a truth buried beneath the surface, one she couldn't quite ignore.

Waverley chuckled softly, a sound tinged with self-mockery. "Yeah, a ghost. It's like the perpetrator is just... invisible. I've been out all night, checking around, talking to anyone who might know something, but he keeps slipping away. The police are on it almost every day, but nobody's been caught. The CCTV's been down, and there are no witnesses. This is supposed to be an elite neighborhood. What else could it be, if not a ghost?" The frustration in his voice was palpable, the absurdity of the situation gnawing at him like a relentless phantom.

"Why would a ghost be stealing money and jewelry?" Sprite asked, forcing a laugh that felt brittle against the weight of the conversation. The attempt at humor felt shaky, like trying to balance on a tightrope stretched too thin, but she wanted to lighten the mood, if only a little.

"Yeah, maybe not a ghost," Waverley replied, a wry smile tugging at his lips, "but someone with some sort of special abilities. It's like they can slip in and out without a trace, a shadow in the night." His voice dripped with frustration, the idea hanging in the air like a challenge he was desperate to solve.

"Special abilities?" Sprite echoed, her eyebrow arching in skepticism. She couldn't help but picture some kind of supernatural thief, a figure out of a bad horror novel, slipping through the cracks of reality with a sinister grace. The thought was absurd, yet it hung in the air, tantalizingly ludicrous.

"Yeah, special abilities," Waverley mused, his voice tinged with nostalgia. "It's rare these days, but back in my grandfather's neighborhood, he used to spin tales of thieves who could just vanish into thin air. I'm half-believing it and half-doubting, you know? But with everything that's been happening, it feels like anything's possible." The words slipped from his lips, an eerie blend of wonder and disbelief, as if he were grasping at shadows.

"No wonder the police haven't found anything yet," Sprite murmured, her voice laced with an unsettling mix of belief and skepticism. She wasn't one to dismiss the mystical; she had long held the conviction that the supernatural danced around them, filled with beings possessing abilities beyond comprehension. Waverley's tales of poltergeists, shadow thieves, and phantom pilferers resonated with her, tugging at the edges of her imagination. Yet even without those otherworldly powers, she knew all too well that humans could be terrifying enough on their own. The darkness in their hearts often surpassed anything conjured by the supernatural.

Their conversation meandered into idle chatter about the weather and Mr. Salene's rental property, which was slowly inching toward a sale to developers. This small talk was nothing more than a thin veil, barely concealing the tension lurking beneath the surface as they navigated the inevitable changes sweeping through their neighborhood. Each mention of the shifting landscape felt like a quiet acknowledgment of the loss they both sensed—a creeping dread that their familiar world was on the brink of vanishing, replaced by something unrecognizable and cold.

Mr. Salene, the landowner, was a man of considerable wealth and generosity, yet his life was a tangled web of troubles. One of the juiciest bits of gossip swirling around town was the bitter feud among his children over the inheritance—a family drama that unfolded with all the suspense of a gripping novel, each accusation sharper than the last, like daggers thrown in the dark. The whispers of betrayal and greed crackled in the air, hinting that this was no ordinary family squabble; it was a saga that threatened to tear apart the very fabric of their lives.

"Even with his father still alive, his kids are already at each other's throats over the inheritance," Waverley muttered, his voice low, laced with a bitter irony. It was a sad truth that money had a way of corrupting even the tightest of family bonds, turning love into venom and laughter into war cries.

Burdened by the relentless bickering of his children, Mr. Salene teetered on the edge of selling off the bulk of his land. Developers, slick and hungry, were circling like vultures, eager to transform the property into a sprawling, opulent shopping center that would loom over the South Bronx housing development, promising luxury and convenience while threatening to erase the very soul of the neighborhood.

Waverley explained that this ambitious project aimed to establish a glittering economic hub for the wealthy, necessitating the acquisition of land all around the housing area—much of it belonging to Mr. Salene for generations. The entire scheme loomed over the town like a dark omen, a harbinger of change that threatened to reshape the familiar landscape into something unrecognizable, stripping away the very essence of what made the place feel like home.

"I know this because I got it straight from an insider," Waverley said, his voice low, as if the mere act of speaking the words might summon unwanted attention.

Sprite nodded, but her thoughts drifted away from the gossip. She had no appetite for idle chatter about Mr. Salene. The old man had shown her nothing but kindness, and that kindness wrapped around her like a cloak of quiet loyalty, keeping her distant from the swirling rumors.

Several times, when she struggled to keep up with her rent, Mr. Salene had been nothing short of understanding, granting her extensions with a patience that felt almost saintly. His leniency had been a lifeline, a rare mercy amid the relentless grind of her life, offering a glimmer of hope in her darkest moments.

If she had rented from anyone else, she'd likely have faced eviction by now. As Sprite and Waverley's conversation began to fizzle out, two women ambled past the front of her apartment building, casting curious glances their way. Their looks were enough to stir a simmering unease in both Sprite and Waverley, igniting worries about the whispers that might follow. After all, a married man and a woman conversing alone, without their spouses, could easily become prime gossip material. A twinge of guilt gnawed at them, intensifying the discomfort that hung in the air like a thick fog.

Waverley rushed through his farewells, downing the last of his water in one swift gulp before rising from his seat. As he stood, his gaze drifted to the window, where the empty birdcage lurked in the corner of the living room. A pang of regret shot through him—a bitter reminder of the birds he'd let slip through his fingers, a missed opportunity that felt like a wound that wouldn't heal.

Sprite sat in silence, her thoughts whirling like a storm.

Waverley was wrestling with financial troubles, yet here he was, fixated on the idea of buying birds. It struck her as strangely out of place, a surreal quirk of his that felt almost like a ghost haunting the harsh reality of his struggles.

Besides, Sprite felt little regret over the birds' absence. In fact, she found a strange relief in their departure, as if their absence had lifted a weight she hadn't realized she was carrying.

Doctor, the starling, had been a constant cacophony, its relentless screeching grating on her nerves and leaving her perpetually on edge, like a raw nerve exposed to the world.

"Oh, right," Waverley said, gathering his things to leave. "Any idea where Ajee's working these days?"

At last, the question slipped into the air, lingering like a ghost, haunting the space between them.

Sprite had been dodging that question for ages, desperately trying to sidestep it. Truth be told, she was genuinely stumped about how to answer. She hadn't the faintest idea what Ajee had been up to lately, yet he always seemed flush with cash. It was unsettling, not knowing what her own husband did for a living. The strangeness of it gnawed at her, particularly for a couple who shared the same roof and crossed paths daily.

"Yeah, he's just picking up odd jobs, moving from place to place," Sprite said, forcing her tone to stay as steady as she could.

"Oh, I see. The other night, I saw Ajee walking alone near the housing area. I tried to call out to him, but he didn't seem to hear me."

Sprite's heart raced, pounding in her chest like a warning drum. What had once felt like idle concern now loomed disturbingly close, a shadow creeping into her thoughts. An ache tightened in her chest, a cold twist of anxiety curling around her heart. What was Waverley suggesting? Did he harbor suspicions about her husband?

"Yeah, Ajee's been working nights lately," Sprite replied, her voice steady despite the tumult inside her.

For a few seconds, Waverley was silent, his gaze boring into Sprite as if he were searching for secrets hidden deep within her. Each second stretched into an eerie silence that hung in the air, thick and oppressive. Sprite's heart raced, pounding like a frantic drum in her chest, until Waverley finally took a deep breath and forced a smile back onto his face.

"Just give him a heads-up. Tell him to watch his step," Waverley said, his tone dropping to a serious murmur. "Things are pretty tense right now."

His tone was devoid of any suspicion or accusation, smooth and neutral like the glassy surface of a still pond, hiding whatever currents might lie beneath.

He turned and walked away, tossing over his shoulder, "Catch you later."

"See you later."

After Waverley zipped away on his scooter, disappearing around the corner, Sprite rushed inside. She slammed the door shut, bolted it tight, and drew the curtains with a sharp flick, each movement fueled by a growing urgency. Her heart raced as she made a beeline for the bathroom, tension coiling tighter with every step toward the laundry bucket.

She pulled Ajee's shirt from the laundry, her hands trembling as she scrutinized the red stain for what felt like the hundredth time. But there it was—no trace of crimson, just the crisp, clean white of the fabric staring back at her. The stain was gone. The shirt was spotless.

She tried to calm herself, reminding her mind that she was spiraling out of control. Maybe she was reading too much into it; the red stain was just a smear from the pasta with chicken and tomato sauce Ajee had for lunch. Or was it? No, it couldn't be—maybe it was from a sausage hero, a slice of New York-style pizza, or a White Castle slider. The possibilities tumbled in her mind, each one more unsettling than the last.

12

Last night, Sprite tossed and turned, chasing sleep that never came. It wasn't the nightmares scratching at the edges of her mind, or the constant itch of mosquito bites gnawing at her skin. No, this was something deeper, something darker, sliding through her thoughts like a shadow with no face, leaving her trapped in a nameless dread that clung to her like the humid air. Restless, she lay there, haunted by a fear that refused to show itself but wouldn't let her go.

Instead, every few minutes, Sprite jolted awake, the eerie strains of a violin cutting through the dark, creeping in from the living room. She couldn't remember when Ajee had taken up the instrument, or when he'd learned to play it like this—like someone possessed. But there it was, a melody both haunting and alive, twisting inside her like a knife. One moment, it bled sorrow so deep it felt like an open wound; the next, it screamed with a terror that made her want to crawl out of her own skin. Each note clawed at her mind, a ghostly echo gnawing away at her sanity.

At first, Sprite tried to shove the unsettling violin music into the background, hoping it would fade into the murky edges of her half-sleep. She knew her husband was in one of his strange, almost otherworldly states again, and she'd learned to live with that. Ajee's quirks had always been more charm than chaos, little eccentricities that made life with him feel oddly magical. But tonight, this music was different. There was something relentless in its eerie, creeping melody—something that burrowed under her skin and refused to let go. It wasn't just strange; it was wrong, and no amount of reasoning could quiet the chill creeping through her bones.

By the third time she jolted awake, her head thick with that familiar fog, Sprite knew she couldn't ignore it anymore. A cold dread prickled across her skin as she peeled herself out of bed, the warmth of the sheets feeling like the last safe place in the world. Slowly, she crept toward the living room. The apartment lay shrouded in darkness, the only light spilling in from the street outside, casting long, eerie shadows that seemed to twist and shift with every step she took.

As she edged into the room, Sprite saw Ajee standing there, his back to her, an ominous silhouette carved out of the gloom. The violin's mournful strains wrapped around him like a shroud, filling the room with an eerie, oppressive quiet that pressed in from all sides. The music wasn't just part of the silence—it was amplifying it, deepening the unease until it felt like the air itself was holding its breath.

In the murky half-light, Sprite could just make out Ajee's silhouette, a dark, menacing shape that seemed to loom larger than life. The violin perched on his shoulder like some ghostly extension of him, its outline barely visible but unmistakably there. His hand moved across the strings with an eerie, almost mechanical precision, each motion cold and deliberate. It wasn't just a performance—it was something far darker, something that seemed to crawl out of the shadows and pull her into its grip.

"Ajee, come on! Ajee!" Sprite's voice sliced through the thick darkness, sharp with a mix of frustration and rising fear. It hung there in the silence, unanswered, as if the shadows themselves were swallowing her words.

Ajee didn't respond, didn't even flinch. His back remained turned, the violin still singing its relentless dirge. Each note hit like a heavy, gut-wrenching toll, deepening the oppressive weight of the night. The music didn't waver, didn't soften—it just kept rolling, a mournful, unyielding echo that seemed to pull the shadows in tighter, wrapping the room in something darker than darkness.

"Aren't you sleeping?" Sprite called out, raising her voice in a shaky attempt to break through. She tried again, but Ajee remained oblivious, lost in the depths of his music. Taking a step closer, she hoped her presence would somehow pierce his trance. But she froze, heart racing, as she realized just how completely he was consumed by the violin, his eyes unfocused, his expression distant—like a man possessed by something far beyond her reach.

His body swayed rhythmically, shifting from side to side, occasionally stepping forward or back as if guided by some unseen force. His right hand moved with an eerie grace over the strings—sometimes gliding with a whisper, other times striking with a force that reverberated through the darkened room. Each motion was a ghostly dance with the violin, a mesmerizing performance that felt both beautiful and unsettling, as if he were channeling something from beyond the grave.

For a fleeting moment, Sprite caught a glimpse of Ajee's tormented expression through the gloom. His eyes flickered between tightly shut and half-open, revealing a storm of conflicting emotions. His face morphed erratically—one moment a mask of suppressed tears, the next a rigid mask of barely contained rage. Each shift seemed to encapsulate a fragment of the inner turmoil that played out with every mournful note of the violin, a silent battle waged in the shadows, where sorrow and fury collided.

Maybe Ajee truly couldn't hear her, or perhaps he simply didn't want to be disturbed. Whatever the reason, Sprite's instincts whispered a chilling truth: the safest course of action was to retreat, to let him remain ensnared in his own shadowy realm. The very air around her felt charged with unspoken tension, urging her to slip back into the safety of the darkness rather than risk disturbing whatever dark dance he was caught up in.

Sprite trudged back to the bedroom, clutching a pillow to her ears in a desperate bid for silence. Yet even as she buried herself beneath the covers, the mournful strains of the violin seeped through, wrapping around her like a chilling embrace—a haunting soundtrack to her restless night. The music lingered in the air, a ghostly reminder that some things couldn't be escaped, no matter how deep she tried to bury herself in the dark.

She didn't know much about music, but the haunting melody that clawed through her attempts to sleep gnawed at her insides, filling her with a creeping unease that wouldn't let go. It seeped into her thoughts, a relentless whisper that twisted her stomach, amplifying every shadow and whisper in the dark. No matter how hard she tried to shake it off, the unsettling tune wrapped around her like a cold fog, refusing to dissipate.

13

Sprite woke up feeling like someone had taken sandpaper to her eyes, the ache sitting just beneath the surface, nagging but never fully fading. Her stomach snarled, empty and feral, demanding to be fed. She cracked her eyes open and caught the scent of green tea, not the weak, flavorless stuff she usually settled for, but something richer, deeper. It curled through the room, thick and inviting, a promise of something better just out of reach.

She glanced at the table by her bed and blinked. There, waiting like an unexpected gift, was a steaming cup of green tea, the scent still curling in the air, alongside avocado toast arranged with precision on a plate. It wasn't the kind of breakfast she'd make for herself—too put-together, too thoughtful—like someone had slipped a small surprise into her day, something just off enough to make her wonder.

Normally, she reached for oatmeal or cereal, something simple and predictable, the kind of breakfast that made the world feel steady. But today felt different, like the universe had tilted just a fraction. Maybe it was the gnawing hunger twisting in her gut, or the rich scent of the tea curling around her, but that avocado toast—vivid green and almost glowing—had an unnatural pull, as if it were calling her. It looked so tempting, it might as well have been served on a silver platter, a royal offering to start this strange, off-kilter day.

She took a slow sip of the tea, feeling its warmth seep through her veins, steadying her, before biting into the avocado toast. Poached eggs, smoked salmon, and a sprinkle of microgreens—each bite felt like something straight out of a soap opera, a touch of luxury she'd never let herself enjoy before. It was a far cry from Julyssa's peanut butter sandwiches by that busy intersection, but somehow, just as satisfying. As she savored the indulgence, her eyes wandered to the wall clock. The short hand was stuck at six, the long hand frozen at four. Monday. A small, insignificant detail that only deepened the eerie, dreamlike quality of the morning.

Sprite nearly choked on her bite, hastily swallowing it down with a gulp of tea. She shot out of bed, but the moment her feet hit the floor, a dizzying wave crashed over her, sending her reeling back onto the mattress. Groaning, she pressed her fingers to her forehead, as if she could massage away the thick fog settling in her brain. Time was slipping through her grasp, and the looming specter of explaining herself to her boss crept closer. For just a moment, the thought of blowing off work flashed through her mind—wild and reckless, but oh, so tempting.

She could fake an illness—put on a scratchy voice, cough into the phone, spin some excuse for Mr. Gegge—but the thought of it made her stomach twist. The idea of dragging herself to the clinic for a doctor's note, pretending to be sick when she wasn't, filled her with a creeping sense of dread. And it wasn't just the hassle. She couldn't afford to lose this job. Not now, not ever. The stakes were too high, and she knew it.

She had no idea what Ajee was up to these days or how long his erratic income could keep her head above water. That uncertainty gnawed at her. Abandoning her half-eaten avocado toast and tea, she grabbed a towel and rushed to the bathroom, scrambling for a halfway decent excuse for being late. In her mind, Mr. Gegge's sour face was already forming—more than just sour, it was mean-spirited, the kind of expression that made you feel two inches tall. Her boss was a jerk, plain and simple, and dealing with him was just another grind in an already hard morning.

If it weren't for sheer necessity, she would've thrown in the towel ages ago. As Sprite fumbled with her uniform, her hands moved too fast, and she botched the buttons—twice. Frustration bubbled up, but she pushed it down. Ajee wasn't anywhere to be seen, but she was sure he'd prepared her breakfast. He always had a knack for those small, thoughtful gestures. If only he could be that reliable all the time. He had the makings of a sweet, understanding husband, but his quirks—those damn unpredictable quirks—kept her guessing, kept her on edge.

It might've sounded crazy, even to her, but it was a wish she couldn't shake. She genuinely longed for it—a life with less uncertainty, less chaos. Slinging her bag over her shoulder, she caught a glance at her phone. Two missed calls from Thyme stared back at her, cold and accusatory, a nagging reminder of whatever loose thread she'd left dangling in the wind.

She could see it clearly—Thyme pacing, her face tight with worry, pleading with the driver of the pickup van to wait just a little longer. Her voice would've cracked with urgency, each call to Sprite more frantic than the last. But with no answer on the other end, there was nothing left to do but give up. Eventually, they'd driven off into the morning haze, leaving behind the weight of unanswered calls and the gnawing sense that something had already slipped through their fingers.

Sprite sprinted toward the front entrance, her heart pounding as the realization hit her: the public bus was her only lifeline. The prospect of getting caught in the inevitable traffic jam set her emotions ablaze, a simmering rage bubbling just beneath the surface of her anxiety. But when she flung open the door, her panic morphed into confusion, her mind racing to process the scene unfolding before her.

She spotted him instantly—a figure clad in a full-face helmet and a black leather jacket, perched on a throbbing motorcycle that vibrated with a menacing growl, its engine already alive with restless energy.

He locked onto her through the visor, his gaze piercing despite the obscured view. When he twisted the throttle, the engine roared to life, a low, impatient growl that seemed to echo the tension between them.

"Hop on," he said, nodding toward the back seat with a sharp jerk of his chin, the words almost lost in the rumble of the engine.

Sprite stood frozen, confusion swirling around her like a thick fog as her gaze fixed on the surreal scene before her. It took a heartbeat for recognition to sink in until he lifted the visor of his helmet in one swift motion. There he was—her husband. Her mind flickered back to a time when motorcycles like this were the epitome of cool, when every hip guy had one and every trendy girl was seen perched on the back, living in the moment, unburdened by reality.

"Stop wasting time. Get on already," Ajee urged, his voice laced with impatience, a sharp edge cutting through the tension in the air.

Sprite obeyed his command without hesitation, clambering onto the motorcycle and perching on the back seat. At first, she felt awkward and clumsy, struggling to adjust to the bike's height, but Ajee's patience never wavered. Once he was sure she was settled, the motorcycle roared to life. They didn't head straight through; the bike couldn't squeeze between the narrow alleyways of the buildings. Instead, they were forced to take a crowded detour, and Sprite found herself ducking under the curious gazes of the neighborhood. Women strolled along the sidewalks, grandmothers watched their grandkids play, workers hurried to their jobs, and schoolchildren on their way to class all turned to gawk. How could they not? Here was Sprite's husband, a man who rarely ventured out and had been jobless, now cruising down the street on a sleek, luxury motorcycle with her still in her work uniform, clinging tightly to the back.

Sprite forced a smile as she passed, trying to play it cool, but she could almost hear the whispers swirling in their heads, each thought slicing through the air like a sharp knife.

"Just a cleaning service job, and yet she's riding around on a fancy motorcycle? What's she doing on the side, besides tailoring? Isn't her husband unemployed, just hanging around at home or wandering aimlessly? They said he'd found a new job, but what kind? Maybe he came into some money, but if that's true, why splurge on a luxury bike? Shouldn't they be settling their debts first?"

"Whose bike is this?" Sprite asked, her voice tinged with curiosity, a hint of apprehension lurking beneath the surface.

"Our bike," Ajee replied tersely, glancing at Sprite in the rearview mirror, the corners of his mouth twitching with an unreadable expression.

Sprite longed to ask where the money had come from, but the question hung in the air like a thick fog, pressing down on her chest, too daunting to confront. Deep down, she dreaded the thought that the answer might shatter her fragile hopes. Maybe it was better left unasked, a way to avoid the burden of knowing. Her teacher had once said ignorance wasn't a sin—sometimes, not knowing was a blessing in disguise.

Once they finally hit the main road, Ajee gunned the engine, a futile gesture in the face of the looming traffic ahead. No matter how fast they went, the route to Sprite's workplace was notorious for its gridlock—a relentless snarl of cars that seemed perpetually stuck in place, like a living, breathing thing refusing to budge.

But then, to Sprite's surprise, Ajee veered off onto a quieter route, heading in the opposite direction. It was an unexpected shift, slicing through the usual chaos with an eerie calm, as if they'd stepped into an alternate reality where the frantic rush of life faded into the background.

Sprite knew this route wasn't leading to her job. "This isn't the way to my workplace," she said, her voice laced with confusion and a flicker of concern.

"I know. Who said I was taking you to work?" Ajee shot back, his tone sharp, as if the question itself was a challenge.

"Then where are we going?"

"Just going for a ride," he replied, a hint of mischief creeping into his voice.

Sprite's heart raced at his reply, a mix of exhilaration and dread coursing through her veins.

She strained to catch a glimpse of Ajee's face in the mirror, but his expression remained elusive. "A ride? I've got work, and I'm already running late," she protested, anxiety tightening in her chest.

Ajee's laughter erupted, oddly muffled by his helmet, yet it resonated with a deep, unsettling satisfaction that sent a shiver down Sprite's spine.

Sprite could sense the dark edge in his amusement, even without seeing his face. It wrapped around her like a cold fog, hinting at something unsettling beneath the surface.

"The road's clear now. Hold on tight, babe," he said, his voice low and steady, as if the words were a warning wrapped in an affectionate guise.

The motorcycle roared to life, surging ahead with a fierce rush. They sliced through the traffic, zooming past towering trucks, massive containers, and a parade of private cars, the world around them blurring into a chaotic streak of metal and motion, each moment stretching like a rubber band ready to snap.

Sprite felt a strange surrender wash over her, an involuntary release as she succumbed to the pull of the moment. She slumped against the passenger seat, her usual need for control slipping away like sand through her fingers. Maybe it was easier—perhaps even better—to let herself drift along with the tide, embracing the uncertainty that lay ahead.

She wrapped her arms around Ajee's waist, not out of fear, but from a deep-seated longing she'd harbored for ages. The thrill of racing down the highway, holding him close from behind, was a rush she had longed for. Adrenaline surged through her with each sharp turn, and she fought to maintain her composure, savoring the raw intensity of the ride like a drug that coursed through her veins.

She had no idea where they were headed, but she reveled in the ride. The entire day felt like a rebellious escape, like a schoolgirl cutting class for the first time, tasting the intoxicating freedom of life beyond the stifling walls of routine, each moment a sweet defiance against the mundane.

Ajee drove her to a quaint breakfast spot nestled within a hotel, a place that seemed to whisper promises of a slow, indulgent morning, where time itself paused to savor the moment.

Once again, Sprite found herself relishing a meal in an environment that felt entirely new and indulgent. The spread before her was a global feast, brimming with dishes from every corner of the world, and she could indulge until she was utterly satisfied. Around her, vacationing foreigners and impeccably dressed office workers mingled, likely there for a meeting or seminar, creating a vibrant backdrop of chatter and clinking cutlery that enhanced the luxury of the moment.

Amid the crowd, she felt like an outsider, a lone woman in a worn cleaning uniform, her presence a jarring contrast to the polished elegance surrounding her.

"Don't sweat it, babe. No one's gonna judge you for what you're wearing here," Ajee said, his voice a steadying balm against her insecurities.

Sprite nodded absently and took a sip of her mimosa. The bubbly citrus burst through her like a jolt—she'd already had breakfast this morning, the one Ajee had prepared himself. So why was she here, indulging in breakfast all over again? The realization crept in slowly, a wry smile tugging at her lips. *Ah, yes.*

Maybe Ajee had uncovered her secret devotion to potatoes, a love affair she indulged in at every meal. Perhaps he had caught her sneaking them at work, and this breakfast was his way of addressing the truth. It all clicked into place—why else would a plate of eggs Benedict sit in front of her, lavishly adorned with crispy hash browns, rich truffle oil, and exotic mushrooms oozing decadence?

After they finished breakfast, Ajee whisked her around the city once more. The traffic jams were relentless—an unyielding maze of idling cars and impatient horns. As the hours dragged on, they finally ducked into a salon, seeking a refuge from the urban grind, a quiet oasis amid the chaos.

She had often seen scenes like this on television, those glossy *Unpolished* shows where female celebrities began their days at the salon, indulging in cream baths, facials, manicures, and pedicures, sometimes even sinking into a full bath if necessary. A stylist examined her hair, shaking her head with a smirk as she remarked on its natural beauty, though woefully neglected, like a wildflower choked by weeds.

Here she was, living out the very scenes she'd once watched on TV—scrubbed, groomed, and lavishly pampered. By the end of it, Sprite looked so transformed that her reflection seemed almost otherworldly. She stared at herself in the salon mirror, awe-struck, barely able to process the sight before her. Astonishingly, she was beautiful. A deep blush crept over her cheeks as the realization sank in, a mixture of disbelief and delight flooding her senses.

"This is the real you," Ajee murmured from behind her, his voice low and earnest, a gentle affirmation that wrapped around her like a warm embrace.

Was this truly the person she was?

Maybe she really did deserve this after all. Yet it felt like a bitter twist of fate that she was only experiencing it now. As they stepped out of the salon, an unsettling realization washed over her. Her face glowed, her hair perfectly styled, but something was still off. The worn, drab uniform clung to her, robbing her of the allure she'd just been gifted.

Ajee glanced at his watch—eleven o'clock already. He proposed they head to the nearest mall, a place Sprite had never set foot in before, a realm of consumerism that felt utterly alien to her.

She had never even entertained the idea of stepping onto its cold, imposing floors. Unlike the modest mall near her home, this place exuded an air of exclusivity that was impossible to overlook. The sprawling structure, the store names flashing on massive screens at the entrance, and the well-dressed elite flowing in and out each day made her feel small and intimidated, as if she had wandered into a world meant for someone else.

She couldn't shake the nagging feeling that the security guards would toss her out the moment she stepped inside. But as it happened, her fears were utterly unfounded.

Hand in hand with Ajee, she stepped into the mall with an unexpected sense of ease. As she wandered through the hushed space, she couldn't help but marvel at the opulent decor, absorbing every lavish detail with a childlike wonder.

Ajee urged her to choose any clothes and shoes she desired, offering her the opportunity to finally shed the drab work uniform that still clung to her like a reminder of her old life.

Sprite hesitated, a flicker of doubt creeping into her mind. Was this really happening?

After over an hour of browsing, Sprite finally settled on a gray turtleneck mini dress. She'd been tempted by a flowing gown, but practicality won out; the last thing she wanted was to wrestle with fabric during a motorcycle ride. In the fitting room, uncertainty gnawed at her. Was the dress too short? Even with the long sleeves, her thighs felt exposed. Would Ajee mind her wearing something so daring? Her doubts evaporated the moment he flashed her a thumbs-up from outside. Once she slipped into her new outfit, spontaneity took hold—they decided on a whim to catch the latest movie at the mall's cinema, a plan neither had anticipated but both welcomed.

For the first time, Sprite sat in a nearly empty cinema in the middle of the day, the space feeling like her own private theater. Outside, the world was trapped in the grind of a Monday, with people trudging through the workweek they dreaded most.

Yet here she was, luxuriating in a day of leisure as if work were a distant memory, as if she belonged to the world's elite one percent. But even as she savored this rare escape, a heavy guilt clung to her, a leaden weight in her chest that made it hard to fully unwind.

She shouldn't be here, she thought, a knot tightening in her stomach. What about her colleagues? Were they left to scramble in the aftermath of her sudden disappearance? And her boss—was Mr. Gegge fuming at the office, tearing through papers, his anger echoing through the halls at her unannounced absence?

But Ajee kept reassuring Sprite that everything was going to be okay. "Don't let yourself get all wound up in it, babe. You're free," he murmured outside the cinema, his voice a steady anchor amid her swirling thoughts.

As the afternoon stretched on, their adventure began to wind down. They watched the city's daily chaos unfold: people trickling back from work, some ensnared in traffic, their curses and angry shouts rising above the clamor. Scuffles erupted on the crowded streets, while others squeezed into public transportation, fending off harassment and dodging pickpockets in the frantic scramble.

Ajee turned the bike around, steering toward a quieter route that offered respite from the bustling crowds. They ventured into a calmer part of the city, where the air grew warmer, and western red cedars began to punctuate the landscape, their fragrant presence promising a momentary escape from the chaos.

Sprite caught the faint, salty tang of the sea, intertwining with the fresh scents of her new surroundings. Before her, the ocean sprawled out, reflecting the reddish hue of the fading sky. A handful of souls dotted the beach, either lounging on the sand or strolling along the water's edge, immersed in their own world of twilight tranquility, blissfully unaware of the day slipping away.

Ajee guided the motorcycle to a secluded stretch of the beach, the engine rumbling softly before he cut it off and parked. The sudden silence wrapped around them like a comforting blanket, a stark contrast to the chaos they had left behind.

Sprite dismounted the motorcycle, the soft beach sand sinking beneath her shoes. She kicked off her work shoes, wanting to avoid the nuisance of sand in them later. Yet, even as she walked barefoot along the shore, a restlessness gnawed at her—an incessant reminder of the job she had left behind without so much as a word.

She had never missed work a day in her life. "Is it really okay for me to just skip work like this?" she asked, clutching her shoes in hand, uncertainty creeping into her voice.

"You need a break. They call it *healing* or something these days. You've been carrying too much weight on your shoulders. I don't want to see you stressed all the time, coming home drained or dozing off on the way to work. And if there's trouble at the office? Just take it as a win," Ajee said, stretching his arms and savoring the fresh sea air.

"But what if I don't work—"

"I work," Ajee interjected, a glint of mischief in his eyes. He paused, letting the words hang in the salty air, then added, "when I feel like it."

Sprite fell silent, the weight of Ajee's words settling over her like a shroud. Ever since his transformation, their meanings had morphed into something unsettling, an ambiguity that gnawed at her insides yet remained unexamined. Fear clung to her like a shadow, a paralyzing grip that had tightened for far too long. The waves lapped at her toes, washing away the footprints she and Ajee had left behind, as if the sea itself sought to erase their passage from memory.

She recalled the dreams she once held close—a beachside honeymoon, a sun-kissed vision woven into the fabric of their married life. But the old Ajee had dismissed that idea in an instant, as if it were nothing more than a fleeting whim.

He believed it was wiser to invest in new furniture for their apartment instead of squandering it on a honeymoon.

Sprite had accepted that decision, rationalizing it as practical, but the yearning to leave their footprints in the sand lingered like an unshakable shadow. "So, what exactly do you do for work?" she finally mustered the courage to ask.

Maybe this was the right moment; after all, Ajee had just brought up work himself, as if inviting her to peel back the layers of his enigmatic life.

"Freelance work. I pick it up when I feel like it. But I've got a knack for making money when I need it. It's a bit tricky to explain—might not be your cup of tea."

Another elusive answer, like a ghost fading away just as she reached for it.

Sprite's patience was wearing thin, her nerves unraveling like old thread. This whole situation had spiraled into a level of strangeness that was becoming impossible to overlook.

Ajee clasped Sprite's hand, his eyes searching hers. "What's got you so worked up?" he asked, a hint of concern threading through his voice.

Sprite yanked her hand away, locking eyes with Ajee. His gaze glinted with an unsettling reddish hue as the sun sank below the horizon. Whether it was real or a trick of her mind, she saw a chilling blend of beauty and dread in those depths. In the twilight, with the sprawling beach sky as a backdrop, Ajee loomed larger than life, towering over her like a figure plucked from a dream—or a nightmare.

"So," Sprite whispered, her voice barely a breath, "who are you really?"

A heavy silence settled between them, punctuated only by the relentless crash of waves and the distant, ghostly murmur of voices drifting on the breeze.

If she concentrated, she could almost hear the frantic thudding of her own heartbeat, a relentless drum echoing in the stillness. In that moment, Ajee's smile began to unfurl, widening with an unsettling slowness, as if his lips could stretch to his ears. Then, from his mouth, a sound trickled out—a whisper so faint it might have been the wind, yet each word was unmistakably clear to Sprite.

"You already know who I am," he said, a trace of amusement lacing his voice. "You're the one who reached out to me."

The sun had dipped below the horizon, surrendering the sky to a deepening twilight, while the moon lingered shyly in the background. The beach, once alive with laughter and chatter, now began to empty. It wasn't a holiday, and the looming responsibilities of everyday life pulled at those heading home, each one burdened by the weight of another workday waiting to begin.

Ajee appeared utterly oblivious to the dwindling crowd, immersed in his own world. He peeled off his shirt and tossed it onto the sand with a casual disregard, followed by his pants. Like a child discovering the ocean for the first time, he sprinted toward the waves, breaking through the surf with a reckless abandon. With a wild, exhilarated leap, he plunged into the deeper water, leaving the remnants of the day—and all its weight—behind him.

Sprite stood rooted at the shore, her eyes wide with disbelief as she watched his wild, carefree antics unfold before her.

"Hey, come on in!" Ajee shouted, waving her over with a grin that was both inviting and mischievous.

Sprite shook her head, her refusal resolute. She had no intention of shedding her clothes here, not with the waves crashing like a wild beast. Fear simmered beneath her surface; the water unnerved her, an expanse of uncertainty waiting to swallow her whole.

She couldn't swim, and the mere idea of stepping into those churning waves filled her with a quiet dread, as if the ocean itself were a living thing, ready to pull her under the moment she ventured too close.

Ajee splashed back to shore, water cascading off his body, the boxer shorts clinging to him like a second skin. Wet sand clung to his ankles as he reached out, seizing Sprite's wrist with an eager grip, his eyes sparkling with mischief and the thrill of the ocean.

She yanked her hand back, instinctively resisting, but his grip held firm, unyielding. "My clothes will get soaked!" she protested, panic lacing her voice as the waves crashed behind her.

"So what? It's no big deal," he replied, giving her a light shove at the waist, his playful grin betraying the urgency of the moment.

Sprite resisted, but the water's chill crept up her legs as her clothes began to soak through. Ajee's push had an unsettling power, a strength that sent a shiver down her spine, making her feel like he could drag her into the depths if he wanted to.

With a sudden, unsettling strength, Ajee hoisted Sprite over his shoulder, as if she were a mere feather, the world tilting beneath her in a dizzying rush.

"No! Stop! Put me down!" Sprite shouted, her voice trembling with a mix of fear and indignation.

A handful of people scattered across the far side of the beach heard her scream but merely smiled, dismissing it as nothing more than a playful squabble between lovers.

Ajee quickened his pace, dragging Sprite toward the deeper part of the sea. When he reached what he deemed the right depth, he didn't just toss her—he slammed her into the water with a force that felt far more deliberate than playful.

Sprite was utterly shocked as the cold, salty seawater soaked through her clothes, seeping into every inch of her being. For a brief, disorienting moment, her face was submerged, her mouth filling with the briny liquid, a taste of panic mingling with the salt.

She scrambled to her feet, gasping for air, the taste of salt clinging stubbornly to her tongue. Her chest tightened, weighed down by a heavy fear, each breath a struggle, as if the very air had conspired against her.

She fought for every breath, her mind racing with the chilling thought of drowning in the relentless sea. The waves conspired against her, each surge intensifying the choking fear that she might be swallowed whole by the ocean. It gnawed at her, tightening its grip with every gasping inhalation.

Ajee laughed, a gleeful sound that echoed over the waves as he watched Sprite flail around like a frantic swimmer caught in the deep end, even though the water barely reached her chest. "It's not that deep, you know. You can stand up," he teased, a grin spreading across his face like a Cheshire cat.

For a moment, Sprite wrestled with Ajee's words, her mind racing in a chaotic swirl. Then, the truth crashed over her like a wave, and embarrassment flooded her cheeks, leaving her feeling both exposed and foolish.

She ceased her frantic thrashing, focusing instead on steadying herself and finding her footing in the churning water.

He was right—she wasn't sinking. The realization washed over her, mingling with the saltwater that clung to her skin.

But still, she thought, if a big wave rolled in, it wouldn't take much to knock her down. "I'm having trouble breathing," Sprite managed to say, her voice trembling and strained, as panic gnawed at the edges of her composure.

The seawater felt like a suffocating weight, pressing down on her lungs, a relentless reminder of her vulnerability in the vast, uncaring ocean.

A sudden wave of panic washed over her as she remembered her asthma—a lurking shadow that rarely reared its head but was always poised to pounce.

"I know," Ajee said, his voice unruffled, as if he could sense the storm brewing inside her. "I know your chest feels tight. You've been carrying so much weight, burying all those emotions. Now's the time—let it all out."

Sprite struggled to grasp Ajee's words. When she said her chest felt tight, she meant it literally—the seawater pressing against her felt like a vice, making every breath a battle, nothing more.

But Ajee interpreted it differently, seeing her struggle as a deeper metaphor, a reflection of the weight she carried within.

And while his words weren't wrong—eerily accurate, in fact—Sprite felt utterly at a loss. Letting go of the burdens crushing her chest? The thought was as perplexing as it was daunting. How was she even supposed to begin?

Am I really supposed to start talking to the waves, like some kind of Dear Diary *nonsense?*

Ajee's hands settled on Sprite's shoulders from behind, a firm grip that, rather than sending her into a panic, wrapped her in an unexpected cocoon of safety.

"Now, just follow my lead, okay? You're with me, right?" Ajee said, his voice steady and reassuring, cutting through the chaos that swirled around them.

Sprite nodded, trapped by the weight of the moment. It felt as if the very tides had conspired to force her hand, leaving her little choice but to follow along, ensnared in the current of events beyond her control.

"Just take a deep breath," he urged, his voice steady, slicing through her panic like a lifeline thrown into turbulent waters.

Sprite inhaled deeply, the kind of breath that felt like it could stretch her lungs to their very limits, a whoosh that echoed in her ears like the distant roar of the ocean.

"Focus on everything that's been stirring up your anger or frustration," Ajee urged.

Sprite's mind resembled a dark, tangled web. Each grievance and source of discontent paraded before her like specters haunting a life she barely recognized. Her parents' stern expressions, her boss's relentless demands, the suffocating monotony of her job, the indifference of friends and neighbors, and even Ajee—her husband—swirled together in a tempest of resentment and frustration.

"Just shout it out—everything. Let it go, let it fly out to the horizon," Ajee urged, his voice steady and full of encouragement, like a lifeline tossed into turbulent waters.

When Sprite opened her mouth, all that came out was a ragged, "Ah...ah...ah..."—a feeble sound that barely echoed above the crashing waves, like a whisper lost in a tempest.

Her mind swelled with a flood of thoughts, thick and tangled, refusing to break free in a single rush. They pressed down on her, suffocating her, trapping her emotions in a painful, stuttering silence that echoed in the depths of her chest.

"One at a time, babe," he said gently, his voice a soothing balm. Ajee resumed massaging her shoulders, his hands gliding across her back with a tender familiarity. "You've got a close friend, don't you? Focus on what you don't like about her."

"Bootlicker," Sprite mumbled under her breath, the word barely escaping her lips, as if afraid it might summon the very spirit of her frustration.

"Speak up! Don't just whisper it—let it rip!"

Ajee's hands dug into her shoulders with a firm, insistent rhythm, each press awakening her dulled senses. His touch sliced through the fog of her self-doubt, shaking free the fears that had clung to her like barnacles for far too long.

"Bootlicker," Sprite spat, her voice laced with a simmering blend of disdain and frustration.

"Keep going," he urged, his voice a steady anchor amid her storm, blending encouragement with a commanding firmness.

"Thyme, you're such a bootlicker—hypocrite, fake, and a slut!" she shouted, unleashing her pent-up frustration like a torrent. Taking a deep breath, she pressed on, "I know you've been messing around with the office staff in the restroom."

Sprite's breath came in ragged gasps, not from the waves battering her chest, but from the effort of releasing her long-suppressed emotions. Just as her breathing began to steady, a towering wave surged toward her, an unexpected giant crashing from the deep. It felt out of place, like a monster from a nightmare that had finally decided to reveal itself.

Sprite couldn't shake the chilling thought that the wave was a manifestation of the secrets she'd just unleashed—a physical embodiment of the hidden rage she had hurled into the horizon. As the towering wave approached, fear gripped her, its menacing crest promising to engulf her in its watery depths.

She was certain she would drown, swallowed by her own bitter resentments. This was the fate that awaited those who harbored such darkness within. As the wave crashed over her—first her face, then her chest and legs—its sheer force felt unstoppable, threatening to drag her under and never let go.

Sprite surrendered to the inevitability of the wave's might, feeling utterly helpless against its overwhelming force. But then, like a sudden spark in the dark, it struck her—Ajee was still behind her.

She couldn't quite grasp how, but Ajee had become her anchor, holding her steady against the relentless pull of the ocean. As the massive wave's fury receded, it left behind smaller, less menacing swells. Each new wave whispered against her skin, a soft murmur compared to the roar of its predecessor, a reminder that the storm had passed.

Sprite suddenly realized Ajee's arms were wrapped tightly around her, drawing her from the tumultuous sea into the calm eye of the storm. In that moment, the chaos of the waves faded, replaced by the steady, reassuring pressure of his embrace, a sanctuary amid the swirling chaos.

He enveloped her from behind, cocooning her in an unexpected refuge amid the turmoil, a fortress of warmth and safety against the raging chaos of the sea.

When Sprite turned her head, she caught Ajee's smile—a slow, knowing grin that seemed to say everything without uttering a word. His nod felt like a silent pact, an understanding shared in the depths of their tumultuous moment.

"We're just getting started," Ajee said, his tone steady and unwavering. "So, what's the story with your boss?"

Sprite squeezed her eyes shut for a moment, as if to shut out the chaos of the world and concentrate. This question felt easier to face.

She despised her boss, and she suspected Ajee was well aware of that. "Asshole. Asshole. Asshoooole!" she shouted, the words tumbling out like a dam breaking.

"Be more specific," Ajee urged softly, his voice steady as if drawing her deeper into the conversation.

"Arrogant, pretentious jerk. Your eyes are always wandering, and I want to stab them out. Your words are revolting, and you think you're a big shot, but your ego's the only thing that's truly massive. I saw you when you were peeing, and let me tell you, your equipment's smaller than a booger. And don't you dare harass me again. You'll regret it. You'll die," Sprite shouted, her voice dripping with venom, and she caught the hint of Ajee's soft chuckle behind her.

A deafening roar erupted from the far end of the sea, a sound that felt almost mocking in its ferocity. The waves surged and churned, growing larger and more menacing with each passing moment, as if preparing to swallow her whole. If that wave were a person, it would be laughing at Sprite, reveling in the sight of someone so oblivious to the seething hatred she'd carried within her. Now, it seemed, she was destined to drown in the very bile she'd harbored in her heart all along. For a fleeting moment, fear crept back into Sprite's chest, a cold whisper threatening to undo her. Yet Ajee's solid presence behind her served as a warm shield, a comforting weight that anchored her against the rising tide of dread.

As the wave surged closer, Sprite fought the instinct to shut her eyes. Instead, she kept them wide open, determined to confront it head-on. This was her hatred, personified, and she would meet it without flinching. The wave crashed into her with nearly double the force of the last, a brutal reminder of the fury she had unleashed. Salty water surged down her throat, a relentless torrent churning in her stomach, demanding release. An intense wave of nausea washed over her, and despite her desperate attempts to fight it, she couldn't hold back.

In the next moment, she was heaving into the roiling chaos of the ocean, her body betraying her with every violent expulsion. Each convulsion felt like a surrender, an unwilling tribute to the tempest that mirrored her inner turmoil.

"That's it," Ajee urged as the massive wave rolled past, its fury ebbing. "You've got more in you. There's still time to unleash it all."

Beyond the distant beach houses, where their occupants were tangled in their own dramas, the stretch of water around Ajee and Sprite felt hauntingly empty. The rising tide seemed to drive away any would-be swimmers, while the stark, unyielding signs—No Swimming Allowed—stood as solemn sentinels, their warnings echoing against the relentless advance of the waves.

Sprite felt the relentless onslaught of water crashing against her, each wave acting as a catalyst for the emotions she had buried deep within. They erupted with a ferocity that surprised even her—a tumultuous flood of long-suppressed feelings spilling out into the sea, raw and unrestrained.

One by one, she let them go—her feelings about her parents, the endless disappointments with her neighbors, the betrayals from school friends, the bitter memories of Iron, her ex-boyfriend, and his insufferable wife, even the tangled emotions tied to Ajee, her husband. Each sentiment slipped away like a shadow retreating from the light, leaving behind an unexpected sense of liberation that washed over her.

Ajee leaned in, his voice low yet insistent, like a whisper in the dark. "So, what's the deal with your husband? What do you really hate about him?"

Sprite felt utterly drained, her voice reduced to a mere whisper, yet the unsettling edge of the question lingered in the air, impossible to ignore.

Sprite turned to Ajee, her eyes narrowing at his unshaken calm. "It's about you," she admitted, the words heavy on her tongue.

"About Ajee Arizin, your husband," he said, the hint of a challenge dancing in his voice.

His response came without hesitation, as if he had severed all ties to the Ajee of old, leaving behind a ghost of who he once was.

Sprite recalled the Ajee she had known—the one who rarely smiled, never spoke the words *I love you*, and remained an enigma, shrouded in shadows she could never quite penetrate.

Now, Ajee appeared to her as someone entirely different—at least, that's how it felt. Memories tugged at Sprite's heart: the early days of their marriage when he worked tirelessly to provide, and that brief period right after he was laid off, when his spirit still flickered with hope before it all but vanished into the shadows.

But Sprite clenched her teeth, forcing herself to rein in the flood of emotions. She needed to be sure of what she wanted to say—those words she had locked away for so long. If she hesitated now, they would slink back into the dark corners of her mind, lost forever, swallowed by the very shadows she was trying to escape.

Sprite inhaled deeply, as if preparing to blow up a balloon so enormous it might burst. "Ajee, I don't love you. I've never loved you. And I never will." The words felt heavy in her chest, but she pushed them out, each one a jagged shard she'd finally set free.

The declaration didn't trigger a thunderous roar or a wave crashing from the horizon. Instead, a low rumble rolled from the brooding clouds above, and the air chilled, whispering of an impending downpour, as if nature itself recoiled from her words.

Ajee reached out, gently patting Sprite's head before planting a soft kiss on top. "Is there anything else you need to get off your chest?" he asked, his voice low and steady, as if inviting her to dive deeper into the tempest brewing inside her.

Sprite shook her head, nestling closer against Ajee's chest. Her eyes brimmed with moisture, and she couldn't quite decipher whether it was sadness or relief that swelled within her, a confusing mix that left her feeling both raw and strangely unburdened.

Suddenly, a chill began to creep into her bones, curling around her like a vengeful spirit. Her body trembled, fingers wrinkling and turning blue at the tips, each pulse of cold reminding her that she was still alive—still caught in the tumult of her own unraveling emotions.

Ajee took Sprite's hand, his grip steady and reassuring, guiding her toward the shore. With each step, the sand shifted beneath their feet like a living creature, making them feel as if they were wading through a dream. The distant hum of the ocean closed in around them, an all-consuming backdrop that pulsed with the weight of unspoken words and buried fears.

14

"So, where'd you end up going yesterday, Mrs. Arizin?" Mr. Gegge leaned in closer, his eyes narrowing like a predator locking onto prey, watching her every twitch, every blink, as if the truth was hidden just beneath her skin.

The room plunged into a taut, suffocating silence, the kind that made you feel like the air had been sucked clean away. The ticking of the wall clock swelled, a relentless, maddening drumbeat, each tick burrowing into Sprite's skull with a precision so sharp it made her want to scream just to drown it out.

She was alone with her superior in the dim, suffocating room. The walls seemed to close in, pressing the air out of her lungs. Just minutes ago, she'd been ripped from her routine and dragged into this grim showdown, summoned for what could only be called a brutal inquisition. The crime—she'd disappeared from work the day before, not a word, not a hint, like she'd vanished into thin air.

Sprite squirmed on the hard, unforgiving chair, every shift only digging her deeper into discomfort as that relentless gaze bore into her, slicing her open like a scalpel. Dark fantasies flickered through her mind—grabbing a pen from the desk and driving it into one of those accusing eyes. But it wasn't just the fierceness that rattled her; there was something predatory about them, something that crawled beneath her skin and made her feel hunted.

Sprite was painfully aware of those eyes—always tracking her every move, lingering a little too long when she bent down to pick up a bucket or stretched to wipe down the glass. And then there were the times she had to clean the men's bathroom, where Mr. Gegge would inevitably appear, stretching out his time at the urinal in some grotesque pantomime, as if hoping she'd catch a glimpse and—God help her—find it intriguing. The whole thing made her skin crawl, revolting in a way words couldn't fully capture.

"My husband's not feeling well, sir," Sprite said, her voice trembling just enough to give her away. She wasn't much of a liar, never had been, so she stuck with a half-truth, hoping it would be enough to slide by unnoticed. But even as the words left her lips, she could feel them hanging in the air, flimsy and brittle, ready to snap.

It wasn't a complete lie, was it? The question gnawed at her, though, like a splinter buried too deep to pull out. She'd told herself it was close enough to the truth, just bent a little. But now, in the silence that followed, the doubt twisted in her gut, reminding her that even half-truths have sharp edges.

Ajee was, in a twisted sense, sick—though she had no intention of digging into the details. One of the more peculiar symptoms of her husband's *condition* was a compulsive urge to cook her lavish dinners and whisk her off to the beach, like some romantic fever had gripped him. It was a diagnosis she had no intention of explaining, not here, not ever.

"So, what kind of illness are we talking about here?" he asked, his tone casual, almost too casual, but those eyes were anything but. They were digging, searching for cracks, for any slip that would unravel her story.

It didn't take a genius to predict that question was coming. The air between them was thick with it, heavy like the humid stillness before a storm, the kind where you can feel the tension building, just waiting for the sky to crack open.

In a moment of sheer foolishness, Sprite had neglected to prepare a response for such an obvious question. Instead, she offered up the closest thing to the truth she could muster, deftly sidestepping the real answer. Maybe she'd picked up this knack for half-truths from Ajee in recent days; after all, lying had its own twisted artistry, a dark craft she was beginning to understand all too well.

"Fever, sir," she said, keeping it brief and to the point, as if the simplicity of her answer could shield her from the deeper questions lurking in the shadows.

Mr. Gegge's eyebrows shot up, thick and bristling, a wild forest stark against the smooth, bald expanse of his forehead. It was as if those two features were locked in a silent, unbalanced duel—one brimming with unruly defiance, the other resigned, bare, and vulnerable, as if it knew it had already lost.

For a fleeting second, he resembled Homer Simpson—minus the charm and innocence, of course. "Just a fever?" he asked, cracking a half-smile that barely masked the chuckle lurking just beneath the surface, as if he found her explanation more amusing than concerning.

What kind of superior would take any satisfaction in hearing that a subordinate's family member was sick? It was a question that gnawed at the edges of her thoughts, a dark, unsettling notion that hovered like a shadow, refusing to fade away.

Sprite couldn't shake the thought that even the thickest-skinned individual would at least wear a façade of sympathy for appearances' sake. How in the hell could this man be her superior? Hadn't he ever been trained in the basics of leadership—how to be a decent human being, how to communicate with the people beneath him? It was a mystery that gnawed at her insides, twisting like a worm burrowing deeper.

Oh, yes, Sprite recalled with a jolt that Mr. Gegge was still tethered to high-ranking company officials by some twisted family connection. That detail lingered in her mind like a roach scuttling in the dark corners, a whisper of darker influences and tangled webs waiting to ensnare anyone foolish enough to get too close.

He was the type who clawed his way to the top using every dirty trick in the book, a real parasite in the corporate jungle. Mr. Gegge leaned back in his chair, giving it a slow spin, his words dripping with condescension. "If it were me, I wouldn't let my wife skip work just for a fever. A man shouldn't be coddled, you know? But hey, everyone has their own way of handling things. Not all men are tough guys. Especially these days. Lots of folks talk the talk but are nothing but wimps. I've heard from other cleaners—won't name names—but they say your husband's out of work and just lazy."

Sprite nodded, her mind scrambling for a response as she watched Mr. Gegge's face twist into a mocking grin, his taunt so blatant it barely hid the insult. Each derisive word he hurled at Ajee felt like a hot, searing explosion in her chest—a visceral, suffocating burst of anger and hurt that left her reeling, gasping for air in a storm of emotions.

She seethed at the thought that this vile, ugly man—with his filthy mouth—had any business commenting on her husband. Did he really think that because he was clad in a crisp shirt, seated in his sterile, chilly office, he was somehow better than her? The arrogance of it twisted her stomach like a knife, fueling her fury.

There she stood, draped in her drab blue uniform, mop and bucket clutched tightly, while he loomed over her with an air of disdain, as if his office and his shirt somehow elevated him above her. Rage churned inside Sprite, mingled with a deep, stifling sense of helplessness. Didn't he understand that she was the one scrubbing his urinal day after day, the grimy task that kept his world spotless while he sneered from his cushy chair?

"Yeah, sir," Sprite mumbled, her voice barely more than a whisper, a fragile sound that felt like it could shatter at any moment under the weight of his scrutiny.

The answer was unnecessary, a hollow echo in the silence that followed. It hung there, weightless and pointless, like a forgotten line in a play that no one cared to remember, drifting into the void as if it had never been spoken at all.

For reasons she couldn't quite grasp, she blurted it out anyway. It slipped from her lips like a secret too heavy to keep, an impulsive confession she hadn't intended to make but couldn't stop herself from voicing, as if the words had a will of their own, bursting forth before she could rein them in.

"Listen, Mrs. Arizin, just a heads-up. You're on a contract, and it's up for renewal next month. I could make sure it doesn't get renewed if I wanted to. So, you still want to stick around?" He leaned in closer, his voice dripping with a casual menace that made her skin crawl.

Sprite's mind drifted, ensnared in the haze of her own thoughts. Did she really want to keep working here? The answer loomed before her, as clear as it was unsettling: of course not. Yet the weight of her situation pressed down on her, leaving her trapped in a web of necessity and dread.

From the beginning, she'd worked out of sheer necessity, a grim survival instinct propelling her forward. But now, as she pondered her situation, she wondered: did that same necessity still cling to her, or had it faded like a ghostly echo, leaving only the haunting remnants of what once was?

I work when I feel like it—when the mood strikes, not a moment sooner.

Ajee stood on the brink of liberation, ready to break free from the chains that had held him captive for far too long.

Somehow, a strange certainty settled in her bones, a quiet but undeniable shift. It was as if the burden of slogging through work just to scrape by had been lifted. The thought crept in: maybe she didn't have to endure this grind anymore—maybe her struggle was coming to an end.

Not that she was itching to trade it all in for a life as a full-time housewife—there were no kids to tend to, after all. Deep down, she resisted the notion that a woman's life should be confined to the drudgery of household chores. She harbored aspirations, dreams that felt like they were gasping for air. If she didn't have to work anymore, she could finally pursue them. That thought ignited a fierce, almost primal urge to stand up, spit in Mr. Gegge's face, and hurl every filthy curse word she could dredge up from the depths of her memory. Her knees trembled, and her teeth ground together as she fought to keep that raw, consuming impulse in check, the urge clawing at her insides.

If she acted on that impulse, Mr. Gegge might fire her on the spot, without so much as waiting for her contract to run its course. Strangely enough, that thought brought a rush of relief; it was precisely what she hoped for, a swift escape from this suffocating existence.

"Got it, Mrs. Arizin?" he asked, his tone sharp, slicing through the tension like a knife.

Sprite nodded, though the gesture felt heavy, weighed down by an unseen gravity, as if an invisible burden pressed firmly on her shoulders.

Mr. Gegge rose from his chair, ushering her toward the exit of the claustrophobic room with a forced politeness that felt almost mocking. As they reached the door, he extended his hand for a handshake, the gesture dripping with hollow formality, like a wolf in sheep's clothing.

Sprite took his hand, her mind racing with a desperate need to escape this stifling place. His handshake was firm and rough, like gripping a piece of sandpaper—a tactile reminder of the uncomfortable encounter she was all too eager to leave behind.

She wasn't shocked; a big, burly guy like him was hardly likely to have delicate, soft hands. But what caught her off guard was how his handshake wasn't just strong—it was downright unyielding, as if he were trying to squeeze every ounce of willpower from her, draining her resolve with each punishing grip.

He had stopped merely shaking hands and had moved on to a vice-like grip, his fingers clamping down with a predatory intensity that made her heart race and her skin crawl.

Sprite flinched as a sharp pain shot through her hand, the sting so sudden it felt like he had squeezed a live wire through her fingers, electrifying and paralyzing all at once.

"I've dealt with plenty of folks like you, Mrs. Arizin," he said, his voice dropping to a low whisper, thick with malice. "I have a knack for spotting a liar just by looking. And you? You're not good at it. You're weak, unable to lie outright—just skilled at dodging the truth like a scared rabbit."

"Let go of me, sir," Sprite said, her voice trembling with barely contained emotion, as if the words themselves were a fragile dam ready to burst.

Her voice trembled, not from fear but from a deep well of shame. Mr. Gegge's words had struck her hard, sinking into her chest like a dull blade twisting in slow motion, a painful reminder of her own insecurities.

"Yeah, I can let you go now, but I can just as easily free you from this job, too. Listen, Sprite, it's your call: which one do you really want to escape?"

His grip tightened, becoming a vise that pulled her in until their bodies collided. The space between them dissolved, and Sprite could feel the heat of his breath, a palpable tension coiling tighter with each passing second.

In a disturbingly swift motion, Sprite was ensnared in his embrace, his arms closing around her before she could fully grasp the reality of what was happening.

With brutal quickness, he spun her around and slammed her against the wall, the icy surface digging into her back as his grip pinned her in place.

In the pit of her stomach, she couldn't shake the gnawing thought: how many times had Mr. Gegge pulled this same stunt? How many others had found themselves cornered like this, victims of his predatory routine?

"How's that? No need to talk if you're too proud," Mr. Gegge whispered, his voice slithering like a snake. "If you're scared, just close your eyes. Don't worry about making a sound. Just relax."

The man's gaze was a razor-sharp blade, slicing through the air toward Sprite. His smile twisted into a grotesque leer, a grin so lecherous it seemed to mock decency itself, a taunt against the very fabric of what was right.

He carried himself with an air of supreme confidence, as if this little performance was his specialty and he'd never once failed to dominate with that chilling stare. But was Sprite afraid? Was she threatened? Not anymore. His gaze paled in comparison to Ajee's steely look when he had compelled her to join him for a candlelit dinner. His smile was a weak imitation of Ajee's enigmatic grin on the beach. This man, all swagger and bravado, was nothing more than a shadow, a flickering illusion against the solid reality of her true strength.

He was nothing more than a repugnant, aging buffoon who fancied himself important. He strutted around like he had it all figured out, but in reality, he was just a bumbling amateur—a pathetic fool who deserved nothing less than to be spat upon. His self-importance was a thin veneer, barely concealing the desperation beneath, and Sprite couldn't help but relish the thought of tearing that façade to shreds.

She recalled her furious outburst on the beach, and without a second thought, she unleashed her anger. With a swift motion, she spat directly at Mr. Gegge's face, her thick, glistening saliva striking his nose and trickling between his eyes before oozing down his cheeks like a vile, sticky waterfall. His expression transformed into one of stunned disbelief, crumbling like a wall that had suddenly collapsed, the remnants of his arrogance scattered in wild disarray.

He looked utterly foolish, like a man who had just stumbled into his own trap, wide-eyed and bewildered, caught in the absurdity of his own design.

Sprite plunged her hand into the man's groin, her fingers digging into the tight fabric of his cotton pants as she seized his testicles with a grip fueled by raw adrenaline. It felt as if years of scrubbing floors, washing windows, and hauling groceries had transformed her hands into instruments of fierce retribution, unyielding and resolute.

A surge of strength coursed through her, an exhilarating rush that made her feel as if she could effortlessly crush his testicles. Mr. Gegge's eyes bulged alarmingly, teetering on the brink of bursting from their sockets, as if they might roll across the floor like marbles escaping a child's grasp.

Without realizing it, Sprite let out a laugh at the sheer horror etched across the man's face. With her spit still dripping down his cheeks, Mr. Gegge's once ironclad grip suddenly faltered, crumbling like old plaster, as if all the strength had been siphoned from his body.

He was genuinely stunned, and that shock peeled back his defenses, exposing his vulnerability like a raw, bleeding wound.

Sprite shoved him with surprising ease, watching as he stumbled back into the chair, teetering like a puppet with its strings cut. She knew that if she hesitated even a moment longer, Mr. Gegge's shock would transform into a tidal wave of fury. Despite the surge of newfound courage swelling in her chest, she understood she wouldn't stand a chance in a physical confrontation with that man. So, she wasted no time. She burst through the exit door and sprinted away, heart racing. As she slipped into the elevator, a piercing scream erupted from the room—a guttural, enraged roar that echoed through the building like a death knell.

She should have been terrified, her body quaking with fear, but instead, she found herself laughing softly as the elevator descended. When the doors opened to the lower floor and she spotted Thyme emerging from the bathroom, her emotions twisted dramatically. The disgust she'd tried so hard to hide now seeped out of her, raw and unfiltered, like a stench that couldn't be masked.

"What's wrong, Sprite?" Thyme asked, concern etched on her face. Maybe she'd caught a glimpse of the redness and tears pooling in Sprite's eyes, a telltale sign that something had gone horribly awry.

"It's nothing," Sprite muttered, shrugging her shoulders as she turned her back, the words falling from her lips like an insincere mask she desperately tried to wear.

Thyme clamped a hand on Sprite's shoulder, spinning her around with a force that demanded attention. "Hey, if something's wrong, you've got to tell me. You're acting really strange."

"I'm fine, Thyme," Sprite insisted, her voice sharp. "You should hurry upstairs. Mr. Gegge's probably itching to see you."

Thyme's face fell, as if an invisible arrow had struck her. Her mouth fell open, lips trembling, and the light in her eyes dimmed, leaving her gaze hollow.

Sprite was startled by her own words. Guilt gnawed at her insides, but there was also an unexpected, almost illicit sense of relief—like she'd just cast off a heavy weight, shedding the last remnants of a burden that had long been too much to bear.

"What do you mean by that?"

Sprite didn't answer. She spun on her heel and hurried away from Thyme, striding across the lobby and out of the office building. As she passed, a few colleagues cleaning the windows glanced up, their eyes betraying a silent curiosity—questions that lingered in the air but remained unspoken.

She trudged a long way to the station, each step heavy with the weight of the day's events. As she walked, her mind replayed the unfolding drama, each footfall a reminder of her own transformation.

She wasn't merely changing; she was unveiling the self she'd kept shackled for too long. Now, she felt like she was soaring, ready to prove she was anything but the weak person she had always seemed. Standing at the station, waiting for the subway, Sprite glanced at her phone. Missed calls from Thyme and a string of text messages from Mr. Gegge flickered on the screen, each one a silent echo of the chaos she was leaving behind.

She clutched her phone tightly, the device feeling like a vise around her anxiety. Hesitation gripped her as she considered opening Mr. Gegge's texts, her gut churning with the unsettling certainty of what awaited her inside.

15

The subway rumbled into sight at last, dragging its iron weight like a reluctant beast, five minutes late, ten—felt like a lifetime. The guy behind her snarled, "Move it! No time to waste!" His breath was hot on her neck, the kind of breath that makes you wonder if people still brush their teeth.

Sprite slid into the window seat, the vinyl cold against her spine like a morgue slab. At this hour, the city felt like a ghost town, the subway nearly empty, the usual crowd already chewed up and spit out by the day. But then, a few minutes down the line, the damn thing stopped again—idling at some godforsaken station, waiting for ghosts that hadn't even bothered to show. Sprite's feet jittered, her fingers twitched as if some unseen current was running through her, and her breath came in short, jagged bursts, like she was waiting for something bad to happen—maybe it already had.

At last, she summoned the nerve to open one of Mr. Gegge's messages, and there it was, coiled like a snake ready to strike. The screen lit up, flashing the vilest, most venomous string of insults she'd ever laid eyes on—words that crawled right under her skin, cold and cutting, each one worse than the last.

Not even Ajee, on his darkest days, had ever spit venom like this. Her chest tightened, like an icy hand had clamped around her heart and started to squeeze. But for the first time, fear wasn't in the driver's seat. It had been shoved aside by a firestorm of rage, burning so hot it felt like molten steel coursing through her veins. The anger wasn't just rising—it was about to explode.

16

The afternoon had plenty of life left when she stood in front of Bronx Heritage Suites, the sun cutting across the sky, throwing long, lean shadows that crawled toward her, like fingers straining for something just out of reach.

Without a shuttle car, Sprite had no choice but to trudge the long haul from the station, the subway roaring past like some caged beast beneath the streets. The heat clung to her, thick and relentless, her clothes sticky with sweat, each step making her feel like the city was closing in, squeezing her tighter with every breath.

She didn't care anymore; the uniform was just dead weight now, something she was more than ready to dump. Who knew what waited for her once she quit? It didn't matter. The future was a blank page, and a part of her almost welcomed it, even if there was a little fear hiding in the margins.

She shoved the thought aside, not ready to deal with it yet. As she walked by, she felt their stares—two security guards, their eyes locking on her like hawks zeroing in on wounded prey, suspicion thick in the air like a bad odor. She didn't know these guys. They weren't from the neighborhood, not the faces she'd learned to tune out. It was obvious someone new was running the show when it came to security in this building now.

Sprite forced a smile their way, even though she didn't feel like smiling. It was a reflex, a habit—like slipping on a mask she'd worn so many times it almost felt natural, even when everything inside her screamed to rip it off and let the darkness show.

"Good afternoon, ma'am," one of the guards said, his dark skin and muscular frame making him loom next to Waverley. He offered a quick nod, raising his hand in a brief, casual salute that felt both friendly and unsettling.

Sprite caught the name on his uniform: Stylian. "Afternoon, sir," she replied with a quick nod, already plotting her escape.

Her emotions were a tangled mess, leaving her utterly disinterested in small talk—especially with a stranger. The mere thought of it felt like dragging nails across a chalkboard; she simply didn't have the energy for that kind of nonsense.

"Hold up a sec, ma'am. Can I see your ID?" the other guard asked, his lighter skin and taller frame making him loom even more.

His name was Darlo.

He moved closer to Sprite, positioning himself to block her path, like a wall closing in around her, leaving no easy way to slip past.

"ID?" Sprite shot back, her tone sharp and direct.

The two guards exchanged a glance, a silent conversation flickering between them, before Stylian let out a long, weary sigh that echoed the tension hanging in the air.

"Just need to see your ID card, ma'am," Stylian said, his voice steady but edged with something unspoken.

Sprite fumbled through her bag, grappling with a tangle of coins and crumpled receipts, her fingers slipping in the chaos. Each moment stretched out, as if she were reaching through a thick fog, desperate to find something solid.

When she finally unearthed her ID card, she handed it to Stylian, relief mingling with annoyance at the disarray that had slowed her down.

He studied the ID with hawk-like intensity, the photo and Sprite's face locked in a silent standoff. His eyes roamed over every detail, as if hunting for a hidden clue in the subtle differences between them.

Sprite forced a smile, trying to replicate the one in her ID photo. It was a weary smile, reflecting the exhaustion that weighed her down now.

She recalled that day—how she'd dressed up and practiced her best grin, only to watch it fade after hours spent waiting in line at the office. All that effort had crumbled into exhaustion, leaving only the hollow echo of her attempts.

"You don't live around here, do you?" he asked, his tone laced with both curiosity and skepticism.

"No, sir. I'm just passing through; my place is on the next block," Sprite replied. "I know Waverley—he used to work here."

The mention of Waverley's name didn't faze the two guards in the slightest. They stood as impassive as statues, their faces revealing no hint of recognition—no sign that they had ever laid eyes on Waverley. Maybe they simply didn't know him, or perhaps the name meant nothing to them at all.

"Starting tomorrow, you won't be able to pass through here anymore," Darlo said, his tone as firm as if he were reading from a rulebook.

"Why?" Sprite asked, her voice cutting through the air with sharp curiosity.

"They're blocking off the road. Too much crime. You know that, don't you?" Darlo said, handing Sprite back her ID with a look that suggested he wasn't surprised she hadn't heard.

A prickly blend of irritation and offense bubbled up inside Sprite. The two new guards watched her with cold suspicion, their faces as unyielding as stone, not a hint of a friendly smile between them. Was it her appearance that had set them off? They had no idea that if she'd worn the same clothes and makeup from the day she skipped work, she would've blended right in with the young women who actually lived in the building.

Still, Sprite understood. The pressure on these new guards had to be crushing. The whole community, the cops, even the media were all watching them. And let's not forget, their own safety was on the line just for taking this job.

"So, I can't pass through here anymore? Should I find another way around?" Sprite asked. She hadn't meant for it to sound sarcastic, but her frustration slipped through anyway.

Darlo and Stylian fell into silence, each lost in their own thoughts, the pause stretching out like a heavy fog settling over them. Then, out of nowhere, Stylian's smile appeared—so faint it was nearly invisible. It seemed even the effort of lifting the corners of his mouth was a battle he could barely muster.

"You can still pass through for now," Stylian said. "The road closure kicks in tonight."

They stepped aside, granting Sprite passage, their silent concession hanging in the air like a reluctant truce.

She thanked them and hurried on, doing her best to keep her composure and avoid looking suspicious. Not that she thought she deserved any suspicion, but the harder she tried to act normal, the more awkward she felt. Bronx Heritage Suites, once a refuge she had cherished, now felt different. Nothing had physically changed—the roads and sidewalks remained neat, clean, free of litter and dry leaves. The atmosphere still held a peaceful air, with only a few cars passing by, one speeding just a bit too much. The wind whispered faintly, drowned out by the daytime hum and the scattered noises drifting from every direction.

But Sprite couldn't kid herself—something had definitely shifted. The endless news reports on the radio, TV, and in the papers had transformed this place into something unsettling, an undercurrent of fear pulsing through what had once felt so ordinary.

When Sprite reached the road beside the apartment that led to her neighborhood, she stopped. This might be the last time she'd pass this way.

She turned and crossed the street, her eyes lingering on the back gate, now more heavily guarded. No one without proof of residency would get through. Visitors had to be checked and monitored, their destinations tracked before they could even step foot inside.

She watched as a taxi was pulled over for inspection, two security guards combing through the trunk with hawk-like intensity. The killer was still out there, lurking somewhere in the shadows.

He could easily blend in, posing as a resident, stowing away in the trunk of a car, or scaling the wall under the cover of darkness—like a shadowy ninja slipping through the cracks.

She understood why the residents here lived in fear. If she called this place home, she'd be scared too. The thought of guarding so much wealth, knowing how many people might try to take it by force, sent a chill down her spine—a fear she'd never really entertained before. The closest she'd come was on a crowded bus or train, watching helplessly as someone got pickpocketed, unable to do a thing about it. But this—this was on a whole other level.

Every time she passed here at night, she never dared to look beyond the back gate. It always felt like peeking into someone else's world—a line she didn't want to cross. Just walking along their sidewalks had always felt like enough. But now, it was too late.

She had an uneasy feeling that this would be the last time she'd ever come this way. After a thorough scan with a metal detector, the taxi was finally waved through. The two guards, strangers like Stylian and Darlo at the front, cast a glance in Sprite's direction from a distance.

She could feel their eyes on her, as if they were sizing her up, probably thinking all sorts of things. Sprite took a slow, steady breath and moved cautiously. The last thing she needed was for them to grow suspicious and decide to come after her. That would be a nightmare.

Deep down, Sprite was grateful she was a woman. There was no way they'd believe a brutal robber and murderer could look as harmless—fragile, even—as she did. That was her one saving grace.

Sprite kept walking, doing her best to appear normal, her steps steady as she moved toward the road. At least this time, she didn't have to dodge any sewer rats. Just a few yards from her apartment, a thought struck her—one she should've had earlier. How was she going to tell Ajee she'd quit her job? Should she lay it all out, detailing the harassment and the moment she snapped, spitting in the guy's face?

17

Everything went smoother than she'd ever imagined—so smooth, in fact, it was almost eerie. The way the world fell into place, each piece clicking with a precision that felt too perfect, too neat. Like something was waiting in the shadows, holding its breath, ready to remind her that perfection always has a price.

That night, Ajee cracked open a bottle of wine, the cork popping with a sound that seemed to echo too loudly in the stillness of the rooftop. He poured the deep red liquid into two glasses, the wine catching the dim light as they settled onto the roof deck. As they sipped, their eyes were drawn to the full moon, hanging there like a ghostly sentinel, trapped between the shadows of the looming apartments and the skeletal branches of trees. It watched over them, distant and cold, as if it knew their secret wouldn't stay hidden for long.

Sprite had gotten used to the drink, starting to understand why so many people were hooked on it. It burned a little less now, and she could almost appreciate the warmth spreading through her. "So that's the deal," she finished, her voice casual, but her eyes flicked to Ajee. Quick, sharp, like she was trying to catch him off guard—see if he'd slip, give something away. But his face was unreadable, and that only made her more uneasy.

His face remained eerily serene, devoid of any flicker of anger or disturbance as Sprite finished her tale. It was unsettling, the way he just sat there, listening like she'd been telling him a bedtime story. His expression was too calm, too still, like a mask glued in place. It felt unnatural, as if nothing could touch him—or maybe he just wasn't human enough to care.

In her heart, Sprite couldn't shake the nagging doubt that maybe her story just wasn't enough to crack through his indifference. Maybe, to Ajee, her experience was nothing more than the dull humdrum of everyday life, barely worth a second thought. She wondered if, to him, her words were just background noise—something to fill the silence, nothing that could stir anything real. It gnawed at her, the possibility that what she'd lived through wasn't gripping enough to even register.

"It's all good," Ajee said, his tone as casual as if they were discussing the weather. "You did the right thing, seriously. If I were in your shoes, I'd probably have done the same—or maybe gone a step further." His words were smooth, reassuring, but there was something unsettling in how easily he said them, like he'd thought it through before. Like going a step further was already a line he'd crossed in his mind.

"But I'm totally gonna get fired," Sprite said, her voice flat, like she'd already made peace with it. She shrugged, a gesture so casual it almost masked the tension beneath, but not quite. It was the kind of resignation that came from knowing the axe was already swinging, and all she could do was wait for it to drop.

"So what?" Ajee said, leaning back, his voice carrying an edge of defiance. "Who says you even have to work?" There was a challenge in his words, like he was daring her to see things his way. The kind of question that sounded simple but hung heavy in the air, threatening to unravel everything she thought she knew.

"So, what am I supposed to do then?" Sprite shot back, her frustration bubbling just below the surface. The question hung in the air, heavy with uncertainty and unspoken fears. It was a challenge wrapped in desperation, as if she were teetering on the edge of a decision that could change everything, and she was desperate for a lifeline.

"What do you want?" Ajee asked, his voice cutting through the tension like a knife. It was a simple question, but it carried a weight that felt almost unbearable, as if it could shatter the fragile façade they were trying to maintain. He stared at her, searching her eyes for answers, wondering if she even knew what she wanted—or if she was just as lost as he was.

"If I'm not working, I want to focus on sewing and study fashion design," Sprite said, her voice firm but tinged with nostalgia. She drifted back to her teenage days, when she'd fill the margins of her notebook with wedding dress sketches, her dreams spilling out in ink. The thought of designing her own wedding dress had always sparkled in her mind, a shimmering hope that had dimmed over the years. It was a dream that never took root, leaving her with a bittersweet ache that lingered long after the ink had dried.

"That's awesome. I'm totally behind you on this," Ajee said, pouring more wine, the deep red liquid catching the light as it flowed into the glass. "If you need to, you can take courses or dive into fashion design. You're still young, after all." His words were encouraging, but there was an undercurrent to his tone, a hint of something unspoken. Like he was trying to keep the moment light while grappling with the shadows of their reality, hoping his support could light the way out of the darkness.

"Really?" Sprite asked, a note of surprise creeping into her voice. The word hung in the air, fragile and uncertain, as if she couldn't quite believe what she was hearing. It was a flicker of hope, and she clung to it, wondering if maybe—just maybe—this time would be different.

If Ajee was serious, then maybe—just maybe—her dream was within reach. The thought sent a shiver of cautious hope through her, like a flickering light in the suffocating darkness. It was a fragile spark, but it warmed her nonetheless, whispering promises of possibilities that had long felt out of reach.

All this time, she'd been convinced her life was a dead end—a hopeless mess with no chance of redemption. But the recent turn of events had planted a seed of doubt in that bleak certainty, a whisper of possibility that stirred in the depths of her despair. Maybe, just maybe, it wasn't too late for things to change after all. The thought felt both terrifying and exhilarating, like stepping onto a tightrope with no guarantee of safety, but the thrill of it was enough to keep her from looking down.

"Yeah, I'll give it a shot, but..." Ajee began, his voice trailing off as doubt crept in, wrapping around his words like a cold fog. The hesitation hung in the air, heavy with the weight of unspoken fears. He wanted to believe in the possibility of change, but the thought of failure loomed over him like a dark cloud, threatening to snuff out the flicker of hope that had just begun to glow.

"But what?" Sprite pressed, her tone teasing but laced with genuine curiosity. The question hung in the air, a challenge wrapped in a smile, urging him to break through the hesitation that held him back. It felt like a dare, as if she was asking him to confront the shadows lurking in his mind, to expose the fears he was desperate to keep hidden.

"I'm not totally sold on it yet," Ajee admitted, the words slipping out with a hint of reluctance. Doubt hung in his voice like a dark cloud, casting a shadow over his fragile hope. He wanted to believe in the possibility, but the weight of uncertainty pressed down on him, anchoring him in place as he struggled to shake off the lingering fear of failure.

"What do you mean?" Sprite asked, leaning in slightly, her interest piqued. The question was simple, yet it cut deeper than he expected, probing at the uncertainty he was trying to mask. Her gaze held him, demanding answers, as if she could see the tangled mess of thoughts swirling in his mind and was determined to unravel them.

"I'm worried I might end up being the old Ajee again," he confessed, his voice barely above a whisper. The admission hung in the air, heavy with unspoken fears, as if he were unearthing a ghost from his past. It felt like a fragile truth, a crack in his carefully crafted façade, revealing the turmoil beneath—a fear that the changes he craved might slip through his fingers, leaving him stranded in a life he thought he'd outgrown.

Sprite's heart seemed to freeze, caught in a suspended beat, when she heard Ajee's words. The silence that followed hung thick and oppressive, as if the air itself were holding its breath alongside her. It felt like a moment stretched to its breaking point, where every tick of time echoed in her ears, amplifying the weight of his admission until it pressed down on her chest like a heavy stone.

She furrowed her brow, her mind racing at the thought of her husband slipping back into his old ways. The idea that her dreams might not only be accepted but actually supported felt almost laughable—a cruel jest of fate that twisted in her gut. It was as if the universe were mocking her, dangling hope just out of reach while the specter of the past loomed closer, ready to pull him back into the shadows.

"I don't know what changed you," she said, her voice steady but laced with vulnerability, "but I like the Ajee you are now—even if it scares me sometimes." The words hung in the air, a delicate balance of admiration and trepidation. She felt the truth of her feelings ripple between them, both a comfort and a challenge, like walking a tightrope between the past she knew and the uncertain future that beckoned.

"Then you gotta get rid of the old Ajee," he said, his voice dropping to a near-whisper, as if the weight of his words might shatter the fragile moment. "Like, totally." There was an intensity in his gaze, a fierce determination that sent a shiver down her spine, as if he were daring her to confront the ghosts of his past. It felt like a challenge, a call to action that resonated deep within her, urging her to let go of the shadows that threatened to pull them both back into darkness.

Sprite replayed her words from that day on the beach, the anger in her voice ringing clear as she declared she had never truly loved Ajee. But the Ajee she had condemned in that shout was the man from before—the one who had married her when she was a mess, the one who had never offered praise or support, the rigid figure who had resigned himself to their fate. This Ajee was something else entirely, a transformed version of the man she had always wished for, one who sparkled with potential and promise. The contrast twisted in her chest, a bittersweet reminder of the shadows that had once consumed them both.

"How?" Sprite asked, her curiosity ignited like a spark in the dark. The single word was loaded with questions, a breathless invitation for him to unveil the mystery. She leaned in slightly, anticipation thrumming in the air between them, eager to grasp whatever revelation lay ahead.

Ajee opened his mouth to answer, but his words were abruptly sliced off by the passing figure of Rashunda, one of their neighbors. The woman drifted by, her presence an unwelcome intrusion that sliced through the moment like a knife through fog. Rashunda's gaze flickered over to them from the street, her smile stretching wide, a mask of forced cheerfulness that didn't quite reach her eyes. Ajee and Sprite returned the gesture, their smiles taut and practiced, as they exchanged obligatory pleasantries. Beneath the surface, an uneasy tension simmered, thickening the air with unspoken words and lingering questions.

Sprite felt a twinge of anxiety, fearing one of the neighbors might catch a glimpse of what they were drinking. Luckily, the bottle was concealed beneath a pile of clutter, and the drinks in their glasses looked nothing more than the innocuous remnants of Christmas grape juice. That deceptive appearance offered a thin veil of normalcy, barely masking the reality of their situation. Just as Sprite was about to resume the conversation, a sudden jolt startled her—a vibration that sent a shiver through her phone. The cell buzzed insistently, its tremor a sharp, unwelcome interruption that sliced through the air like a sinister whisper, demanding her attention and shattering the fragile bubble of their moment.

She glanced at the screen and saw the caller's name: Mr. Gegge. A cold certainty settled in her gut, a creeping dread that told her she knew exactly what he was about to say. The thought hung in the air like a dark cloud, heavy with the weight of impending trouble, casting a shadow over the fragile moment they had managed to carve out for themselves.

He wasn't calling to apologize. No, this call was destined to be a reprimand, or worse—a thinly veiled threat. The anticipation of his harsh words loomed over her like a shadow, darkening the moment with an oppressive sense of dread that settled heavily in her chest. It was the kind of dread that wrapped around her throat, tightening with each passing second, suffocating the fragile hope she had nurtured.

She let the phone continue its relentless vibration, the buzz a persistent reminder of the looming conversation. Each tremor felt like a countdown, a rhythmic thrum that matched the growing anxiety in her chest. It pulsed through her, echoing the dread that hung in the air, demanding her attention while she desperately wished to ignore it.

Ajee reached out, as if he had a sixth sense about who was calling through the buzzing phone. "Here, let me take this," he said, his voice steady but laced with an undercurrent of concern. There was an urgency in his movement, a sense that he understood the weight of the moment more than she did, as if he were bracing himself for the storm that was about to break.

"Don't. It's really not necessary," Sprite said, pulling her phone away from Ajee's grasp. The gesture was instinctive, fueled by a mix of defiance and dread. She felt a surge of protectiveness over the device, as if it held not just a conversation but the fragile remnants of her composure. Ajee's eyes searched hers, a silent plea for understanding, but all she could focus on was the electric tension between them, a storm brewing just beneath the surface.

"It's cool, don't worry about it," Ajee said, giving Sprite a reassuring nod, his gaze steady on hers. There was a calmness in his voice, a deliberate effort to pierce through the swirling anxiety that clung to the air. But beneath that reassuring façade, she sensed the tension simmering just out of sight, a reminder that the real storm was still brewing, waiting for the right moment to break.

Reluctantly, Sprite handed her phone over to Ajee, a chill creeping down her spine as she braced for the inevitable clash. The thought of the argument to come sent shivers coursing through her; when men began hurling curses, it was only a matter of time before things turned ugly. The air thickened with tension, as if the very walls were holding their breath, waiting for the explosion that seemed poised to shatter the fragile peace they had fought so hard to create.

Sprite dreaded the idea of the conflict spiraling into a physical showdown, the mere thought of it twisting in her gut like a coiled snake. Unease settled over her, thick and suffocating, as images of chaos flickered through her mind. She could almost feel the tension crackling in the air, a warning that something dark and unpredictable was lurking just beneath the surface.

She couldn't bear the thought of anything bad happening to Ajee or of his newfound efforts to turn his life around being derailed. The stakes felt painfully high, as if the fragile progress they were making was suspended by a thread so thin it might snap at any moment. Every ounce of her being screamed for him to stay safe, to keep moving forward, but the lurking dread felt like a dark shadow, waiting to snatch it all away.

Ajee answered the call, his silence a deliberate choice, a shield against the storm brewing on the other end. He let the other party's words tumble out in a relentless stream, his calm demeanor barely flickering as he absorbed the barrage. The roof deck seemed to hold its breath, the air thick with unspoken tension, as if it were a witness to the impending clash, waiting for him to find the right moment to respond and unleash the storm brewing inside him.

Sprite leaned in, straining to catch the murmur of Mr. Gegge's voice on the other end. The conversation was shrouded in a veil of ambiguity, his words slipping away like smoke through her fingers, swallowed by the static of her own growing anxiety. Each syllable felt distant, echoing in her mind as her heart raced, amplifying the tension that wrapped around her like a vice.

She could sense the simmering hostility beneath the surface, but the specifics eluded her, each word a ghost slipping through her fingers. Mr. Gegge's voice came through faintly, distorted and garbled, as if he were speaking through a mouthful of marbles or gargling with gravel. The unpleasant sound twisted her stomach, deepening the sense of dread that hung in the air like a thick fog, suffocating and inescapable.

After nearly five minutes of listening to the call, Ajee's interest began to wane. The words blurred together, a monotonous drone that felt like a weight pressing on his chest. He hung up and handed the phone back to Sprite, his expression hardened. "Forget about it," he muttered, the dismissal laced with an edge of frustration, as if he were trying to shake off the lingering shadows of the conversation.

18

Sprite jolted awake, heart thudding in the oppressive silence of the night. The room was smothered in darkness, so thick it felt alive. She glanced toward the wall clock, its hands nothing more than vague smudges swallowed by shadow. One o'clock? Two? It didn't matter. In that black, airless void, time was a ghost—slipping just out of reach, mocking her from the edges of her mind.

She stumbled out of her room, fingers scraping along the wall like blind, skittering insects, her eyes refusing to cut through the suffocating dark. The need to hit the bathroom clawed at her gut—too many drinks, too late. But as she shuffled into the hallway, a chill prickled up her spine. Ajee wasn't there. He wasn't curled up in his usual spot. It'd been a long time since she'd thought about Ajee's nightly disappearances, but now the absence gnawed at her, the kind of forgotten fear that creeps out of old corners when you're not looking.

She found a strange comfort in her own ignorance, or maybe it was just the act of pretending not to know. Ignorance was easier, safer. But as she shuffled toward the bathroom, the fragile quiet shattered. Footsteps—soft but unmistakable—and then the slow, deliberate scrape of a chair from the living room, the one where she kept her sewing supplies. Her stomach turned, a knot tightening inside her. Someone was in there, and it sure as hell wasn't Ajee.

She assumed it was Ajee, though what he was up to remained a mystery she wasn't ready to unravel. She'd deal with it later. After a quick trip to the bathroom, the house seemed too quiet—unnervingly so. The strange sounds echoed in her head, refusing to fade. Had she imagined the rhythmic whir of the sewing machine, or had it been real? The doubt gnawed at her, creeping under her skin like something alive, something waiting in the dark.

Moving with deliberate care toward the living room, Sprite hoped not to disturb Ajee. But then she heard it—a muffled groan, low and unfamiliar, sending icy fingers crawling down her spine. The living room lay dim and cloaked in shadow, the familiar shapes of her belongings barely discernible: the radio on the table, the sewing machine huddled in the corner, the clothes hanging neatly. Everything seemed in its place—except for one thing.

Waverley's daughter's white dress, which had been hung with the others, now draped over a chair in the center of the room. No, not draped—worn. Someone—or something—was inside that dress, the fabric swallowing its head, leaving only a grotesque silhouette in the gloom. It slumped in the chair, its movements slow, jerky, accompanied by those muffled, guttural groans that seemed to ooze from the very shadows.

Sprite's heart pounded like a hammer in her chest, breath snagging in her throat. She stared, frozen, trying to make sense of the nightmare tableau before her. What kind of twisted vision was this, lurking in the suffocating dark, waiting for her to make the next move?

She edged closer to the figure, each step dragging her deeper into the suffocating air, thick and heavy like the weight of a nightmare. The groans sharpened, cutting through the silence, gaining an unsettling clarity as the shadowed form solidified in the dim light. A white cloth veiled the figure's face, obscuring any hint of identity. Was it Ajee? Or something far darker, something she didn't want to face? Her breath hitched, a cold lump of dread coiling tighter in her chest with every inch she moved, each step pulling her closer to whatever horror waited beneath that dress.

With trembling hands, Sprite yanked at the cloth, her fingers fumbling against the damp fabric. It came away in slow, reluctant layers, each fold peeling back like a whisper of some long-buried secret. The pieces drifted to the floor, ghostly remnants of something far worse than she'd imagined. Her scream lodged in her throat, frozen there as she stared at the face beneath—one she despised with every fiber of her being. Wide, terrified eyes stared back at her, pleading, the only sound escaping its lips a series of strained, muffled groans, barely audible under the smothering cloth. This was no longer just a nightmare; this was her darkest hatred made flesh.

"Mr. Gegge," Sprite whispered, her voice barely more than a breath, trembling on the edge of disbelief. She shook her head, her mind scrambling to convince itself this wasn't some twisted dream she'd stumbled into, some half-formed nightmare bleeding into reality. But the dread clung to her, heavy and real, sinking into her bones. No, this was happening—whether she wanted to face it or not.

The groans swelled, rising from the shadows like something alive, more insistent with each passing second. They clawed at the air, jagged and desperate, as if they were trying to drag themselves out of the suffocating darkness, out of some hidden place where nightmares fester.

Maybe he was fighting to call out to Sprite, his muffled pleas for help tangled in the suffocating darkness, reaching for her through the veil of his own terror. Just as she teetered on the brink of deciding Mr. Gegge's fate, a voice sliced through the shadows behind her, freezing her in place and sending a chill rippling through her bones.

"Got one last gift for you, babe."

Sprite spun around, and there he was—Ajee, looming in the shadows, as if he'd been conjured from the darkness itself. He pressed himself against the wall, his movements deliberate and unnervingly calm. With a flick of his hand, he pressed a button, and in an instant, the room erupted with harsh, blinding light, banishing the oppressive shadows that had clung to every corner like unwanted memories.

Mr. Gegge squeezed his eyes shut against the sudden blaze of light, his face contorting in a grimace of pained adjustment. Then, from beneath the tight seal of the cloth, a higher-pitched groan escaped him, laced with raw, unfiltered agony that cut through the air like a knife.

Sprite was now utterly convinced this was all real. "What did you do to him?" she asked, her voice trembling as dread twisted in her gut.

"As you can see. Sorry if you got any of this guy's blood or spit on your clothes. Waverley still hasn't picked up his order, has he?"

Sprite shook her head. "Not yet." The words came out as a whisper, heavy with an unspoken weight.

Ajee stepped closer, looming over Mr. Gegge as he yanked the man's hair back, forcing him to tilt his head so Sprite could see the sheer terror etched on his face. "This guy wanted to rape you. You understand that, don't you?" Ajee's voice was cold, laced with a twisted sense of satisfaction.

Mr. Gegge struggled to shake his head, but his efforts were futile, his movements helplessly trapped in the iron grip of Ajee's hand. Each desperate twist only deepened his sense of confinement, as if the shadows themselves were closing in around him.

Sprite faced the awful truth, the realization crystallizing in her mind. What Mr. Gegge had attempted during their last encounter was unmistakably an attempt at rape—a grotesque violation etched into her memory like a scar. After she spat in his face, a fire of fury ignited in Mr. Gegge, his eyes blazing with rage and humiliation.

He erupted in a torrent of vile threats and obscenities, his rage distorting his words into a venomous snarl that dripped with malice.

She had no idea what Mr. Gegge had told Ajee on the phone, but deep down, she was certain of one thing: his intentions to rape and harm her were all too real, a chilling promise she couldn't afford to ignore.

Without warning, Ajee drove his right knee into Mr. Gegge's face with brutal force. The sickening thud made Sprite flinch, yet a twisted satisfaction coursed through her as she watched the man she despised bleed. Fresh blood streamed from Mr. Gegge's shattered nose, dripping steadily and splattering onto Ajee's black pants, the dark fabric barely revealing the crimson stains.

Sprite recalled the red stain on Ajee's white shirt, the one she'd always convinced herself wasn't blood. She had become so skilled at deceiving herself that the line between truth and fiction had blurred beyond recognition. But now, the truth was undeniable. The blood was real. The murders and robberies were real, etched into her mind with a cold, inescapable clarity that left no room for denial.

"Pretty wild, huh?" Ajee said, a laugh bubbling beneath the surface, as if he were struggling to contain a dark sense of amusement.

Mr. Gegge's groans had morphed into desperate cries, tears streaming down his face, mingling with the blood pouring from his shattered nose. The grotesque blend of anguish and blood painted a grim portrait of his suffering, a haunting testament to his pain.

"You don't need to be scared," Ajee said, releasing Mr. Gegge's hair and walking over to Sprite. He took her shoulders in his hands, squeezing gently as if to anchor her. "You've earned all of this, my beautiful wife. You want me to stay like this, don't you? You don't want me going back to who I was before, do you?"

Sprite still wasn't entirely sure about the whole connection, but if she had to choose, she'd take the cool, romantic Ajee over the boring one she'd never liked. Still, the idea of diving into this darker side of him filled her with unease. "No choice," she murmured to herself, resigning to the grim reality of the situation. She felt Ajee's grip on her right hand tighten, then gently open her palm, as if offering her something unspoken.

A cold, unyielding metal object pressed against her palm—a fork, likely pilfered from the kitchen. The chill of the steel contrasted sharply with the warmth of her skin, a subtle reminder of the harsh reality closing in around her like a vice.

"Do you remember what you hate about this guy?" Ajee asked, his voice low and probing, like a knife teasing at an old wound.

Sprite nodded, trembling. "His eyes," she replied, the words barely escaping her lips, heavy with dread.

Ajee gently prodded Sprite's back, nudging her toward Mr. Gegge, granting her the freedom to act on her darkest impulses. It was a bitter truth: Sprite harbored a deep-seated loathing for those lecherous eyes. Now, however, those eyes had transformed into quivering orbs of sheer terror, locked in a horrified gaze at what lay before them. The cries from his throat grew more frantic, rising in a chilling crescendo that echoed in the room like a death knell.

Sprite felt a gut-deep certainty that if the cloth were ripped away from his mouth, this man would wail like a frightened child. Her breath came in shallow, rapid bursts, and her heart pounded like a wild drum. Her eyes darted nervously between Mr. Gegge's contorted face and the fork clutched tightly in her right hand. It might be the same fork she'd once used to cut steak with Ajee, but now it was transformed into a tool of her own dark purpose, and for the first time, she was finally allowed to wield it.

As the grim reality of what was about to unfold sank in, Mr. Gegge clamped his eyes shut with desperate force. He writhed violently, trying to hurl himself free from the chair, but beneath the layers of the dress he wore, a rope constricted him tightly, holding him in a merciless grip. The futility of his struggle only deepened the horror of his situation, leaving him trapped in a nightmarish tableau.

"Don't let yourself be trapped," Ajee said, his grip on Mr. Gegge tight and unyielding, a silent reminder of the power he wielded over the man's fate.

19

"Do whatever you want. It's your choice."
Ajee's fingers clamped around Mr. Gegge's skull like a steel vise, the bones beneath his skin quivering with each thudding pulse.

He didn't squeeze—no, not yet—but the threat loomed, coiled in the tight strain of his knuckles, like a storm waiting to split the sky. Slowly, deliberately, Ajee peeled back Mr. Gegge's left eyelid, exposing the eyeball—round, defenseless, a target begging to be crushed.

Mr. Gegge thrashed like a fish on a hook, panic jerking through his limbs, but Ajee had done this before—too many times to be rattled.

He knew the exact spot where fear bled into pure, raw agony, and he wasn't about to cross it—not yet. There was a cold patience in the way he moved, a slow, practiced cruelty that whispered he'd done this before. Many times. Too many.

Sprite inched the fork closer, the tines quivering like a leaf in a gale, but still pushing forward. Mr. Gegge's left eyeball, wide and glistening, mirrored the cold metal as it approached. Closer. Closer. Then, just as the tip hovered a breath away from piercing that fragile surface, it froze—suspended like death itself, weighing whether today would be the day.

Sprite stared into her own reflection in Mr. Gegge's eye, and what she saw chilled her to the bone—a stranger. Her breath caught, her heart stuttering in her chest. What was she doing? Was she really about to cross that line, to become a murderer? A monster? The questions pounded in her head like rapid gunfire, each one louder, more urgent, stirring something deep within her—a buried part she thought long forgotten. Before she could even consider pulling her hand back, Ajee's fingers tightened around her wrist, firm but steady, just like when he'd guided her through the fine points of dining etiquette. Only this time, the lesson was darker.

He pressed her hand forward, slow and deliberate. For a moment, there was slick resistance, a hesitation in the flesh, but Ajee added just a bit more pressure, and then—*Pop!*. The fork's tip sank into Mr. Gegge's eye, breaking through with a soft, sickening sound that lingered in the air like a bell tolling doom.

Sprite felt it—the sickening, slick give of soft tissue beneath the fork, yielding in a way that twisted her stomach into knots. It was too real, too alive, a sensation that crawled up her arm and lodged itself in her mind, refusing to let go.

Ajee didn't flinch. He pressed the fork deeper, and with a sickening squelch, fresh blood began to ooze from Mr. Gegge's eye. The room filled with two desperate, muffled screams, choked by the sheer horror of the moment, the sound barely piercing the suffocating tension that hung in the air.

Sprite should have been screaming—loud enough to shake the walls and rattle the neighbors—but her breath was trapped, like a vice clamped around her throat. It felt as if she'd plunged into a waking nightmare, where her voice had betrayed her—silenced, unable to utter even the simplest cry for help or whisper a prayer. The horror paralyzed her, leaving only a desperate, silent scream trapped inside.

She yanked her hand free and stumbled backward, but her escape was clumsy. She crashed to the floor, limbs flailing—a helpless heap of terror and confusion. The cold, hard ground rushed up to meet her, the shock of the fall jolting her back to the stark reality of the nightmare she had just witnessed.

Meanwhile, Mr. Gegge slumped to the floor, the chair clattering down with him in a tragic cascade of metal and flesh. Blood poured from his ruined eye socket, spilling out in a slow, grim stream that snaked across the tiles, painting the floor with a dark, living horror.

"Hey, what's up?" Ajee asked, leaning in closer to Sprite, who lay sprawled on the floor, still reeling from the chaos.

"I don't want this!" Sprite yelled, struggling to rise, her legs betraying her with their weakness. She twisted around and crawled, desperate to escape Ajee's grasp. "I don't want to be like you!"

Ajee's grip tightened around Sprite from behind, his hands steady on her trembling body.

He yanked her head back by the hair, the rough motion jerking her upward as his fingers tangled cruelly in her strands. A jolt of pain shot through her, an ugly reminder of the control he wielded with callous ease. Panic surged in Sprite, and a sharp scream escaped her lips, but Ajee's hand was there in an instant, clamping over her mouth with suffocating force. The sound was cut off abruptly, swallowed by his cruel grip, leaving her in a paralyzing silence punctuated only by the frantic pounding of her heart.

"I gave you freedom, and you just tossed it away," Ajee growled, his voice gravelly and laced with fury.

Sprite fought with the last vestiges of her strength, her elbow driving into Ajee's chest with a desperate jolt. Pain flickered in his eyes, and for a moment, his grip loosened. But instead of weakening him, that sudden pain seemed to invigorate Ajee; a twisted grin spread across his face as he laughed, the dark thrill of the struggle igniting something savage within him. As Sprite staggered away,

Ajee's boot slammed into her back, sending her crashing face-first to the floor.

He lunged to grab her hand, but Sprite fought back with the last of her strength. They tumbled across the cold ground in a desperate, frantic struggle. But it was a losing battle—Sprite's body and spirit were already spent, each movement a grim testament to her defeat. Amid the chaos, Ajee's laughter rang out—a dark, twisted melody of enjoyment that seemed to fuel his cruelty. As they writhed on the floor, Sprite's head slammed into a chair, and through the haze of pain, she caught sight of Mr. Gegge's eyeball rolling toward her, its ghastly movement a grotesque mockery of life. Terror clutched her chest, and in that instant, everything dissolved into an all-consuming blackness.

20

In the shadowed confines of its cage, the bird had spent its entire life. Cold metal bars were all it had ever known, a boundary so permanent it couldn't even fathom the idea of flight. The sky, the open world, was as alien to it as the surface of the moon. Why think of escape? Its owner was a dependable provider—food, water, a healer in sickness, a protector from unseen dangers. Every day, the bird sang its heart out, filling the air with a melody meant to please, to survive. It had come to believe this was its fate, and with time, it convinced itself that contentment lay within those bars.

But every now and then, its sharp eyes caught slivers of the world beyond: chickens scratching in the dirt, cats prowling in the dark, wild birds soaring freely through the air. A flicker of something stirred deep inside—was it longing? Fear? The outside world wasn't without its terrors. Birds got crushed under tires, torn apart by predators, their bodies limp under the indifferent sky. In those moments, the bird reassured itself. The cage was safety, it was certainty.

Until one day, a wild bird landed near the cage. It sat there, wings unruffled by fear, and the caged bird's world began to shift.

The wild bird cocked its head and said, "Hey, sis. I see you've been stuck in that cage a long time. I've been there, too—felt the same way, trapped behind bars. But don't worry. I know how to get that door open. I'll set you free, and you'll feel the wind under your wings, flying like you were meant to."

In a twist that cut against all reason, the pet bird—after a lifetime of confinement—turned away from the wild bird's offer of freedom with a cold, eerie finality. Its refusal felt inevitable, as if some dark force had already sealed its fate long ago. The open door, the promise of soaring skies, wasn't met with hope but with a deep, unsettling denial, as though the bird had made a choice it couldn't unmake—one that sent a shiver through the air.

"My brother, I can't leave this cage. I'm sorry, but I just can't. I know you're trying to help, and I appreciate it, I do. But I love my owner, and I know he loves me. He takes care of me—makes sure I'm fed, keeps me safe. We've got something, a bond. Trust, respect. And honestly? I don't want to leave him. I just... don't."

The wild bird's feathers bristled with irritation, a sharp ripple of disbelief. How could a prisoner willingly reject freedom? It was as if the cage had warped the pet bird's mind, twisting it into some cruel parody of loyalty—a dark game of Stockholm Syndrome. The idea of choosing captivity over the open skies gnawed at the wild bird, its patience fraying. There was something sickly surreal about the whole thing, a twisted irony that felt almost too bitter to swallow.

"Look, sis, don't kid yourself. If he really cared about you—if he truly trusted you—why keep you locked in that cage? Think about it. Why not let you fly around the yard, perch on his trees when you want? He could still feed you, you could still sing for him. That way, you'd have your freedom, and he'd still have you by his side. Doesn't that make more sense?"

The pet bird sank into a heavy silence, the wild bird's words hitting a nerve it had long tried to ignore. These thoughts weren't new—they'd echoed through its mind more times than it could count. It had wrestled with them, over and over, like shadows that refused to give way to light. But no answers ever came, just murky suspicions and half-formed beliefs, clinging to its heart like a fog that refused to lift. The clarity it craved remained elusive, always just out of reach.

"Listen, my wild brother," the pet bird said, its voice tinged with a quiet resignation. "Humans—they don't understand us, they don't hear what we're really saying. They think I'll try to escape the second they open this cage. That's why they keep it locked. Sure, it's not perfect, not even close. But it's something I've learned to live with."

The wild bird circled the cage in restless agitation, its wings slicing through the air with a frantic energy. Each pass around the bars felt like a silent taunt, a cruel reminder of the prison that held its kin. The relentless rhythm of its flight was a dance of frustration, a pulse of helplessness that said more than words ever could. It was as if the wild bird's very presence mocked the metal bars, daring them to bend, to break, but knowing full well they wouldn't.

"That just shows he doesn't really trust you," the wild bird insisted, its voice sharp as a beak. "Your love for him isn't mutual, sis. Why stay loyal to someone who doesn't treat you right? It's not fair, and you know it. Deep down, I bet you want freedom just like I do."

"No, I'm not looking for freedom," the pet bird replied, its tone steady but heavy. "I'm looking for peace."

"Alright, then," the wild bird said, the resignation heavy in its voice.

With a sudden explosion of energy, the wild bird pecked furiously at the locked cage door. Its beak struck with relentless urgency, tugging and clawing at the bindings that held the iron bars in place. The pet bird's heart raced, jolted by shock and alarm, its calm shattered by the wild bird's frantic, chaotic assault on its prison.

"What are you doing? Get out of here!" the pet bird cried, panic lacing its voice.

"I'm trying to open this door for you," the wild bird replied, its determination fierce despite the chaos.

"But I already told you, I don't want to leave this cage," the pet bird insisted, a tremor of defiance in its voice.

"I'm not making you leave, sis. I'm just giving you a choice—something your human master never bothered to do."

"What are you talking about?" the pet bird asked, confusion flickering in its eyes.

"Now the door's unlocked. Here's how you open and close it," the wild bird explained, demonstrating the mechanism of the cage door. "You can stay as long as you want—or leave whenever you like. Got it?"

After uttering its final words, the wild bird soared into the sky, disappearing behind the tangled branches of a tree of heaven. With its departure, a wave of overwhelming anxiety crashed over the pet bird. Huddled in the corner of its cage, it shrank away from the now-unlocked door, as if it were some monstrous beast. An internal struggle raged within—a fierce battle between the comfort of familiarity and a repressed longing for freedom, each side vying for dominance. This conflict gnawed at the pet bird, stripping away its appetite and leaving its once-plump body gaunt and trembling. It cursed the wild bird, the very gift of choice that had upended its peaceful existence. Before the wild bird's visit, life had been a serene routine. Now, its mind was a chaotic storm of dread and confusion.

Finally, one restless night, the pet bird resolved to confront its fears. It recalled how the wild bird had shown it to open the door. With hesitant pecks and tentative tugs, the door swung wide open. A rush of relief, previously unimaginable, surged through its chest. Its wings quivered with the promise of liberation as it stepped out of the cage. It envisioned soaring freely through the sky like the wild bird. But having never used its wings before, they felt stiff and foreign. The moment it attempted to fly, it plummeted to the ground, the impact jolting through it like a cruel reminder of its limits.

As it lay there, darkness unfurled around it, revealing a predator's gaze. A cat, its eyes glowing with a sinister hunger, prowled through the underbrush, closing in with lethal intent. The realization struck the pet bird like a cruel joke—the freedom it had yearned for now felt like a death sentence. In its terror, it no longer chirped but screamed, a raw, primal cry that echoed into the void as the shadows closed in, the cat's presence looming ever closer.

"Help! Somebody, help! Master, please! I'm sorry—I swear I won't try to leave again! Just help me!" The words tumbled out in a frantic plea, desperation threading through each frantic note.

The bird's desperate cries didn't go unanswered for long. Footsteps echoed in the distance, growing nearer, each step resonating with urgency. Just as the cat coiled, poised to strike, a bundle of broomsticks came crashing down, slamming into its face. Startled and wild-eyed, the cat let out a yowl of terror, spinning on its paws before bolting over the fence and vanishing into the neighbor's yard, leaving nothing but the faint rustle of leaves and a bird gasping for breath.

"How'd you end up out here?" the owner asked, scooping up the bird and gently placing it back in the cage. "Huh, looks like the door's busted."

The owner repaired the cage door, clicking the lock shut with a finality that echoed in the stillness. Inside, the bird let out a cry—not of despair, but of sheer relief. Its life had been spared, and oddly enough, it found comfort in the familiar confines of its prison. It was safe, back where it belonged. The next day, the wild bird returned, circling above, eager to see what had become of its sister.

"Thanks to you, I almost got eaten by a cat," the pet bird snapped, its voice sharp with irritation.

"Eaten by a cat? Why didn't you just fly off?" the wild bird asked, eyeing the cage door now locked tight.

"Did you forget? I can't fly like you. My life is here; my place is in this cage. Don't compare me to you," the pet bird shot back, its voice laced with frustration.

"That's nonsense. How could you not be able to fly? You probably just panicked," the wild bird retorted, its tone incredulous.

The wild bird moved to tamper with the cage door lock again, its beak poised to pry at the metal. But the pet bird intervened, blocking its way. This wasn't about the lock anymore; it was about something deeper—something the wild bird couldn't begin to understand.

"Get outta here. Stop messing with my life!"

The wild bird flew away, a heavy sense of disappointment weighing on its feathers. It couldn't shake the feeling of pity for the pet bird, whose spirit seemed utterly hollowed out, scrubbed clean of any true desires or dreams. The wild bird gnawed at itself with self-reproach, haunted by the thought that it had failed to teach its sister how to fly before cracking open the cage.

Ajee snapped the notebook shut and set it down on the drawer with a soft thud. He grabbed the glass of water he'd left sitting on the table, downing it with urgency, his throat parched from just a few pages of reading. The cool liquid revived him, as if it coursed through his veins, awakening something long dormant.

Once he drained the glass, he stood up and turned his gaze to Sprite, sprawled on the bed. Her hands and feet were tightly bound to the corners, her mouth gagged and sealed with tape. Only her eyes were free, darting around in a desperate attempt to convey her emotions—a silent scream trapped within her frantic gaze.

"How's it going, sweetheart? Enjoying my story? Why aren't you asleep yet? Is it too intense for you?"

Sprite's muffled moans seeped through the tape, a haunting echo of Mr. Gegge's own groans when he had endured a similar fate. The sound was disturbingly familiar, a cruel reminder of the helpless cries that once haunted the dark corners of her memories.

She had no idea what had become of him, never catching a glimpse of his fate again, and the silence that followed his disappearance loomed over her like a dark cloud—just as unsettling as the torment she now faced.

"Yeah, the story's just fiction, not a perfect match. But I get how that wild bird felt. I should've taught you how to fly before I opened your cage. I'm sorry. I'll make it right."

Sprite writhed against the ropes binding her hands and feet, each twist and pull only deepening the bite of the bindings. With every desperate tug, the fibers dug mercilessly into her skin, a relentless grip that refused to loosen. The more she fought, the tighter they became, a brutal reminder of her utter helplessness.

Ajee hovered nearby, glancing in every few minutes to ensure she remained trapped. "What's wrong, sweetheart? Want to escape?" he taunted. "I told you, I can't let you go just yet. First, I have to teach you how to fly."

21

Sprite's hands and feet were bound tight, and she'd barely scraped together a few hours of fitful sleep—midnight to three a.m., if she had any sense left. Every time she cracked her eyes open, that godforsaken clock on the wall blinked back at her, its cheap instant coffee logo staring her down like a bad omen, mocking her. Maybe it was the logo that kept her awake, or maybe it was the memory of her twisted, sadistic husband, his ghost still haunting her like a shadow in her brain, making sleep impossible. Awake, Sprite's thoughts spun out of control, a twisted, wild carousel of desperate plans for escape.

She'd long since given up on fighting the ropes that cut into her wrists, her strength drained to nothing after hours of struggling and begging, every ounce of hope wrung dry. Now, she was just a hollow shell, filled with nothing but dread and exhaustion. The cloth gag was tight against her mouth, plastered over like a cruel joke—she couldn't scream even if she had the strength. The early morning was suffocatingly silent, save for the eerie sound of a violin somewhere in the darkness. Its mournful notes slashed through the quiet like a knife, haunting, chilling. Ajee's violin. That same sorrowful melody she'd heard a few nights ago, threading its way into her mind. She didn't know a thing about music, especially not classical, but this tune... this damned tune was different. It twisted something deep inside her. As if the Ajee playing it wasn't her husband at all, but a stranger—a shadow wearing his skin, a ghost with a violin bow.

She'd spent days trying to convince herself that Ajee's strange, erratic behavior was just the result of some mental disorder—stress, maybe depression, something she could rationalize, explain away. Something human.

After all, he'd had those bouts with high fevers, times when he'd collapse, burning up and delirious, and losing his job had struck him like a sledgehammer. That much made sense. But now, as the haunting melody floated through the air, it twisted something inside her. It made her see the truth she'd tried to ignore: the man playing that violin wasn't the man she married. Beneath the surface of her husband was someone else, something darker, something she barely recognized.

He wasn't just another side of Ajee; he was someone else entirely, with a different past, different memories, different ambitions. Dissociative identity disorder? Maybe. But it felt deeper than that, like an entirely new person had taken root inside the shell of the man she used to know. A stranger with a dark, twisted backstory, hiding behind her husband's face, harboring intentions she couldn't even begin to guess.

Sprite had seen this kind of thing before, played out in the flickering glow of horror movies: one personality sweet and charming, the other a monstrous beast, clawing for control. But with Ajee, it wasn't that simple. Both of his personalities were equally vile. The first was a thick-headed brute, numb to anything resembling empathy, barreling through life with a total lack of sensitivity. There was no charm, no mask to peel away—just different shades of the same loathsome creature.

Sure, he never hit her, but his words were weapons, sharp enough to cut deeper than any blow. He unleashed a relentless barrage of verbal and psychological terror on Sprite, day after day. The Ajee she faced now wasn't just despicable—he was a full-blown monster, a creature of malice and twisted intent, hiding behind the familiar face of her husband. The mask had slipped, and what lay beneath was something far darker than she ever imagined.

Once, he'd been the very picture of kindness and gentleness, a charming prince in a world of darkness. But beneath that façade lurked a ruthless predator, someone who felt no hesitation about inflicting pain or even snuffing out lives. And now, look at what that so-called romantic man had done to her. The transformation was sickening, a cruel betrayal of everything she thought she knew.

Deep down, Sprite had known all along. From the very beginning, she'd sensed that malevolent presence lurking within the new Ajee. She wasn't blind; she wasn't deaf. The darkness had always been there, hidden but unmistakable, its chill creeping up from the depths of his soul, wrapping around her like a cold hand. She had felt it, that quiet dread whispering in her ear, a warning she'd been too afraid to fully acknowledge until now.

Ajee was right—deep down, she had quietly accepted it all. She had allowed the horror to seep into her life, like a slow poison, numbing her senses and dulling her instincts. It was easier to pretend everything was fine than to confront the truth. But now, as the darkness closed in around her, that quiet acceptance felt like a betrayal, a shackle binding her to the nightmare she could no longer ignore.

She'd struck an uneasy truce with the darkness, content to linger in the murky shadows of her own fear. She didn't care where Ajee's money came from or what crimes he committed in the world beyond their door. All that mattered to her was the illusion of a romantic dinner, the glimmer of glittering jewelry, the allure of stylish clothes, and the adrenaline rush of racing a motorcycle. It was a dangerous game she played, but for a moment, it was enough to drown out the whispers of dread lurking just beneath the surface.

She was a hypocrite, drowning in the intoxicating haze of her own denial. Sprite sobbed uncontrollably, her tears a torrential flood of anguish. It wasn't just the fear for her life or the suffocating prison her husband had trapped her in—it was the crushing weight of self-blame. If only she had gone to the police from the start, if only she'd spoken up after that candlelit dinner when he had given her that eerie necklace. Each thought felt like a knife, slicing deeper into her chest, leaving her gasping for air in a world that had turned upside down.

Maybe, just maybe, she could have spared countless lives from this unfolding nightmare. The weight of that possibility sat heavy on her shoulders, a relentless specter haunting her every thought. What if her silence had fed this darkness? What if she had acted sooner, pulled the thread that could unravel it all? Each unspoken word felt like a betrayal, echoing in her mind, a constant reminder of the lives that hung in the balance because she hadn't found the courage to speak up.

Maybe if she'd acted sooner, Waverley wouldn't have lost his job, his child might have walked down the aisle, and Sprite wouldn't be bound hand and foot, trapped in this waking nightmare. The thought gnawed at her like a relentless rat, each regret a sharp bite. Every missed opportunity felt like a chain link, binding her tighter to this horror, a stark reminder of the lives shattered because of her inaction.

In her lonely confinement, she tore into herself with even more venom. *You're no different from him,* she hissed through her gag, the words bubbling with bitterness. *You didn't just grip that fork tightly—you craved the thrill of plunging it into that bastard Mr. Gegge's eye.* The thought twisted inside her, a dark pleasure she couldn't shake, a sick fantasy that danced on the edge of her desperation.

Her scream was muffled by the gag, emerging as a pathetic, sibilant hiss that seemed to dissolve into the shadows. It was a sound that echoed her desperation, a feeble cry swallowed by the oppressive silence, lost in the void of her confinement.

She pictured herself screaming the truth over and over, even as a massive wave crashed before her. *I really did want to poke his eye out. But I didn't actually want to do it.* Unlike Ajee, she was merely an observer—like a bird in a cage, savoring the idea of wild freedom without ever daring to reach for it. She was like someone relishing a theme park ride, thrilled by the sensation of falling while remaining safely strapped in. A horror movie junkie craving terror without facing the chase, a bookworm eager to dive into the twisted minds of deranged characters while sidestepping their burdens.

And as if on cue, Ajee's violin swelled, its eerie notes saturating the room with an oppressive dread. Over time, it felt as though the strings were scraping against her very bones, a relentless, gnawing pain that burrowed deeper with each passing moment. What had once been a mournful melody morphed into a frenetic, high-pitched barrage—like the soundtrack of a thriller where the hero is relentlessly pursued by an unfeeling, invincible killer. Then, just as abruptly, the high notes cut off in a jarring climax—like a string snapping under unbearable tension. With that, the room plunged into an oppressive silence, heavy and suffocating.

Sprite drifted into a restless sleep, her mind sinking into the murky depths of unconsciousness. It was a dark, formless void where nightmares lurked, waiting to drag her deeper into a world she desperately wished to escape. Each moment of slumber felt like a surrender, a fleeting respite from the horror that awaited her when she opened her eyes again.

In her dream, Ajee sipped her coffee and muttered, "This coffee's terrible. Did you put cyanide in it or something?" His voice dripped with mockery, a chilling blend of humor and menace that sent a shiver down her spine. The casual cruelty in his tone twisted the mundane moment into something sinister, a reminder that even in her dreams, there was no escape from the darkness lurking just beneath the surface.

22

Sprite woke up craving the sweet comfort of a horchata latte and a pernil sandwich, a small mercy she longed for. But if that was too much to ask, she'd settle for waking up with her hands free. She'd make her own damn breakfast, maybe even brew Ajee his bottomless pot of coffee, regardless of the churning in her gut and the thick fog in her head. She wouldn't complain about breaking her back to keep food on the table while her husband played unemployed king. She could handle it all—as long as she wasn't dragged back into the nightmare of serial murders. Hell, she'd crawl back to her cage if she had to, as long as she wasn't stalked by some prowling beast with blood on its mind. But was that really the deal here? Ajee's laughter echoed in her skull, bouncing off the walls of her mind like a loose screw rattling in a tin can. It wasn't just a sound; it was a presence, a shadow creeping into the corners of her thoughts, and she couldn't shake the feeling that something was coming for her.

She could hear it even in the dead silence of the room, a haunting reminder that no matter how far she ran, no matter how much distance she tried to create, Ajee was still in there—laughing, always laughing. The sound curled around her like smoke, persistent and inescapable, taunting her with the truth that no matter where she hid, his laughter would always find her.

First, I have to teach you how to fly. It's not just about spreading your wings; it's about knowing the weight of the world beneath you and how to soar above it, defying gravity and fear.

That voice suddenly crawled out of her head and stepped into the real world. The door creaked open from the outside, slow and deliberate, and there he was—Ajee, grinning like a snake that had just cornered its prey. His smile slithered across his face, a mix of charm and menace that sent a chill skittering down her spine. The air thickened, the shadows deepened, and she knew, in that instant, that whatever game he was playing, she was the unwitting player, trapped in a chilling dance with a predator.

He stepped in, carrying a tray like it was some kind of offering, a plate precariously balanced beside a bowl and a glass that trembled with each cautious step he took. The whole setup felt more like a ritual than breakfast, each item on the tray laden with unspoken significance. The weight of it hung heavy in the air, suffocating her with the sense that this was no ordinary meal—it was a calculated performance, and she was the unwilling audience, bracing for the act to unfold.

She had no clue what lay hidden under those covers, but her stomach didn't care—it growled like a wild animal, loud and needy, drawn to the thought of food and drink like a moth to a flame. Hunger had a way of overriding everything else, even fear, gnawing at her insides until it eclipsed the dread that lingered in the corners of her mind. In that moment, survival eclipsed all else, the primal urge to eat clawing its way to the forefront of her thoughts, demanding attention as if it were a monster of its own.

"Morning, babe. Sorry the breakfast's a little late," Ajee said, setting the tray down on the edge of the bed before sinking into the mattress beside her. His voice was casual, almost too smooth, as if the delay were just a minor inconvenience rather than a prelude to something darker. The way he settled next to her sent a shiver down her spine, a reminder that his charm often masked the lurking shadows beneath.

Sprite looked at Ajee, and it struck her how his face hadn't changed at all since that first night. It was unsettling—whether she was tied up or free, it seemed to make no difference to him. His expression remained the same: cold and indifferent, as if she were just another piece of furniture in the room, an object to be overlooked. The realization clawed at her insides, a creeping dread that he saw her not as a person, but as a mere accessory to his twisted game.

She glanced at the bowl on the tray, a thin, soupy mess sloshing inside. Soup. The word rolled through her mind like an old memory, distant and faint, evoking a sense of longing that twisted her gut. It had been ages since she'd tasted soup, and now here it was, staring back at her like a forgotten ghost from a life she barely remembered—a comforting reminder of normalcy that felt hauntingly out of reach. The steam curled upward, filling the air with a scent that stirred something deep within her, a flicker of warmth in the cold shadow of her reality.

She was beyond sick of steak, sandwiches, and pizza, and the thought of sipping warm soup felt like a small, stolen luxury. But did this mean Ajee would finally take off her mouth cover? The hope clung to her like a last shred of sanity in a world that seemed to have forgotten what kindness meant. It was a fragile ember in the oppressive darkness, flickering but refusing to die out. If she could just taste that soup, maybe it would remind her that humanity still existed, buried beneath the layers of fear and despair.

If he wanted her to eat, he'd have to take off the cover. Maybe—just maybe—this was the first crack in the wall, the faint glimmer of a path toward freedom. The thought sent a rush of adrenaline through her veins, igniting a flicker of hope that she hadn't dared to entertain before. It felt dangerous, almost reckless, but in this twisted reality, any sign of mercy could be the turning point she desperately craved.

She could almost taste it—a fleeting hint of freedom, like a dream that was just within reach. She pictured it vividly: once he pulled off the cover, he might—just might—start loosening the bindings on her hands and feet, piece by piece, turning it into a cruel game with the tantalizing promise of escape. The thought danced in her mind, both exhilarating and terrifying, as if each loosened knot held the potential to unleash her from this nightmare. But she knew better; hope was a dangerous thing in a place like this, where every glimmer of light was shadowed by the threat of darkness.

"If you want to eat, then I've got to take off your mouth cover first, right?" Ajee asked, his voice smooth and casual, as if he were discussing the weather rather than the key to her survival. The words dripped with an unsettling nonchalance, making her skin crawl. It felt like a game to him, a twisted negotiation where her hunger was just another pawn on his chessboard.

Sprite nodded, her heart thudding in her chest. This was the moment she'd been holding her breath for—the thin sliver of hope she'd clung to in the suffocating dark. Each beat echoed in her ears, a frantic reminder that this fragile chance might slip away if she didn't seize it. In that instant, the world around her faded, and all that mattered was the possibility of freedom, shimmering just out of reach.

Ajee rubbed his chin, glancing up at the ceiling as if he were deep in thought. "If I take off your mouth cover, are you going to scream?" he asked, leaning in close to Sprite, his breath brushing against her skin. The question hung in the air, thick with tension, and she could feel the weight of his gaze, searching for the answer hidden behind her fear. In that moment, she was acutely aware of how precarious her situation was, teetering on the edge of danger with every heartbeat.

Sprite knew she had to play her cards right this time. Gone was the naïve, trembling version of herself; she had to be sharp and fearless, a warrior forged in the fires of her own desperation. She couldn't afford to falter now; every decision was a high-stakes gamble, and she needed to be ready to bluff her way through the darkness. With each breath, she steeled herself, reminding herself that survival required more than just instinct—it demanded cunning.

She shook her head slowly, a deliberate gesture that served as a quiet signal of resolve in the murky game of survival she found herself tangled in. Each movement was measured, a defiant stand against the chaos that surrounded her. In that moment, she understood that strength came not from the absence of fear, but from the decision to confront it head-on, even when the odds were stacked against her.

"Promise?" Ajee asked, his voice laced with a mock sincerity that sent a chill down her spine. The word hung in the air, a thin veil over a darker intent, as if he were sealing a pact she wasn't sure she wanted to make. His eyes searched hers, probing for any hint of weakness, and she felt the weight of his gaze like a noose tightening around her throat.

This time, Sprite nodded, her movements slow and deliberate, each one weighed down by a heavy, ominous sense of foreboding. It felt as if the air itself thickened around her, pressing in with the weight of unspoken consequences. Each nod was a silent acknowledgment of the danger lurking just beyond the edges of her fragile hope, a reminder that every choice could lead her deeper into darkness.

23

Ajee peeled the plaster from Sprite's mouth, slow and careful, like he was scared her skin might come with it. He did it as gentle as he could, but still, a sharp sting lit up Sprite's cheek—a mean little reminder that no matter how soft the touch, pain had a way of sneaking in, finding its mark.

Then he yanked the cloth from her mouth, the one that had been stuffed in there who knows how long. It hit the floor with a wet slap, and that's when it clicked—Sprite recognized the fabric. It was torn from right under her sewing machine. The second she was free, a ragged, desperate gasp ripped from her throat, like her lungs had been waiting a lifetime to taste air again.

Without missing a beat, she screamed with every bit of strength she had left. "Screw you! You bastard!"

The cloth was shoved back into her mouth before she could catch another breath, rough and fast, like they were trying to wipe her scream from existence.

Ajee slammed his palm down, pressing the cloth tight against her mouth. It smothered her screams, leaving only faint, tortured groans slipping through, like the whispers of a soul trapped deep inside.

When the screams finally dried up in her throat, Sprite was left wrestling with a gnawing confusion. Why hadn't she screamed for help? Shouted "Thief!" or "Fire!"—anything that might've drawn someone's attention? Instead, all she'd managed was "Screw you!"

and "You bastard!" The bitter irony settled in, and with a sinking dread, she realized she hadn't changed a bit—still caught in the same naïve, emotional spiral, lashing out when she should've been fighting to survive.

Ajee's laughter spilled out, cruel and jagged, as he kept stuffing the gag in her mouth. His shoulders shook with each chortle, and his grin stretched wider, twisting his face into something grotesque, almost unrecognizable—a mask of sick amusement that made him look more like a monster than a man.

"Feels better, don't it?" Ajee asked, not expecting an answer. "Better to curse than sit there grumbling, right? Grumbling don't get you nowhere. And all that talk about water crystals?" He let out a snort. "Total crap—pseudoscience."

At those words, a chill slithered down Sprite's spine.

She couldn't shake the suspicion that Ajee could read her thoughts—or at least, he once had. Had the thing inside him been some kind of ghost before? A spirit drifting through her life, lurking in the shadows, eavesdropping on the private corners of her mind? The thought twisted in her gut like a knife, digging deeper with every passing moment.

Sprite stopped fighting. She needed to conserve what little strength she had left. She tried to slow her breathing, but her stomach growled, deep and hollow, hunger gnawing at her insides. It hit her—she hadn't eaten or drunk anything for nearly a day. Maybe that was why her body felt so drained, her voice just a rasp in her throat. Weakness had crept in silently, stealing the fight right out of her.

Ajee's voice dripped with a casual menace as he spoke. "Even if you tried to scream for help with that weak voice of yours, nobody would hear you. Alhric, the guy next door, has been off in Portland with his wife for the past week, and the apartment on the left is still empty. But honestly? I'd rather you didn't scream at all. Just in case.

I don't want you straining your throat." He lifted a bowl of soup and inhaled its steam with exaggerated pleasure, closing his eyes as he savored the aroma for Sprite's benefit. "So, do we have a deal? No more screaming?"

Sprite hit her breaking point. She had no strength left to fight; struggling felt like a futile exercise in agony. Her body was leaden, each movement a torturous reminder of just how powerless she'd become.

She nodded over and over, each motion a weary concession. A single tear slipped from the corner of her eye, the starkest sign of her surrender, as if that tiny drop of emotion was the last vestige of her fight. Ajee's smile spread, cold and satisfied, like a predator relishing its victory.

He set the bowl back on the tray with deliberate slowness, savoring the moment. Then, with methodical ease, he peeled the gag from her mouth, as if it were just another step in his twisted ritual.

Once more, Sprite could draw a full breath. This time, she kept her mouth shut, the lesson of her previous mistake etched firmly in her mind. She inhaled deeply, trying to steady the frantic pounding of her heart. But as Ajee leaned in and pressed a kiss to her sweat-drenched forehead, her pulse quickened again, fear intertwining with the unsettling intimacy of the gesture.

He ladled rice and broth into her mouth, one spoonful of each, as if he held some bizarre belief they shouldn't mingle. To her surprise, the meat soup was rich and savory, its flavor almost luxurious, a cruel reminder of the comfort she'd long been denied.

She couldn't tell if Ajee had splurged on a fancy meal from some swanky joint or if her ravenous hunger was turning each bite into a rare indulgence. Just then, Sprite began to cough, having swallowed too quickly, the harsh reality of her situation crashing in on her fleeting moment of pleasure like a wave.

Without missing a beat, Ajee thrust a glass of water into her mouth, his movements sharp and deliberate, as if he feared the momentary relief would slip away just as quickly as it had come.

Sprite let out a relieved sigh as the cool water soothed her throat. "Aren't you worried about the cops?" she asked, disbelief threading through her voice.

"Nope," Ajee said, scooping more rice onto his spoon. "I'm not scared of anything." His tone was casual, but there was a hard edge beneath it, like a steel blade hiding behind a veneer of nonchalance.

"You've actually killed someone. You're going to end up in prison," Sprite shot back, her voice steady but laced with disbelief.

"You talking about those people from the news? Chill out, babe. I've got it all sorted. They might nab someone else, if they can," Ajee said, shoveling another spoonful into Sprite's mouth. "Even if they catch me, so what? I don't care. I'm going to do what I want while I can, and they're welcome to try and catch me—if they're up to the task." His voice dripped with defiance, a challenge thrown into the air like a gauntlet.

"But I don't want any part of this. I'm not a killer," Sprite whispered, struggling to keep her voice steady.

"Ever get the feeling you've actually killed someone? I told you to stab someone in the eye, and you were shaking," Ajee taunted, a cruel smirk creeping across his face.

"But Mr. Gegge is dead, right? Where'd you stash his body? In this apartment?" Sprite asked between bites, her voice laced with concern. She wasn't sure what had happened to Mr. Gegge after she'd stabbed him, but she was pretty damn sure Ajee had finished him off.

With a wound like that, keeping him alive would have been more trouble than it was worth. It was a mess no amount of effort could fix—a grim reminder that sometimes, death was the simplest solution.

Maybe she hadn't delivered the fatal blow herself—she remembered seeing Mr. Gegge writhing in agony, his eye a bloody mess, just before she panicked and tried to escape. But the truth loomed like a shadow: her fingerprints were all over that fork. Sprite's mind twisted with dark imaginings, each one darker than the last.

Each time Ajee vanished into the night, she pictured him out there, burying or hiding the bodies of his victims. Their apartment had no yard—so where was he stashing them? In someone else's house? Out in the open park nearby? The possibilities churned in her mind, each one more horrifying than the last, twisting like a dark spiral into madness.

"Yeah, I hid him in this apartment," Ajee said, a smirk creeping across his face. "More specifically, he's inside your stomach right now." The words hung in the air, chilling and grotesque, like a dark joke that wasn't funny at all.

Sprite's chewing came to an abrupt halt. A sickening wave of nausea churned in her stomach and chest, a gut-wrenching realization crashing over her. This wasn't mondongo.

She should have seen it coming from the start. "This, this..." She couldn't even form the words, her throat tightening as the reality set in.

Her stomach twisted violently, as if everything inside her—even her heart—was trying to claw its way up and out of her mouth.

"That's right, babe. And it's not the first time, either. Remember that steak we had on our anniversary?" Ajee grinned, a mischievous glint in his eyes. He fished out a round object from the soup and held it up for her to see, the gesture dripping with dark amusement.

At first, Sprite mistook it for a meatball or maybe a quail egg. But as Ajee brought it closer, the sickening truth dawned on her—it was an eyeball. Mr. Gegge's eyeball. The realization crashed over her like a cold, suffocating wave, twisting her insides with horror.

"This is the eye you stabbed," Ajee said, nodding eagerly, as if he were showcasing a grotesque trophy.

Sprite reached her breaking point. She heaved, the remnants of her meager meal erupting violently from her stomach. The vomit spilled over her neck and dripped onto her clothes, a grotesque mess that clung to her like a cruel, sticky reminder of her helplessness.

"I'm not eating this." The words escaped her lips like a desperate vow, laced with defiance and horror.

"If you're not eating this, then you're not eating anything else. I can't cook anything else—I only do this kind of meat," he replied, his tone casual, as if he were discussing the weather rather than the grotesque choice before her.

Sprite's tears broke free, streaming down her face in a silent cascade of despair.

She felt trapped in a nightmare, each moment more surreal than the last, with no idea how to claw her way out of the suffocating darkness.

"Keep screaming, and I'll gag you again," Ajee warned, his voice slicing through the air with a sharp edge of menace.

"What do you want from me? Just tell me what you need, and I'll do it. Just let me go," she pleaded, desperation threading through her voice like a frayed wire ready to snap.

"Come on, babe, what's the matter with you? Isn't it obvious what I want?" Ajee said, his voice dripping with mock concern. "First things first—finish your food. If you don't eat, you're gonna get sick, and I don't want that." He coaxed Sprite to open her mouth, then slipped Mr. Gegge's eyeball inside, a twisted offering of compliance.

At first, Sprite struggled to spit it out, her instincts raging against the grotesque act. But when she locked eyes with Ajee's chillingly sinister smile, a wave of icy fear surged through her, paralyzing her in place.

Ajee could snuff out her life in an instant, as easy as flipping a switch. If he wanted to, her fate could mirror Mr. Gegge's—an inescapable descent into the cold grip of his will. The promise she had made just moments before echoed ominously in her mind: she would do anything.

Sprite forced herself to chew the eyeball slowly, grappling with the overwhelming urge to retch. Desperation clawed at her, and she twisted her reality with frantic fervor: This was just a meatball. Just an egg. Just mondongo. Anything but what it truly was.

As her teeth sank into the object, an unnerving softness met her bite—like rubber yielding beneath her pressure. Determined to escape the horror, she swallowed quickly, feeling it slither down her throat, a grotesque sensation that clung to her insides like a dark secret refusing to let go.

Ajee pressed another kiss to Sprite's forehead, a chilling gesture of approval. A good wife, an obedient wife. The kiss landed like a twisted brand of submission, sealing her forced compliance with a silent, sinister promise.

He ladled another serving of rice and soup into her mouth, each spoonful a grim ritual, a relentless reminder of her captivity. Sprite's mind raced with dark, harrowing questions: What else had he fashioned from his victims' remains? What was really in the broth? Blood? Urine? Each thought twisted her stomach tighter, a haunting dread clawing at the edges of her sanity.

"Don't sweat it. You didn't do anything wrong. He's the one who messed up—a creep who harassed you. He got what he deserved."

24

Sprite forced down the final spoonful of human flesh soup, her stomach twisting and churning with each reluctant gulp. The taste, thick and vile, clung to her tongue like a living thing, like something that didn't belong inside her, something that shouldn't exist at all.

She'd never, not even in her darkest, most twisted nightmares, imagined she'd become a cannibal. But now she had, and the thing she'd just done—the line she'd crossed—would haunt her far deeper than any nightmare ever could. "Why are you doing this to me? What did I do wrong?" she whispered, her voice thin and raw, as Ajee wiped down the dishes, already halfway out the door, not even bothering to look back.

"Because I love you," Ajee said, his voice low, almost tender. "You've been stuck, babe. Trapped by me, by your own head. You couldn't do what you really wanted, so I had to step in. You weren't happy, and all I want is to see you happy." He set the tray down, his fingers gliding through Sprite's hair in a gesture that should've been comforting but felt like something darker, something twisted.

"So, now what? Do I look happy? Do I look free?" Sprite snapped, her voice sharp as broken glass. She glared down at her hands and feet, bound tight to the bed, the ropes biting into her skin.

"You still don't get it," Ajee sighed, his voice heavy with exhaustion, as if he'd been carrying this weight forever. He shook his head slowly, almost sadly. "Not yet, babe. Not yet. When you're ready, I'll let you go." The words hung in the air like a promise wrapped in chains.

"Ready for what?" Sprite shot back, her voice cutting through the room like a blade, sharp with frustration and fear.

"Ready to live free, with the guts to grab whatever you want," Ajee replied, his voice steady, almost unnervingly calm, as if this twisted logic made perfect sense to him.

"And what if I don't want to?" Sprite shot back, her eyes narrowing, fury simmering beneath her words. "Do I get the freedom to say no?" Her voice was tight, daring him to answer.

Ajee smirked, a slow, cold twist of his lips. "Smart girl. I knew I didn't make the wrong call. But here's the thing—you won't wanna say no. Even if you think you do, that's just cause you don't understand yet." He leaned in closer, his voice dropping to a near whisper. "That's enough questions for now. You need to relax, or you'll burn yourself out before you even see the whole picture."

Sprite's words tumbled out in a rush, just as Ajee reached for the cloth to gag her again. "And if I fight back, are you gonna kill me too?" Her voice was tight, fear laced with defiance, daring him to answer.

Ajee pressed the cloth against her mouth, securing it with tape, his movements deliberate. "You know, death's a type of freedom too, babe," he said, his tone unnervingly calm. Once he ensured Sprite was completely restrained, unable to cry for help, he grabbed the tray and stood up. As he walked out of the room, he nudged the half-open door with his foot, leaving behind a silence that felt heavier than the air itself.

25

Sprite lay sprawled on the bed like a ragdoll tossed aside, the sheets a chaotic tangle around her. Time dripped by, slow and relentless, like a leaky faucet, each minute stretching out into a taffy-like eternity. The room was heavy with a silence that clung to her skin, thick and suffocating, as if the very air was waiting, holding its breath for something—anything—to happen.

By the afternoon, Ajee arrived with lunch in tow, and as Sprite had anticipated, the menu still leaned heavily on meat. This time, it was pollo guisado—a dish so rich and savory it could've fed a small army. The aroma wafted through the air, thick and tantalizing, stirring something deep inside her. It was the kind of meal that promised warmth and comfort, yet felt like a reminder of everything she was trying to escape.

Sprite grimaced at the thought of how a man of Mr. Gegge's bulk could hardly be consumed in a single meal. What really churned her stomach—more than the grim reality of feasting on human flesh—was the undeniable truth that Ajee's cooking was exceptional. It wasn't the human meat that made it so; it was the masterful blend of spices, the way Ajee coaxed out the very best from every ingredient he touched. Each bite was a paradox, rich and flavorful, a symphony of tastes that danced on her tongue while her mind screamed in horror.

He was a maestro in the kitchen, conjuring dishes that could make your taste buds dance, but that was just the tip of the iceberg. Beyond being a virtuoso violinist and a master of seduction, with a smile that could melt ice, he had a darker side—a cold-blooded killer with a heart as chill as the grave. There was a disquieting charisma about him, an unsettling charm that wrapped around you like a velvet noose, leaving you breathless and unsure whether to laugh or shiver. In the end, it was hard to tell which part of him was the performance and which was the true horror lurking beneath.

Moments after she'd choked down lunch, grappling with the queasy knots of guilt twisting in her gut, Sprite turned to Ajee, a question burning in her core. What was he, really? Was he some kind of ghost, drifting in from the shadows of her past? A demon lurking in the recesses of her mind? The uncertainty clawed at her, a relentless itch that refused to be scratched, leaving her teetering on the edge of understanding and madness. She could feel the weight of his gaze, as if he were reading her thoughts, each flicker of his smile deepening her dread.

Or perhaps—just perhaps—he was a figment of her own twisted imagination, a specter that had somehow crawled out of her nightmares and into the flesh-and-blood reality of her waking world. The thought sent a chill down her spine, as if the very fabric of her sanity were unraveling. What if Ajee was nothing more than a shadow, a dark echo of her fears, manifesting in a way she could no longer ignore? The line between reality and nightmare blurred, and she found herself wondering if she was the architect of her own horror.

"Look, I already told you, you're the one who dragged me into this," he said, brushing a stray bit of pollo guisado from the corner of Sprite's mouth. "You might not get it, but I'm always around. I hear your complaints—every last one of them, even the ones you never dared to say out loud. Your quiet mutterings, the things you bury deep inside, and the secrets you scribble in that diary of yours? I know all of it, babe. I've been in your life far longer than your husband ever has." His voice was low and smooth, like honey laced with poison, and it sent a shiver down her spine as the reality of his words sank in.

A shiver crawled down Sprite's spine, leaving icy trails in its wake, like ghostly fingers tracing the path of her dread. The chill seeped into her bones, a visceral reminder of the darkness lurking just beneath the surface of her reality.

She couldn't shake the unsettling thought that all along, as she whispered her deepest grievances into the night, a shadowy figure had stood silently beside her, listening intently. When she scribbled in her diary, she envisioned someone lurking just out of sight, peering over her shoulder—perhaps laying a cold hand on her or brushing her hair with a ghostly caress. And when she slept, she imagined eyes watching her from the darkness, tracking her every movement with a hunger so palpable she could almost feel it, like breath on the back of her neck, a chill that sent her heart racing.

"Is Ajee dead?" she asked, her voice laced with disbelief. The words felt foreign on her tongue, as if summoning a specter she couldn't quite grasp. She recalled how this nightmare of a person had once alluded to wanting to get rid of the old Ajee, and a shiver of unease curled in her stomach. What did that mean? Did she dare to ponder what lay beneath that twisted façade?

Ajee took a deep breath, his gaze sweeping the room as if searching for a buried memory. "I don't know, maybe. Does it even matter? You were the one who said you never loved him. Your marriage was just a deal you got roped into. There was nothing special about that Ajee Arizin. I used him not because he was anything great, but because he was weak—boring and weak. It's honestly a shame you ended up with someone like him." His words dripped with a venomous honesty, each syllable a reminder of the disdain he felt, as if he reveled in the notion that her past was nothing more than a tragic misstep.

"He's not weak," Sprite replied, her voice steady and defensive. The words came out sharper than she intended, a fragile shield against the bitterness that threatened to seep in. She could feel the heat rising in her cheeks, a fierce loyalty igniting within her that pushed back against Ajee's disdain.

He might have been dull as dishwater, but weakness was never his fault. For reasons she couldn't quite pin down, her perception of Ajee began to shift. Out of nowhere, memories of him started to take on a warmer, almost nostalgic glow, casting him in a light she hadn't recognized before. Each recollection seemed to soften the edges of her criticism, blurring the harsh lines of reality, and for a fleeting moment, she found herself wondering if there was more to him than she had ever allowed herself to see.

Ajee wasn't weak; he was merely caught in the eye of a storm that had battered and bruised him. Life had thrown its worst at him, relentless and unyielding, leaving scars that ran deeper than skin. Each blow had chipped away at his spirit, but beneath it all lay a resilience she had never noticed before, a quiet strength struggling to surface amid the chaos.

Maybe, as his wife, she had been too quick to give up on him. The thought made her despise herself, a bitter taste of regret settling on her tongue. Why was she suddenly turning the blame inward? Perhaps it was because the man standing before her now was the ideal Ajee she had always imagined, yet he fell tragically short of the real thing she had wanted. What was this twisted mindset she was grappling with? The contrast between her fantasies and the truth gnawed at her, leaving her feeling unmoored and adrift in a sea of confusion.

She wasn't sure if there was a name for this feeling, but she knew someone, somewhere, had probably labeled it. People had a name for everything, even the strangest of emotions. It was that maddening sensation you got when you ditched your lousy ex, only to discover that your new partner was even worse. Suddenly, your ex didn't seem so bad in comparison, and the weight of your choices pressed down on you like a leaden shroud, making you question every decision that had brought you to this moment.

Then you might find yourself wanting to get back with your ex, or worse, they might come crawling back, all smug and self-satisfied, saying, "Hey, how's it going? Remember how great things were when I was around?" Their casual demeanor would make your skin crawl, a twisted reminder of why you'd left in the first place, leaving you grappling with the unsettling reality that nostalgia can be a treacherous companion.

"He's weak," Ajee said with a shrug, his tone dripping with disdain. "Anyone who just got fired, moping around like a lost puppy, giving up on finding another job, and leaning on his worn-out wife—what else can you call that but weak? A total jerk? He was like that even as a kid." Each word was a sharpened dagger, and Sprite felt the sting of truth behind his words, even if it twisted her gut.

"When he was a kid?" Sprite asked, her curiosity piqued. The question hung in the air like a thick fog, and she couldn't shake the feeling that this creature had been shadowing Ajee for a long time, lurking in the shadows of his past, feeding on his insecurities and regrets. The thought sent a shiver down her spine, and she felt the weight of unspoken history pressing down on her.

Since he was a kid, it seemed a dark thread had been woven into the very fabric of his life, twisting and tightening with every passing year, pulling him deeper into shadows he couldn't escape. Each year added another knot, another burden, and Sprite couldn't help but wonder how much longer he could bear the weight of it all before it threatened to unravel completely.

"Yeah, since childhood," Ajee said with a smirk. "He was just like you—always grumbling to himself, venting into the void. I used to listen to him, mostly laughing at his misery. Maybe that's the only thing you two have in common: you both like to rant at shadows." Ajees chuckled, clearly amused. "You know, when he was a kid, his old man used to beat him up. He hated his father, but he never had the guts to fight back. Then one day, his father just vanished—took off with some new wife—and that only deepened his hatred. He swore he'd never turn out like the old man. Promised he'd be honest, straight, loyal. But look at him now. He's just as rigid and selfish as his father was. Sure, he might be loyal, but that's only because he's got no imagination left. He's been dead for a long time, darling Sprite. Dead, even to himself." Each word dripped with disdain, a reminder of how deeply Ajee relished picking at the wounds of the past.

Sprite was taken aback, her mind reeling. This was the first time the figure had delved so deeply into Ajee's nature, peeling back layers she hadn't even acknowledged. How much did he really know about them, about this place, about the very fabric of their world? The questions gnawed at her, leaving a cold, unsettling itch in the pit of her stomach, like the creeping sensation of being watched by unseen eyes lurking in the shadows.

Before Sprite could voice her curiosity, Ajee silenced her with a dismissive wave, already focused on cleaning up the remnants of her lunch. His movements were methodical, almost mechanical, as if he were performing a well-rehearsed routine rather than simply tidying up. The kitchen felt colder in his silence, each scrape of the plate against the counter echoing with an unsettling finality.

26

Sprite had long since lost track of time; days and nights melded into a murky haze of hunger and despair. The flesh of the unfortunate souls who crossed her path had become nothing more than a grim necessity—a dark, vital sustenance she had learned to swallow with a mix of revulsion and hunger.

She recalled, in a distant haze, some grim tale she'd caught on TV—ancient tribes, wild-eyed and desperate, convinced that devouring their enemies' flesh would bestow upon them a taste of the supernatural. They believed that by consuming the very essence of their foes, they could harness dark, unearthly power, tapping into forces beyond their comprehension. The thought sent a shiver down her spine, mingling dread with an unsettling allure.

As Sprite chewed on yet another piece of meat, its texture indistinguishable from the rancid muck of her nightmares, she couldn't shake the unsettling thought that she was just another lost soul ensnared in some perverse, ancient ritual. She had crossed the line into cannibalism, and with that dark leap, she sometimes daydreamed of acquiring arcane powers—maybe the ability to vanish into thin air or to choke someone with nothing but a thought. The allure was tantalizing. But then reality crashed down on her like a sickening thud: the flesh she consumed was Mr. Gegge's. What kind of supernatural force could that provide? The power to see through clothes? Bulletproof testicles? Instead of wielding any mystical might, all she earned was a relentless, gnawing stomach ache that mocked her every whim.

Maybe she'd caught a chill, or perhaps her body was staging a mutiny against the grotesque fare she'd been forced to consume. The thought sent a shiver through her, as if her insides were trying to revolt, staging their own dark rebellion against the unnatural diet she'd been subjected to. It felt like a twisted uprising, each organ conspiring to protest the horrors she had ingested, urging her to resist the madness that had become her life.

Every morning, Ajee would drag her from the depths of her nightmares, washing her with warm water while the steam mingled with her fear. He wielded a pair of rusty scissors to snip away her tattered clothes, sidestepping the cruel bindings on her hands and feet. After this grim process, he'd dress her in a new set of clothes—garments that seemed to mock her captivity. They were a twisted parody of comfort, adorned with buttons on every conceivable side, allowing him to slip them on without ever touching her bound limbs. It was a daily ritual, a chilling reminder of her unending confinement that left her feeling both exposed and trapped.

Sprite had just come to realize that Ajee had a knack for sewing, though she couldn't help but be critical. His stitches, while functional, were a ragged testament to his skill—if you could call it that. Each thread seemed to whisper a tale of hasty, uneven effort, a clumsy dance of needle and thread that left much to be desired. It was as if he were in a constant rush, each stitch a desperate attempt to keep her together while failing to hide the jagged edges of his craftsmanship.

Ajee would trudge in with a bedpan every time Sprite needed to relieve herself, turning it into a grim ritual that grew all too familiar. This was her introduction to the bedpan life—trapped on the mattress for days on end, a prisoner of her own frailty. Each time she used it, the cold metal was a chilling reminder of her confinement, her world shrinking to the confines of that small, unfeeling vessel. It was a stark symbol of her degradation, a constant reminder that her body had become both her prison and her tormentor.

She'd been hospitalized before for asthma, but back then, with a nurse's help, she could at least shuffle to the bathroom. Now, the stories she'd heard from a friend who'd undergone a cesarean section haunted her thoughts—how her friend had been bedridden for days, unable to move, forced to rely on a catheter. The mere idea sent shivers down her spine, especially now that the scar from her own ordeal still flared up with a persistent, haunting ache. The pain was a constant, cruel reminder of her confinement, a ghost of past suffering that refused to fade, gnawing at her with every passing moment.

Sprite had never endured the agony of childbirth or the aftermath of major surgery, but she had tasted her own version of confinement—bedridden and under the watchful gaze of a cold-blooded killer who might as well have been a ghost. Impatience gnawed at her, and every inch of her body sang a symphony of pain. Her wrists and ankles felt as though they were slowly being crushed in an iron vice, a relentless ache that refused to relent, tightening with each passing moment. It was a torment that blurred the line between physical agony and a deep, simmering despair.

One time, she attempted to move her hands and was immediately jolted by a searing pain from the relentless friction. It was so intense that it seeped into her nightmares, where she dreamed of her wrists and ankles severed from the constant rubbing against the ropes. Each night, the terror became a familiar specter, taunting her with visions of dismemberment, an all-too-real reflection of her torment.

In that grotesque fantasy, she somehow managed to escape, even with her hands and feet mangled beyond recognition. The thought sent a shudder through her; she couldn't bear the idea of it becoming her reality. Her only hope lay in waiting for Ajee to either release her or, at the very least, loosen the cruel bindings that held her captive. His words echoed in her mind, a twisted mantra he droned on about: he'd set her free when he deemed her ready. But what the hell did that even mean? When would the bar of readiness be met? The uncertainty gnawed at her sanity, a relentless, unanswerable question that only deepened her dread and left her spiraling into despair.

She tried to unravel the twisted mindset of Ajee, that enigma of a man. It felt like peering into a murky abyss, struggling to decipher the dark, cryptic motives lurking beneath his cold exterior. His thoughts, elusive and enigmatic, were a riddle she couldn't quite solve; each attempt only deepened the shadows of his warped psyche, leaving her more bewildered and unsettled. It was a puzzle with missing pieces, and the deeper she delved, the more she felt herself lost in the darkness.

Before, he had practically begged her to harm—maybe even kill—Mr. Gegge, the man she loathed with every fiber of her being. The thought had hung in the air between them, a sinister invitation cloaked in his fervent desperation.

She had failed that grim test, her resistance crumbling under the weight of her own hatred. Now, a cold dread gnawed at her, the fear that Ajee might devise another cruel trial, one that would push her even further into the abyss of her despair. Each passing moment felt like a countdown, the looming threat of his next move casting a long, dark shadow over her already fractured will.

Maybe he'd bring a new victim into her hellish prison, forcing her to prove her loyalty by taking that person's life. The thought twisted in her mind like a knife, each possible scenario more horrifying than the last, a grotesque tapestry of torment and betrayal. Each chilling image sent a shudder through her, a vivid reminder of the depths of her own despair and the darkness that Ajee could unleash.

Sprite held her breath, her chest tight with fear. Her heart hammered against her ribs, a frantic drumbeat echoing in the oppressive silence. Could she muster the strength to do it? The question loomed over her like a dark cloud, its answer as elusive and terrifying as the shadows that surrounded her, a constant reminder of the abyss that threatened to swallow her whole. Each heartbeat was a countdown, each passing moment amplifying the weight of her dread.

She faced a grim choice: transform into the killer Ajee demanded, spill blood, and pass his twisted test. Only then would he deem her ready and grant her release from this hell. The thought twisted in her gut, a dark irony that her salvation hinged on becoming the very monster she despised. Each pulse of her heart echoed the weight of that decision, a heavy reminder of the nightmare that had become her reality.

After that, she'd run straight to the police, desperate to trade her freedom for a chance at justice. Sure, there was a risk she might be arrested, charged with murder, and end up in prison for years. But that was still a better fate than rotting away in her own bed, a victim of Ajee's sadistic game. The alternative? To refuse his test and face whatever nightmare awaited her if she didn't comply. All she had to do was convince Ajee she was ready to kill the person he brought, and then she'd need to ask for a weapon—maybe a knife or some other sharp instrument. Once she was free and armed, her plan was to turn the weapon not on the victim, but on Ajee himself, to subdue him and make her escape. It was a plan that tugged at her heart, a flicker of hope amid the suffocating darkness. But her mind rebelled; the risk was immense, the danger too great to ignore, and doubt crept in like a chilling fog, clouding her resolve.

Ajee was a professional killer, and he took his craft seriously. He wasn't the type to let his guard down or underestimate an amateur like Sprite. No, he would be meticulous, anticipating every trick she might try. He'd have layers of protection, safeguards meticulously designed to thwart any attempt she made to deceive or incapacitate him. The thought of slipping through his defenses felt as far-fetched as escaping a steel trap, each mental image of her plan unraveling only deepening her sense of dread. A chilling realization settled in: she was not just a pawn in his game; she was a target, and the odds were stacked firmly against her.

Sprite weighed her options, her body trembling with each dark thought. The idea of killing someone just to save herself felt like a deep, biting cruelty, a moral abyss she couldn't bear to contemplate. Each shiver that ran through her was a cold reminder of the twisted crossroads she now stood at, where survival seemed to demand the sacrifice of her very soul. The choice gnawed at her, a shadowy presence lurking in her mind, whispering that to live meant becoming the very thing she feared most.

Maybe she could strike a bargain with Ajee. Perhaps she could persuade him to modify the first test, make it so she only had to injure or torture someone, rather than kill. The thought made Sprite sigh heavily, her breath a shuddering whisper in the oppressive silence. It was a sickening compromise, yet one her mind, now teetering on the edge, considered. How far had she fallen, to even entertain such a thought? Each grim idea felt like another thread unraveling, pulling her deeper into madness. How much longer could she cling to her sanity before it slipped entirely into the void?

She didn't remember falling asleep. One moment, her thoughts had been racing, tangled in fear and desperation, and then—nothing. It was as if her consciousness had simply flickered off, a sudden, jarring cut to black in the movie of her mind. No slow drift into slumber, just an abrupt plunge into darkness, as if someone had flipped a switch and left her stranded in the void.

One moment, she was caught in the whirlwind of her spiraling fears, and the next, she was slipping into a murky, uncertain darkness, the transition so seamless she barely noticed. Had she really slept? Or had she fainted, her body overwhelmed by stress and hunger? The gnawing ache in her stomach wasn't just from the meat; it was just as likely that Ajee had slipped something into her food, something to drag her into unconsciousness. When she came to, her head swam with disorientation. Blinking through the haze, she realized the familiar ceiling and harsh light bulbs were gone. In their place were dingy walls and an old wardrobe, the unsettling feeling of being somewhere far worse creeping in like a cold draft.

She looked to her right, then to her left, and down. Everything had shifted. The room felt wrong, as if the walls had closed in or the floor had tilted. Her position was alien to her, like she'd been dropped into a space that wasn't her own. It was as if the room had rearranged itself while she was unconscious, the familiar contours now strange and unsettling, leaving her with the creeping dread that nothing here could be trusted—not even reality itself.

She found herself seated in a stiff dining room chair, wrists lashed tightly behind her, feet shackled to the legs. She snorted in frustration, the absurdity of it gnawing at her. How could she have been unconscious while her body was being moved? The thought alone felt ridiculous, and yet... the realization hit her like a punch to the gut—Ajee had untied her, moved her like a lifeless doll, and then bound her again. It was a chilling testament to his calculated cruelty, his control so complete he didn't even need her awareness to carry out his twisted games.

She cursed herself for not seizing that fleeting chance to escape, but deep down, she knew it was a fool's hope. Even if she had been conscious, Ajee would've been two steps ahead, his every move calculated. The thought of slipping through his fingers was nothing more than a desperate fantasy, and she hated herself for even entertaining it.

Ajee had anticipated everything, every move, every desperate possibility. He wasn't just a captor; he was a sadistic mastermind, a professional killer who thrived on anticipation, on cruelty. He didn't just expect her to try and outwit him—he relished the idea, knowing he'd already beaten her before she could even make a move. Every second of her captivity was another turn in his twisted game, and she was trapped, playing by his rules.

She squirmed, shifting her weight, trying to rock the chair backward, just like in those grim kidnapping movies where a desperate lunge could topple the whole thing. But her efforts were in vain. The chair's back was wedged firmly against the bed, locking her in place. It was a cruel mockery of escape—she could struggle all she wanted, but Ajee had thought of everything. Even her futile attempts at freedom were just another part of his twisted design.

Even if she somehow managed to topple the chair to the side, she had no illusions about what came next. The chances of freeing herself were slim to none, and the risk of ending up in an even worse position loomed large in her mind. The chair, ancient as it seemed, was surprisingly heavy, its solid frame a taunting reminder of how trapped she truly was. Each creak under her weight mocked her efforts, as if the very wood conspired with Ajee, silently laughing at her desperation.

Sprite waited in tense, restless silence for what felt like an eternity, her mind swirling with dread. Then, without warning, the bedroom door creaked open, abruptly slicing through the stillness like a knife. The sudden intrusion shattered her fragile calm, sending a fresh wave of panic coursing through her veins.

"Hey there," Ajee said, stepping through the door with a casual ease that sent a chill down her spine. "Look at you, already up." He strolled over to Sprite, taking his time as he circled her like a predator sizing up its prey, each step deliberate and unnerving.

It seemed he was meticulously inspecting every knot and strap, ensuring her bindings were as tight and unyielding as he'd intended. Each movement was deliberate, a grim affirmation of her helplessness that tightened around her like a noose.

Once he seemed satisfied, he leaned in close, his breath hot against her skin as he planted a chilling kiss on her cheek. The touch felt both intimate and sinister—a final, mocking gesture that underscored his control over her, a twisted claim on her very being.

Sprite attempted to turn away, but Ajee's grip on her jaw was like a vice, forcing her to meet his gaze. His touch was cold and unyielding, a brutal reminder of his dominance that sent a chill racing down her spine.

"Tonight, we have a class," Ajee whispered, his breath sending shivers down Sprite's spine as it tickled her ear. "You're eager to attend, aren't you? I heard you're aiming for graduation. Don't sweat it; I'll make sure you pass. But first, you need to attend the class. I'm the lecturer." He leaned back, locking eyes with her, his smile a mask that didn't touch the depths of his cold demeanor.

Sweat began to bead on Sprite's temples, a cold, relentless trickle that mirrored her escalating fear. What fresh hell was Ajee planning? Would he force her to take a life, dragging her deeper into this twisted nightmare? The thought slithered through her mind like a chilling whisper, each drop of sweat a testament to her mounting dread. Her thoughts raced, tangled in the dark possibilities of Ajee's test. If it was as horrific as she feared, what options could she possibly have? The grim reality of her situation twisted in her mind, each potential scenario sinking deeper into despair, darker than the last.

Ajee ran his fingers through Sprite's hair one last time, the touch almost tender yet chilling in its coldness, before turning on his heel and slipping out of the bedroom. The door clicked shut behind him, sealing her in a thick, oppressive silence that felt like a shroud, wrapping her in isolation and dread.

Sprite sat in the oppressive stillness, her mind a battlefield of uncertainty. Every so often, a wave of doubt crashed over her, gnawing at her resolve with the fear that she might not survive this twisted ordeal. The dread was a constant companion, lurking just beneath the surface, poised to rise up and choke her when she least expected it.

She wasn't the heroine of some action flick; she was painfully aware that, both physically and in combat skills, she was little more than a weak, average woman—perhaps even weaker than most. Then came the sound of scraping from outside the door, an unmistakable noise that sent chills down her spine. Something heavy and cumbersome was being dragged, each rasping pull growing sharper and more distinct. It felt as if the scraping resonated not just against the floor, but against the very joints of her tortured body, amplifying her sense of dread with each agonizing scrape.

She yearned to stretch and crack her aching joints, a desperate craving for even the slightest hint of relief. Then, the bedroom door creaked open again, but this time it was a slow, torturous process, each inch revealing more of the dark, foreboding hallway beyond. It felt like a confession, an unveiling of the horrors that awaited her outside, and with each agonizing creak, her heart raced, bracing for what lay beyond the threshold.

Ajee emerged from behind the door, his back to her at first, shuffling into the room while dragging something heavy behind him. The sound echoed ominously, amplifying the dread tightening around Sprite's chest. When he finally turned, her heart plummeted—what he had been dragging was a human body. The figure was obscured, its head shrouded in a black plastic bag, but the posture and clothing were unmistakable. It was Thyme, her closest work friend. A cold certainty settled over her like a shroud as Ajee laid the body before her and slowly peeled back the plastic covering from Thyme's face, revealing the horror beneath.

There lay Thyme Ragsdale, the very woman who had helped Sprite land the job as a cleaner but had also become a relentless thorn in her side, endlessly reporting her to Mr. Gegge.

Sprite had always sensed, lurking in the shadows of her mind, that Thyme had a secret side job at the office. But now, as she looked at the young woman lying unconscious before her, a chill crawled down her spine—could Thyme be dead? The girl's body was unnaturally rigid, hands and feet bound, mouth sealed shut with tape. The parallels to her own situation were haunting. There were no visible wounds on Thyme, yet the chilling resemblance to her own bound state swelled within Sprite, filling her with a creeping dread.

Maybe Thyme had been drugged with something. After all, it didn't make any sense to bind and gag her if she were already dead. The thought gnawed at Sprite's mind, a chilling possibility that only deepened the horror of her situation. Each second that passed seemed to stretch, amplifying her dread as she wrestled with the grim implications of Ajee's twisted game.

"This is your friend—the one you confided in when you couldn't write in your diary," Ajee said, smoothing out Thyme's rumpled work uniform as if preparing her for some grotesque show-and-tell. "But lately, you've realized she's not so trustworthy. She's been spilling your secrets to your coworkers, even those office guys who like to cozy up to her during overtime."

Sprite couldn't quite pinpoint when her feelings for Thyme shifted from friendship to disdain, or when their once-strong bond had decayed into a hollow pretense. But she recalled vividly how, during her frantic job search—after her husband had been fired—Thyme had been the only one who stepped up with a lifeline, offering a solution when all hope seemed lost.

Thyme had boasted about her connections, promising they could secure Sprite a job with a cleaning service. The way she pitched it felt almost too good to be true—a glimmer of hope shrouded in the guise of a simple favor, tempting enough to blind her to the potential pitfalls that lay hidden beneath the surface.

Sprite had laughed it off, certain Thyme was joking. What could a janitor like her possibly know about someone who could help? The notion felt absurd—just another cruel jest mocking her desperation.

A week later, Thyme proved she wasn't just blowing smoke.

Sprite was hired by the company with barely a hurdle. No tests, no fees—just a quick interview with a manager who seemed more interested in her availability than her qualifications. It felt almost too easy, like slipping through a crack in reality, a glitch in the system that whispered of something sinister beneath the surface.

Thyme had been a high school classmate, but they'd never been close. Their paths barely intersected, leaving only the faintest echoes of familiarity—a fleeting smile in the hallway, a nod across the cafeteria. Their connection was so tenuous, it was as if the universe had deliberately kept them apart, preserving the distance that would later unravel in a far darker context.

Sprite remembered Thyme as the girl who glided through the hallways surrounded by a constant swarm of friends, a blur of laughter and chatter that made her feel almost untouchable. She was the embodiment of effortless popularity, her smile a beacon drawing others in while Sprite lingered in the shadows, invisible and alone, grappling with the ache of envy and isolation.

She occasionally found herself hanging out with the guys in the cafeteria, Iron included—her ex-boyfriend. That camaraderie hadn't blossomed until they started working together, forging a fragile bond over shared jokes and half-hearted banter, their past lingering like a ghost at the edges of their conversations.

As the only familiar face in that sterile environment, Thyme quickly became Sprite's sole confidante. She knew all about Sprite's marital struggles—the discontent that hung over her marriage, Ajee's descent into depression after losing his job, and the years of heartache tied to their failed attempts at starting a family. Through it all, Thyme listened with an unwavering calm, her optimistic demeanor a stark contrast to the chaos surrounding them. She would often hold Sprite's hand, spouting Tony Robbins quotes from the TV like mantras, attempting to weave a thread of solace through the fabric of Sprite's unraveling life.

Sprite was perpetually amazed by Thyme's uncanny ability to remain upbeat, as if she were wrapped in a bubble that shielded her from the world's harsh realities, even while her own life crumbled around her.

Thyme had been on the brink of marrying her boyfriend of five years—everything was set, invitations printed, the dress chosen—until it all shattered in a spectacular explosion of chaos.

He'd cheated on her, and just like that, the wedding was off—every ounce of planning, every flicker of hope, obliterated in a heartbeat. Yet there was Thyme, forever wearing that bright, effortless smile, as if heartbreak were just another bad date to shrug off with a laugh.

She recounted the entire story with a startling lack of emotion—no sobs, just a single tear clinging to the corner of her left eye. It had taken Sprite nearly a month to piece it all together; those rumors she'd overheard from the others weren't mere idle gossip—they were true. Whispers around the office suggested that Thyme was more than just a friendly face. Some said she was involved with several higher-ups, including Mr. Gegge. But the rumors didn't stop there. It was rumored that cleaning toilets wasn't her only dirty job; some claimed she moonlighted as a call girl for the office crowd after hours.

Sprite had brushed off the rumors until the night she caught Thyme slipping in and out of the VIP restroom with male employees during late shifts. She told herself it wasn't her business, that she should just look the other way. But deep down, it stung, a sharp reminder of how easily trust could unravel.

She had once admired and respected Thyme, but now that admiration felt like a cruel joke. The betrayal gnawed at her insides, festering until it all erupted during their last meeting, when disappointment bubbled over like a pot left too long on the stove.

Ajee snatched a glass of water from the drawer and hurled it at Thyme's face without a second thought. Her forehead twitched—a slight, almost imperceptible response—but she remained unconscious, like a marionette with its strings severed, lying in wait for the puppeteer to jerk them back to life.

Ajee struck Thyme's face repeatedly, the sharp cracks echoing in the heavy silence. With each brutal smack, her breathing grew quicker—shallow, frantic—as if the air itself were trying to escape her. Gradually, like someone clawing their way out of a suffocating darkness, her eyes fluttered open. They darted around the room, her mind racing to process the twisted nightmare she'd just awakened to.

She turned her head right, then left, her gaze landing on Ajee's face before shifting to Sprite's. Then her eyes fell on the ropes binding her hands and feet. The realization hit her like a punch to the gut, panic surging up like a tidal wave, crashing over her and drowning any remnants of calm.

Thyme thrashed weakly, her body jerking side to side in a desperate, futile fight. Whatever strength she had was spent, drained by more than just the ropes binding her hands and feet. Something deeper was sapping her will, leaving her utterly helpless. Eventually, her struggles dwindled to a pitiful wriggling, like a worm pulled from the dirt, squirming helplessly in the light.

"For tonight's class, Thyme's going to be my assistant," Ajee said, casting a casual glance at Sprite, his words laced with a chilling nonchalance.

Sprite struggled to scream, her voice strangled in her throat as she twisted and fought against her restraints. The cold truth wrapped around her like a shroud—she knew exactly what awaited Thyme. There was no escaping it; Thyme wouldn't walk away from this alive.

Ajee chuckled at the sight of the two women writhing and moaning in tandem, imagining that the moment their bindings were off, they'd collapse into each other's arms, sobbing and huddling in a corner like frightened children.

As that chilling laugh echoed around her, Sprite was hit by a crushing sense of futility. Her frantic struggles had been nothing but a waste of breath, a futile flailing against the darkness closing in around her.

Desperate to steady herself, she drew a deep, shuddering breath and shifted in her seat. What could she possibly do now? And what about Thyme—what could either of them do? The walls of their helplessness closed in tighter, suffocating any flicker of hope.

Ajee rose from his chair and strolled out of the room, humming a jaunty tune that felt grotesquely out of place. In the suffocating silence that followed, Sprite and Thyme exchanged glances, their eyes locking in a wordless exchange of terror and resignation, a silent pact forged in fear.

Sprite could see that Thyme was still grappling with the grim reality of their situation. It was understandable—what could possibly be racing through her mind, waking up to find herself bound, with Sprite held captive by her own husband? The confusion must have felt like a thick fog, wrapping around her thoughts, stifling her ability to grasp the horror unfolding before them.

Thyme might still be clinging to the fragile hope that this was all just a nightmare, desperately trying to wake herself from this horror.

But no, Thyme—this wasn't merely a bad dream; it was a nightmare warped into something infinitely worse. One question gnawed at Sprite's mind: why had Ajee chosen Thyme? Was it because she had cried out her name at the beach, a slip that now felt like a sinister invitation?

Sprite could almost understand Ajee's twisted logic in asking her to stab Mr. Gegge. After all, she had harbored enough hatred for him, even indulging in dark fantasies of taking his life. Yet, deep down, she had never truly wanted to cross that line.

But Thyme was different. The feelings Sprite had for her were tangled in a web of complexities that defied the neat boxes of hatred or revenge. The mere thought of hurting Thyme twisted something deep within her, an unsettling knot of guilt and regret that clawed at her insides.

Thyme had never laid a hand on her, never crossed her in any way that would justify revenge. The mere thought of inflicting physical harm felt like an unthinkable cruelty, a betrayal of everything Sprite had once believed to be right and just. It was as if the very act of hurting Thyme would tear at the fabric of her own humanity, unraveling the last threads of her morality.

Thyme had been nothing but a help to her—and to Ajee, too. If Ajee was really honing in on every name she'd blurted out at the beach, that list would include her father, a handful of friends, and even Ajee's own name. But maybe, just maybe, none of this had anything to do with that. Perhaps Ajee's motives ran deeper, twisted into some dark corner of his mind that had nothing to do with her past blunders, but rather with a plan far more sinister than she could fathom.

Then she heard the footsteps—slow, deliberate, like the ticking of a clock counting down to something inevitable.

Ajee re-entered the room, his grip tight around a meat knife, its blade glinting menacingly in the dim light.

Sprite held her breath, whispering a silent prayer. She felt that only God could save her now, though a gnawing fear lingered—He might be angry for her recent neglect.

Ajee plopped down cross-legged in front of Thyme, his eyes gleaming with a mix of amusement and menace. "All right, Sprite, time for a refresher. You flunked the last lesson on pronging the boss's eye, and your GPA is in serious trouble. If you don't want to get kicked out and still hope to graduate—like you've always dreamed—you need to ace this course," he said, his tone like that of a lecturer ready to enforce the harshest of penalties.

Sprite's entire body trembled, her nerves stretched taut like a wire ready to snap. Was this really happening? Was she genuinely confronting the nightmare she had dreaded most—being forced to kill Thyme?

No, she couldn't do it. Even if it meant her own end, the thought of killing Thyme was unbearable. After weighing her options, her conscience delivered the verdict—she couldn't cross that line.

She knew she had to choose the second option. If Ajee ordered her to use the knife on Thyme, she'd turn it on him instead. Maybe she wouldn't kill him outright—perhaps just slash his legs so he couldn't chase her or stab him in the gut to send him crumpling to the floor. Even if it led to his death, it was still better than the alternative.

She didn't want to kill Ajee Arizin, her own husband, but if it meant ridding the world of the monster he had become, it was the only choice left. Sprite pictured it vividly: the blood, the struggle, the chilling certainty of death if she failed. She and Thyme would meet their end together. This was the last, desperate road she had to walk.

At least she wouldn't have to commit an act that would gnaw at her conscience, dragging her down into the abyss of her own making.

"Actually, sweetheart," Ajee said, a twisted smile creeping across his face, "I considered letting you practice with the knife on your own. But I'm a good teacher, and I know you're not quite ready for that. I wouldn't want you to screw it up again. So, I'll guide you through it, step by step. For now, just sit back and watch."

Sprite's imagination shattered into a thousand jagged shards, each splintered thought cutting deep into her sanity.

She let out a primal scream, a raw sound clawing its way from the depths of her soul. Her bound feet beat furiously against the floor, a desperate rhythm echoing her helplessness.

Trapped in this wretched position, she was powerless to save Thyme. Damn it, she thought bitterly, this monster had crossed every line of cruelty imaginable.

"Keep your eyes wide open," Ajee commanded, his fingers tightening around Thyme's neck. "Don't blink. Pay close attention. If you miss it, you've failed. This is all about observation."

Thyme's struggles dwindled with each agonizing moment, her eyes flitting desperately to the meat knife pressed against her slender neck, the glint of the blade reflecting the dim light as it threatened to sever her from life itself.

Sprite could almost feel the icy edge of the blade slicing through the air, the threat of it grazing her skin sending a tight knot of fear into her throat. Inside her, a storm of inner turmoil raged, a chaotic blend of dread and desperation that threatened to swallow her whole.

She felt utterly powerless to stop Ajee, but the thought of having to witness this horror unfold was almost more than she could bear. Could she endure the weight of such helplessness? The very idea made her stomach churn, tightening her chest with a suffocating dread.

If she wanted to survive this nightmare, to claw her way to freedom, she knew she couldn't look away or close her eyes. It was the only rational choice, but who could bear to witness their friend being butchered right before them? Even a seasoned war veteran, battle-hardened and steeled against horror, might falter at such a gruesome spectacle. The thought twisted in her gut, an insidious dread creeping into her bones.

Sprite was ensnared with no way out. Her mind raced, grappling with how to keep her eyes open without truly seeing, a desperate dance between awareness and denial. It was a chilling paradox, a fragile shield against the horror unfolding before her.

She couldn't afford to shift her gaze; Ajee would catch her, and she'd pay for it. Maybe—just maybe—she could pull off a quick blink at the most gruesome moment. In that instant, she wished for nothing more than to simply go blind, to escape the horror without having to witness a single drop of blood.

"Alright, let's get this show on the road. Keep your eyes peeled," Ajee murmured, his voice low and chilling. He raised the knife high, his other hand clenching Thyme's neck, while his foot pressed down hard against her body, pinning her in place like a bug beneath glass.

Sprite's breaths came in jagged, uneven gasps, each one tearing through her chest like a desperate cry for help, clawing at the air as if to summon a savior from the depths of her despair.

She fought to keep her eyes open, but a dizzying wave of nausea washed over her, threatening to pull her under. Losing consciousness felt almost like a sweet relief now—anything to escape the horror unfolding before her, anything to silence the scream building in her throat.

27

Light always beat sound—that was one of the universe's unwritten rules, as old as time itself. You saw the flash before you heard the boom, the crack of lightning outrunning the slow growl of thunder. But not this time. This time something was wrong, like the world had decided to rewrite its own playbook. Maybe it was just Sprite's mind—tangled, twisted, playing tricks on her in the thick, buzzing air. The sound came first. A wet, sickening noise, like a knife sliding through flesh, over and over, each thrust a brutal rhythm of scrape and press. Then, in a sickening snap of reality, the scene came into focus. Sprite's stomach dropped, a fist of cold horror slamming into her chest, knocking the air from her lungs.

She forced herself to open her eyes, but her body wouldn't play along. It was a stubborn, unbroken animal, bucking against her will. Her nerves were still raw, her emotions still scraping at her insides. Her eyelids stayed clamped tight, tears streaming down her face like a storm that wouldn't quit. In that suffocating blackness, the air was thick with groans—anguished, broken. Those cries twisted together with the sickening squelch of the knife, turning into soft hisses and whimpers, fading like the last gasps of a nightmare. Without meaning to, her eyelids gave way, slowly, heavy as iron.

With a cautious flicker, she cracked her eyelids, just enough to catch a flash of deep, unsettling red. Then she saw it—a body, thrashing, its movements frantic at first, then slowing, weakening, until it began to dissolve into the shadows.

As Sprite's world slipped away, Ajee's murmurs reached her, soft and distant, like a voice echoing through water. The sound clung to the edges of her fading consciousness, barely there, as if it might vanish any second.

"Come on, Sprite, that's weak. Do it again."

28

Sprite thought she had finally reached the pinnacle of her nightmare, but instead, it unfurled like a jagged mountain ridge, steep and merciless. When she regained consciousness, her vision blurred, but through the haze, she caught a glimpse of Thyme's gaping neck—a gruesome sight that knotted her stomach. Thyme's eyes were wide and unblinking, staring into a void, her head half-submerged in a pool of crimson—a disquieting image reminiscent of a sunset sinking into the ocean on some far-off, tropical shore.

Confronted by that haunting scene, Sprite felt her grip on reality slipping away once more, as if the dark waters were reaching out, beckoning her back into their depths. She couldn't remember how many times she had drifted into this abyss; each time she surfaced, her will to live felt halved, a cruel math that gnawed at her spirit. Better to die, she thought, a notion that flickered through her mind whenever she clawed her way back to consciousness, only to succumb again to the void. Yet amid the despair, a flicker of hope remained—those vivid dreams that enveloped her while she wandered in the shadows.

Suddenly, the wail of a siren pierced the air outside her apartment, a mournful cry that clawed at her senses. Then came a man's voice, amplified through a loudspeaker, reverberating with an urgency that sliced through the thin walls of her home like a knife.

It was a sound that demanded attention, a stark reminder that the world outside was still very much alive and tumultuous, even as she remained trapped in her own suffocating silence.

"This place is surrounded, pal. You might as well throw in the towel."

She couldn't be sure if those were the exact words the police used when they surrounded an apartment, but in the fog of her dream, they rang with a chilling clarity. Then came the unmistakable sound of a door being kicked in, splintering wood yielding to brute force. Heavy, deliberate footsteps followed, echoing in a rhythm that felt both ominous and measured, as if the intruders understood the fragile barrier between their world and hers.

She watched Ajee pacing back and forth in front of her, his mind racing with frantic strategies to confront the police. They had no clue he was holding a hostage; their confidence was blinding. As they advanced toward the bedroom, their infrared lights swept across the walls, casting eerie shadows that flickered like restless spirits, illuminating the taut silence that wrapped around them.

Ajee yanked Sprite to her feet, gripping her from behind, the kitchen knife glinting ominously in his hand. "One step closer, and this girl's dead," he warned, stepping back and pressing the blade menacingly against her neck.

A police officer stepped forward, his face eerily reminiscent of Joe Taslim, a striking mix of determination and calm.

He carried himself with an air of authority, like a man poised to slice through the chaos and restore some semblance of order to the madness unfolding. "What do you want? Just state your demands," the officer said, his voice steady and unwavering.

Ajee fell silent, the weight of the moment pressing down on him like a heavy fog. He didn't respond immediately, ensnared in the tangled web of his own thoughts. What did he truly want? The question lingered in the air, a ghostly echo that taunted him as he wrestled with the chaotic swirl of desperation and fear.

He was just a madman, driven by nothing more than a twisted desire to make Sprite like him. In his own rambling confession, he claimed he wanted to liberate her from the chains of her own mind—whatever that cryptic nonsense meant. Perhaps he envisioned a life for her where she could be happy, free to shape her own destiny, chasing after whatever she desired without fear—even if it meant stealing a car or taking a life. But the police would never entertain such delusions; their world didn't bend to the whims of the unhinged.

She found herself relentlessly pulled back by Ajee until his back hit the wall, the cold surface a stark reminder of his predicament. She could feel his breath growing rapid and uneven—a telltale sign of the panic beginning to grip him. Any criminal would be unnerved, cornered as he was by a fully armed police squad that bore all the hallmarks of an anti-terror unit, their steely resolve and tactical precision amplifying the thick sense of dread that hung in the air.

"Look, just state your demands now. We'll consider them, but you need to let the hostage go," Officer Joe Taslim insisted, his tone firm and unwavering.

Ajee drew in a deep breath, the kind that felt like it pulled the very air from the depths of his lungs, as if he were trying to summon courage from the shadows lurking just beyond his grasp.

Sprite could feel the frantic pounding of his heart, a wild thrum that echoed in the silence between them—a rhythm of fear and desperation that resonated deep within her own chest.

He would undoubtedly start screaming and rambling, a frantic outburst that would leave him exposed, giving Joe Taslim the perfect opportunity to put a bullet through his head—a clean headshot. Or perhaps it would escalate into a bare-knuckle duel, just the two of them locked in a primal struggle. Plenty of makeshift weapons lay scattered around; hell, Sprite's sewing machine could easily turn into a blunt instrument in their twisted dance of violence.

"I want coffee. Get me some coffee—right now," Ajee demanded, his voice sharp and impatient.

The police officers exchanged bewildered glances, their confusion hanging in the air like a thick fog. Yet, as the absurdity of the situation settled in, they shuffled toward the kitchen, reluctantly brewing a cup of black coffee for Ajee. The mundane act felt almost surreal against the backdrop of the chaos unfolding around them.

Ajee erupted in laughter, the sound jarring in the tense atmosphere as he loosened his grip on Sprite, setting her free, if only for a moment. He took a sip of the coffee, sheer delight washing over his face as he sighed in satisfaction. With a broad grin, he gave a thumbs-up, praising the police for their surprisingly good brew—a bizarre moment of camaraderie amid the encroaching chaos.

Meanwhile, Joe Taslim led Sprite to safety, ushering her into the police car. For a fleeting moment, it felt as if they might ride off into the sunset, living happily ever after as YouTubers. It was a laughable notion, an absurd dream woven from the fabric of the chaos surrounding them—a surreal twist in a narrative that had taken such a dark turn.

In her dream, Sprite laughed—a haunting blend of joy and sorrow that left her gasping, her laughter morphing into tears that streamed down her face. Then the laughter faded, swallowed by silence, leaving only the salty remnants of her weeping. It should have all made perfect sense, yet the absurdity gnawed at her. How long would she have to endure this nightmare, waiting for the police to finally raid the apartment and shatter the illusion?

Ajee had taken many lives, each one a ghost that clung to the edges of his consciousness, haunting him with whispers of their final moments.

She was certain there were many other victims out there, faces lost in the shadows of Ajee's rampage. No matter how cunning he believed himself to be, there was no way he could erase the bloody traces of all those murders. The community was gripped by fear, living in a state of terror; the police had to be feeling the pressure to act. They could find this apartment with ease, especially since she had been held captive for days. The neighbors must have noticed her absence, their suspicions brewing like a storm on the horizon. Soon, Thyme's family would undoubtedly come looking for her, alerting the police to her disappearance. Yet, even amid these thoughts, her dream felt surreal—not just because of its absurd conclusion, but also due to Ajee's twisted instinct for survival.

Sprite was convinced that Ajee didn't give a damn about her life—or even his own, for that matter. After all, wasn't his body just a hollow shell, a mere vessel devoid of any real worth?

If he felt trapped, she could almost picture him opting for a final escape—a dark gesture of defiance against a world that had turned its back on him. She recalled his chilling words: *Death's a type of freedom too, babe.*

When her tears finally dried, Sprite dared to open her eyes again, hoping Thyme would no longer loom before her. She couldn't bear to witness the remnants of that horror scene again. To her relief, the floor lay empty, devoid of any traces of the chaos that had unfolded. The bloodstains had been meticulously scrubbed away, as if time had passed long enough for the floor to dry completely, leaving no sign of mop marks to betray the nightmare that had once been.

She could have been out cold for a whole day, or maybe even longer. Her stomach churned with emptiness, and her vision swam in a haze, but none of that mattered. It was still a better fate than having to swallow that gruesome human soup again. This time, the chilling thought that the meat might be Thyme's flesh sent a shiver racing down her spine.

Amid her dread, she faintly caught the sound of music drifting from the kitchen—a haunting melody that felt strangely out of place in the shadows enveloping her.

Perhaps Ajee was now busy cooking Thyme's body in a large pot, whistling a cheerful tune that sliced through the air with an unsettling cheerfulness—a grotesque contrast to the horror of what he was preparing.

She swore she wouldn't eat it. If it came to that, she'd let Ajee kill her, resigning herself to becoming the meal instead. But deep down, she doubted her scrawny body would even be appetizing. Just then, she heard footsteps from outside. It wasn't the chaotic sound of a crowd like in her nightmare, but rather the deliberate thud of one person's steps—heavy and slow, each footfall echoing ominously in the silence. Sprite's mind raced with dark imaginings of Ajee bringing in another victim. Who would he choose this time to force her to retake that failed course? Her father? A school friend? Iron? Waverley? As those thoughts churned in her mind, the bedroom door burst open, slamming against the wall behind it with a violent crash.

Sprite summoned the last of her strength to force her eyes wide open. Who could it be?

But as her vision sharpened, she realized the only presence in the room was Ajee.

Ajee stumbled into the room, his movements unsteady and erratic. Was he drunk? The thought clung to her mind, hanging in the air like a thick fog.

He fumbled along the wall, his other hand clutching his head as if trying to hold himself together, each movement teetering on the edge of desperation.

For a fleeting moment, Sprite caught sight of droplets of blood trickling from his hand and seeping down from his forehead, stark reminders of the chaos that clung to them like a bad dream.

He shuffled closer, his head drooping as he dragged his feet forward, each agonizing step a testament to his unraveling sanity. With one hand pressed against the wall for support, he looked like a man caught in a waking nightmare. Then, without warning, he slammed his head against the bedroom wall with a sickening thud that reverberated like a gunshot. Sprite gasped, her breath hitching in her throat as the air thickened with shock.

Ajee lifted his head once more, only to bring it crashing down against the wall again, the sickening sound reverberating through the room like a dark drumbeat, marking the rhythm of his despair.

Sprite struggled to comprehend the bizarre scene unfolding before her, a surreal tableau that felt more like a waking nightmare than reality, as if the world had warped into something grotesque and unrecognizable.

Ajee continued to slam his head against the wall, again and again, until the surface was stained a deep red, blood trickling down his forehead like a macabre stream. After what felt like an eternity of brutal impacts, he suddenly turned his head and whispered, "Sprite."

Sprite remained silent, her gaze locked on Ajee as she sensed something unsettling in his eyes. They revealed no trace of the terrifying darkness she had braced herself for; instead, they reflected a massive, unyielding wall—impenetrable and bleak. The man before her was not the monster of her nightmares, but her husband—the real Ajee Arizin.

"Please, I need help!"

Ajee crumpled to the ground before Sprite, his body slamming against the floor with a dull thud. Blood oozed from the gash on his head, pooling beneath him in a dark, glistening puddle that seemed to drink in the light.

Groaning, he propped himself up, summoning every ounce of strength to rise. His trembling hands reached for Sprite's face, peeling the tape from her mouth with a desperate urgency before pulling free the rag stuffed inside. It slipped away like a long-buried secret, the fabric releasing a stale breath of confinement.

Sprite gasped for breath, a desperate hunger for air flooding her lungs. In that instant, after what felt like an eternity, a flicker of joy ignited within her at the sight of Ajee, a spark of hope in the depths of her despair.

"Ajee," she breathed, the word a desperate whisper. She longed to scream, to throw her arms around him, but all that escaped her lips was the fragile breath of a wish, too tender for the chaos surrounding them.

Ajee stirred again, crawling toward Sprite's back, his hands fumbling desperately in a frantic search for the rope binding her wrists. He tugged at it repeatedly, but it clung to her like a stubborn shadow. Maybe it was the sweat and blood slicking his fingers, or perhaps the last remnants of his strength had drained away like a fading memory, lost in the chaos.

"Ajee, are you awake?" Sprite whispered, her voice a fragile breath in the thick silence.

"I had a dream, Sprite. A nightmare I couldn't wake up from," he said, his voice trembling, each word a struggle as he fought against the bindings.

A deep groan rumbled from his chest, and with one final, desperate surge of effort, he pried the bindings loose from her wrists.

He flung the rope onto the bed, and a peculiar warmth spread through Sprite's wrists, as if the blood, trapped for so long, could finally surge back into her numb fingers, awakening them from their icy slumber. But her arms remained stubbornly immobilized, leaving her helpless to assist Ajee in freeing her legs from their restraints.

"Once I get you free, you need to run—get as far away as you can, Sprite. Find help. Don't wait for me," Ajee urged, his hands working frantically to loosen the bindings.

THE STRANGER AT HOME 233

A tingling sensation spread through Sprite's ankles, echoing the revival in her wrists. Her legs felt heavy and unresponsive, refusing to support her weight. As she braced herself against the back of the chair, her recovering palms found a grip. But just as a flicker of strength ignited within her, a sharp throb shot through her wrist—a cruel reminder of her ordeal. The chair buckled beneath her, sending her crashing to the floor in a cacophony of wood and limbs, the impact jolting her as if the ground itself were rebelling against her desperate attempt to rise.

"Get out of here. Fast! Run, Sprite, run!" Ajee gasped, sitting on the floor, desperation tightening his voice as he struggled to catch his breath.

Sprite fought to rise, but her legs betrayed her again, sending her crashing to the floor. Every bone felt shattered, splintered like glass. Her vision swam in a haze, yet even through the blur, the sight of Ajee twisted her heart, a raw ache that refused to fade.

She couldn't bear the thought of leaving him there, not when he needed her more than ever. "C'mon," she whispered, her voice thick with desperation.

"Nah, you need to go alone. Get moving," he urged, his voice a strained whisper filled with urgency.

Sprite nodded, the weight of Ajee's words settling in her gut like a stone. She understood that she had to escape before the other Ajee clawed his way back to the surface. Summoning every last bit of strength from her weary body, she let out a scream—an unholy sound that echoed through the darkness—and crawled toward the exit, each inch feeling like a marathon. Occasionally, she glanced over her shoulder, half-expecting to see the shadows engulf him completely.

Ajee remained slumped on the floor, cradling his head in his hands as if trying to contain the chaos raging within him. The weight of the world pressed heavily on his shoulders, and each labored breath felt like a desperate struggle against the encroaching darkness.

Sprite finally forced her way out of the room, her heart racing as she glanced around. The silence hung thick in the air, an emptiness that felt suffocating. No one. Nothing. Just the lingering dread that seeped from the walls, whispering secrets of what had transpired. Faint strains of music wafted from the kitchen, but Sprite had no desire to investigate, the melody a mocking reminder of the horror she was desperate to escape.

Just a few steps from the door, she took a deep breath, holding it tight in her chest, and pushed herself up, her fingers clawing at the wall for stability. As she shuffled along the cold, unyielding surface, a flicker of gratitude warmed her; at least her apartment was small, the confined space a cruel comfort in her desperate bid for escape.

She envisioned the lavish palaces from soap operas, racing through endless corridors and gliding down grand staircases swathed in luxurious carpets. With every shred of willpower she could muster, Sprite reached out her hands, the exit still looming like a distant dream. Then, with a surge of desperation, she ran with everything she had, her heart pounding, until her fingers finally closed around the doorknob. At last, she thought. At long last.

She twisted the doorknob and yanked it hard, but the door didn't budge. Locked—just as she had feared. A flicker of hope in Sprite's heart dimmed, leaving her legs trembling beneath her once more. The key was absent, not even a shadow lingering in the keyhole.

She scanned her surroundings with frantic urgency, her eyes darting from the table to the television, then beneath the furniture. But there was no key to be found—just the empty space where hope had once lingered, now mocking her with its absence.

Ajee had to be the one who brought it. It didn't make sense—how could he untie her, urge her to escape, yet leave her without the key? The contradiction gnawed at her, a dark shadow of betrayal lurking just beneath the surface of her desperate hope. It was like standing on the edge of freedom, only to find the ground crumbling beneath her feet.

Sometimes, the greatest battles are not against what stands before us, but what lurks within.

Sprite knew she couldn't pin the blame on Ajee. Just waking up had been a miracle in itself, a fragile thread of hope woven into the dark tapestry of her grim reality. It was a glimmer in the abyss, a flicker of light that could just as easily be snuffed out. In this twisted world, even hope felt like a betrayal, a reminder of everything she stood to lose.

She heaved against the door, pushing and pulling with every ounce of strength she could muster, but it wouldn't budge. The realization seeped into her mind like a cold dread—there was no way she could break this door down. It stood before her like a silent sentinel, mocking her efforts, reminding her just how fragile hope could be in the face of solid wood and iron locks.

Even at her best, she doubted she could have broken that door down, let alone in her current state. Desperation clawed at her, a visceral urge that sent her heart racing as she frantically scanned for another escape. The walls seemed to close in, each shadow a reminder of her captivity, every creak of the house a whisper urging her to keep searching.

"Help! Someone, please help me!" she screamed at the door, her voice a fragile echo swallowed by the oppressive walls. Each desperate word felt like it was trapped in a thick fog, muffled and distorted, as if the very air conspired to keep her cries from reaching the outside world.

Time was slipping away, each second a cruel reminder of her dwindling chances.

In her desperation, she made the agonizing decision to return to the room and plead with Ajee for the key, hoping against hope that he could somehow save her.

Ajee was still conscious, and for a fleeting moment, hope surged through her—he would give her the key, she was sure of it, if only it was within his reach. Now that she could move, however painfully, the trek back to the room felt almost manageable, though every step was weighted with the gnawing dread of what she might find when she got there.

With deliberate caution, she leaned in to peer through the crack in the door. A sharp breath caught in her throat, the chill of fear tightening its grip around her heart. The room was hollow now, an unsettling void where Ajee had once been. Bloodstains smeared across the floor and an overturned chair were all that remained, silent witnesses to his disappearance. Where had he gone? The room felt wrong, off-balance, like the air itself was holding its breath. A heavy sense of foreboding settled over her, warning her to turn back. But like the doomed protagonist of a horror flick, her feet disobeyed, pulling her deeper into the room, the dread swelling in her gut with every step.

Maybe Ajee was crumpled behind the bed, swallowed by the shadows, a broken figure left in the wake of whatever twisted fate had overtaken them. The thought clung to her mind like cobwebs—he could be there, just out of sight, another casualty in this waking nightmare. Yet the darkness felt alive, as though something far worse than silence lurked just beyond the edge of her vision, waiting.

If only the space beneath the bed wasn't crammed with old cardboard boxes, she might've risked a glance, but the clutter sealed off any chance of a clear view. Just as she prepared to check the other side, a shiver clawed its way up her spine. There it was—a cold certainty settling over her. Another figure stood behind her, casting a shadow she didn't dare turn to face.

Sprite whipped around, her heart hammering in her chest, convinced that facing whatever lurked behind her was better than letting it sneak up from the shadows. Her breath hitched as she steeled herself, ready for anything—anything but the empty space that now stretched before her, mocking her with its silence.

There he was: Ajee, slouched against the doorframe, his silhouette stretching ominously in the faint light. Blood oozed from his head, his fingers stained crimson as they pressed against the wound. The sight of him—broken, battered—made her heart stutter. Which version of Ajee was this? The husband who had fought to save her, or the darker force lurking just beneath the surface, waiting to tear her apart?

Sprite couldn't be sure what to think, her mind racing between fear and survival. She kept her distance, eyes sweeping the room for something—anything—she could use if her worst fears materialized. A wooden chair loomed nearby, too heavy to lift in her weakened state, but it called to her nonetheless. In the corner, Ajee's violin stood like a silent observer, its glossy finish catching the light, mocking her with its fragility. And then, coiled on the bed like a sleeping snake, was the rope that had once held her captive—a reminder of her bondage but also, perhaps, a means to fight back. Desperation sharpened her thoughts: in moments like these, even the simplest things could become deadly. The rope was her last hope, a weapon disguised as a tool, ready if she needed it.

"Sprite," Ajee groaned, his voice raw and cracked like broken glass. He stumbled toward her, each step labored, as if the weight of the air itself pressed him down. His movements were sluggish, almost unnatural, as though something far darker than exhaustion was pulling at his limbs, dragging him across the floor.

Sprite took a cautious step back, instinctively widening the gap between them. Every fiber of her being screamed to flee, to put as much distance as possible between herself and the figure lurching toward her. The air grew thick with tension, her pulse pounding in her ears, drowning out the faint sound of Ajee's labored breaths. Something about him was wrong, deeply wrong, and that gnawing dread curled its way around her spine.

"The key," Ajee muttered, his voice thick and slurred, as if each word was a struggle to pull from his lips. He fumbled through his pocket, his bloodied fingers trembling. "I swear, it's right here." His eyes, glassy and unfocused, darted from Sprite to his pocket, as though he himself was unsure of what he might find. The apology slipped out in a whisper, barely audible, weighed down by guilt and desperation. Yet, as he patted his clothes, the empty clink of his fingers told a different story.

At last, his fingers emerged from the depths of his pocket, clutching a jumble of keys that dangled from a Pikachu keychain. The cheerful, cartoonish figure felt like a cruel joke against the grim backdrop of their reality, its bright yellow face standing out starkly against the darkness that surrounded them.

He extended his trembling hand toward Sprite, the keys glinting in the dim light like scattered stars—small, fragile beacons of hope in a world steeped in darkness.

Despite the tremor coursing through her body, Sprite hesitantly raised her hand to grasp the keys from Ajee. Just as her fingers brushed against the Pikachu keychain, his hand shot shut around it, trapping it in his grasp. In an instant, he lunged forward, clamping down on her wrist with a grip that felt like iron, sending a jolt of panic racing through her veins.

Sprite winced as a sudden jolt of pain shot through her wrist, her heart pounding like a drum in her chest, each beat echoing louder than the last.

"Your studies aren't over yet. Where do you think you're going, huh?"

Ajee's voice had transformed, dropping to a lower, rough tone that scraped against her senses like gravel grinding together. Sprite's stomach churned. Was this the true voice of the killer?

Sprite didn't want to find out. With every ounce of strength she had left, she yanked her hand back, but all it earned her was a sharp jolt of pain that shot up her arm like electricity.

Even battered and bleeding, Ajee was still stronger than her, his grip like iron. In an instant, Sprite's confidence crumbled. How had she ever thought she could overpower him?

She fought with every ounce of strength she could muster, twisting and pulling, but Ajee didn't budge. His body wasn't big or muscular; it wasn't built like a wall of concrete. It was just the lean, fragile frame of an ordinary man—yet somehow, he felt unmovable.

She couldn't fathom where the raw strength surging through that thin frame came from. Desperation took over, and with her left hand, Sprite lashed out, striking Ajee directly on his injured forehead. The sickening thud against the bloodied wound made him flinch, loosening his grip just enough for her to draw in a desperate breath.

Sprite took a step back, her instincts screaming for her to flee. But just as she turned to escape, her feet betrayed her, sending her sprawling into the corner of the room. Panic's sharp edges closed in around her, suffocating and relentless.

Ajee groaned softly, his fingers clutching his head as blood flowed steadily, staining his skin. He squeezed his eyes shut, desperate to block out the agony, but the relief was fleeting. When he opened them again, his pupils glinted like the burning eyes of a demon, glaring out from a sea of crimson.

He lunged at her, a blur of motion that sent Sprite scrambling for anything within reach. Her fingers closed around the neck of a black wooden violin, its smooth surface cool against her skin. This was Ajee's violin—the one he'd played so often in the dead of night, filling the darkness with haunting melodies that now felt distant and unreal, like a ghost from a life she could barely remember.

She couldn't recall ever seeing that violin in their home, nor did she know where Ajee had gotten it. But in that moment, none of that mattered. All that mattered was the weight of the instrument in her hand and the palpable threat looming before her, ready to strike like a coiled serpent.

Without a moment's hesitation, she swung the violin with every ounce of strength she could muster, the wood crashing against Ajee's already battered head. The sickening thud reverberated through the room, a brutal echo that underscored the ferocity of her strike, landing another punishing blow to that vulnerable spot.

This time, Sprite swung the violin not just once but twice, the sickening crack of splintering wood slicing through the air as the neck shattered under the weight of her fury. She had no idea if violins were truly that fragile, whether this one had merely succumbed to age, or if her pent-up rage had infused her with a strength she never knew she possessed. She didn't care to find out. What she did know was that with her second strike, Ajee crumpled to the floor, the fight knocked out of him.

He crashed to the floor with a thud, the impact reverberating through the room. The keys slipped from his grasp, clattering and skittering across the floor before coming to rest near the edge of the bed, like fallen leaves in a forgotten corner.

Sprite gasped for breath, adrenaline still coursing through her veins. In her right hand, she clutched a jagged shard of the broken violin neck. Turning it over, she noticed a faint inscription delicately carved in italics: *Jimmi*. But Jimmi who? The name lingered in the air like a ghost, weaving another thread of confusion into the tangled web of her thoughts.

Sprite had no time to dwell on the name. Seizing the moment while Ajee lay incapacitated, she snatched the keys and bolted from the room, her heart pounding like a war drum. Each step toward the living room felt monumental, but she pushed on, fueled by a desperate determination to reach the exit. With the keys clutched tightly in her hand, escape was tantalizingly close. Yet, just as her fingertips brushed the cold metal of the door, a sound sliced through the air—footsteps, quick and purposeful, echoing ominously behind her.

Sprite spun around, her breath hitching in her throat like a fish out of water.

Ajee stood in the doorway, a dark silhouette against the dim light, his presence a storm brewing on the horizon. He towered over her, panting heavily, his face flushed deep crimson, even his mustache drenched in the color. The only remnants of his former self were the whites of his eyes, stark and wide, a chilling contrast to the madness swirling within. His legs trembled beneath him, betraying a precarious balance as he fought to hold himself upright.

For a brief, unsettling moment, Ajee resembled a giant puppet sprung to life, just like one she'd glimpsed at a twisted carnival long ago. A shiver skittered down her spine as his footsteps echoed ominously, each heavy thud drawing nearer, a sinister countdown to an inevitable confrontation.

Had he not been injured, she was certain he would have lunged at her like a predator, his eyes gleaming with a primal hunger that sent shivers racing down her spine. But as they closed the distance to about seven feet, Sprite's gaze dropped to his right hand, where she suddenly realized he was gripping a kitchen knife—the very same one he wielded each day in the mundane ritual of cooking.

She remembered how Ajee had always loathed stepping into the kitchen, avoiding the cooking utensils as if they were cursed. But now, everything had changed so drastically it felt surreal, as if the very air in the room had thickened into something darker, suffocating the remnants of his former self.

Ajee now appeared adept at wielding kitchen tools, a transformation that sent a fresh wave of dread coursing through Sprite. The light glinted off the knife's blade, making her heart race; its shimmer twisted her fear into something palpable and suffocating, like a noose tightening around her throat.

Sprite fumbled with the key, frustration gnawing at her as it refused to fit into the lock. Just when things couldn't get worse, the key slipped from her grasp and clattered to the floor, a cruel joke echoing in her ears. Anger simmered within her—she felt like one of those hapless characters in the films she used to mock. As she bent down to retrieve the key, a prickling sensation crawled up her spine. Ajee's presence loomed behind her, his breath coming in ragged gasps, hot and oppressive against her skin—a jarring reminder that she was not alone in this fraught moment.

When Sprite finally turned, Ajee's face was mere inches from hers, his features twisted in a way that sent ice coursing through her veins.

He lunged forward, the knife aimed straight at Sprite's chest. Time froze in that horrifying instant, and she felt fate's grip tightening around her. Her breath hitched in her throat as she shut her eyes, bracing for the end. What more could she do? Perhaps death was just another form of freedom, an escape from the nightmare that had engulfed her.

She braced for the sharp sting of the blade piercing her chest, but instead of agony, she felt the unexpected weight of a blunt object pressing against her. It was strange—this touch should have been painful, yet it was oddly dull and unthreatening, leaving her bewildered in that fleeting moment.

Sprite slowly opened her eyes to find Ajee hunched over her, his left hand gripping her right shoulder like a lifeline while his right hand rested heavily against her left breast—a disconcerting pressure that sent a shiver of confusion racing through her. She glanced down, half-expecting to see the blade buried in her flesh. Instead, she saw the knife aimed at her chest, but in an odd reversal; the handle pressed against her skin instead of the blade. Had Ajee truly lost his grip on reality to the point of misusing a knife? Or was this some twisted design of his own, a perverse manipulation of their already warped reality?

Sprite didn't waste a moment with questions. In one swift motion, she yanked the knife from Ajee's hand, and to her astonishment, he offered no resistance at all, as if the very will to fight had slipped from him like water through his fingers. It was as if he had surrendered not just the weapon, but a piece of himself, leaving her with an unsettling sense of triumph that felt more like a prelude to disaster.

"C'mon, hurry up! There's no other way!" Ajee whispered urgently, his voice a desperate rasp that felt like a lifeline tossed into turbulent waters.

The knife in Sprite's hand trembled violently, a quivering extension of her surging fear, as if it could sense the terror coursing through her veins.

Deep down, Sprite grasped Ajee's intentions, a dark realization slithering into her mind like shadows creeping across the floor, wrapping around her thoughts in a suffocating embrace.

He wanted her to be the one to end his life. Perhaps Ajee had finally realized that the only escape from the monster gnawing at his insides was death itself. But what if this was just another of those twisted tests he always spoke about? Did he really want Sprite to murder her own husband, the very man who embodied all the loathing she had buried deep in her heart? The thought sent a shiver of dread coursing through her, the weight of the choice pressing down like a leaden shroud.

Sprite locked eyes with the figure before her, grappling to understand who he truly was. The very idea of being asked to kill sent icy tendrils of fear slithering down her spine; she couldn't do it. No matter how twisted their circumstances had become, the thought of plunging a knife into the man she once loved felt like a betrayal too profound to fathom.

If this was another version of Ajee—the killer—she refused to fulfill his twisted desires. She craved freedom, the chance to forge her own path, yet she wouldn't become a pawn for that malevolent force. But if this man was truly her husband, the Ajee she once knew, how could she bring herself to end his life? Sure, her feelings were a tangled mess—love twisting into hatred at times—but that loathing didn't stoke a fire fierce enough to transform her into a murderer.

As long as there was another way, she clung to that hope, fragile yet persistent. But deep inside, a voice howled, slicing through her thoughts like a knife: *There is no other way, Sprite.*

Deep down, Sprite didn't want to admit it, but that voice was right. With trembling resolve, she gripped the knife's handle, its cold weight anchoring her to the moment. It all boiled down to a single, desperate act: thrusting her hand forward with every ounce of strength she could muster. In that fleeting instant, the possibility of escape hung tantalizingly in the air, a slender thread of hope offering a chance to break free from the nightmare that had ensnared her.

Yet before she could plunge the knife, she needed to grasp who it was she was about to kill. It mattered—more than anything—that she knew. The eyes before her flickered, shifting between two distinct lights, each reflecting a different truth, a haunting duality that left her reeling.

Sprite found herself grappling with the most bizarre question she'd ever posed to her husband: "Who are you?" The words hung in the air, thick with the weight of uncertainty, as if unraveling the very fabric of their shared existence.

Her heart pounded in her chest like a trapped animal, frantic and desperate for escape, each beat echoing the chaos swirling in her mind.

She needed to know, needed the truth to slice through the fog of confusion that enveloped her. But the silence clung to them like a shroud, heavy and suffocating; the only reply she received was that same haunting question, echoing back at her with an unnerving intonation that never changed.

"Who are you?" he asked, his voice low and laden with a dark intensity.

Sprite could stall no longer. With every ounce of strength, she plunged the knife into his chest, only to find that flesh and bone were far sturdier than she'd ever anticipated—not the soft give of butter or the easy slice of sponge cake. Desperation consumed her as she stabbed again and again, tears streaming down her face like a torrential downpour, blurring her vision and mingling with the blood that spilled like a dark secret.

Ajee crumpled to the floor, a weak gasp escaping his lips, but no scream broke the silence. Sprite's breath quickened, coming in frantic gasps as she felt the knife still buried in her husband's heart. Blood coated her hands, warm and slick, and the edges of her vision began to fade, blurring into an unsettling haze that swallowed the room whole, leaving only the haunting reality of what she had done.

But she refused to let her consciousness slip away in such a wretched state. Struggling to rise, she clung to the fragile hope that Ajee might still be alive, that the flicker of life remained beneath the crimson tide, a desperate spark in the overwhelming darkness.

He was breathing, even as blood seeped from his chest like a dark promise. Then, amid the horror, a faint smile flickered across his lips—a haunting reminder of the man he once was, a ghost of joy trapped in a nightmare.

"Congrats, babe. You're free now. You're ready to soar," he whispered, his voice barely a breath, like a dying wish carried on the wind.

His words ignited a fire within Sprite, a searing mix of regret and rage that coursed through her veins like poison, turning her blood into a molten inferno.

She screamed, driving the knife deeper, fueled by a primal urge to obliterate the evil that had twisted her life. "Shut up! It's my choice whether I want to soar or rot in a cage! Don't you dare lecture me, you devil!" Sprite yelled, her voice raw and ragged, each word a weapon against the darkness. She pressed on, desperate for the blade to pierce Ajee's heart and vanquish the demon lurking within him. But as his eyes began to dim, she finally released the knife and stumbled back, gasping for breath. Her gaze landed on the key lying on the floor, and she snatched it up, adrenaline coursing through her veins. Rising to her feet, she thrust the key into the lock, the prospect of escape finally within reach now that the threat was gone.

After two frantic attempts, the key finally clicked, turning in the lock with a sound that reverberated through the room like a whispered promise of freedom.

She yanked at the stubborn door handle, and with a reluctant creak, her apartment door swung open. A wave of relief washed over her, as if she had finally stepped into a world free from the nightmare that had clung to her like a shadow.

Before she stepped into the uncertain light beyond, she cast one last, lingering glance over her shoulder—a final look at the darkness she was leaving behind, the shadows that had whispered her fears and wrapped around her like a shroud.

Ajee lay sprawled on the floor, a grim tableau painted in crimson, his stillness a haunting reminder of what had just transpired. He didn't rise, didn't melt into the shadows as she had feared. Instead, his eyes fluttered shut, and Sprite caught the faint, almost imperceptible motion of his lips, as if he were trying to utter something from beyond the veil of consciousness.

She strained to decipher the words, squinting through the thick haze of fear and confusion that clouded her mind like a storm rolling in, heavy and oppressive.

"Sorry about that," he murmured, his voice barely a whisper, laden with a weight that felt both apologetic and ominous.

Sprite had no idea what he was apologizing for or whom he was addressing. Panic surged through her like ice water, and she bolted outside, her scream slicing through the silence, reverberating off the cold brick walls of the narrow corridor.

Brutal Murder Uncovered in Domestic Hostage Situation

Mott Haven, NY — In a shocking turn of events, a local woman, Sprite Karson, 27, escaped from a week-long hostage situation orchestrated by her husband, Ajee Arizin, 33. The harrowing incident unfolded last Friday, August 6, when Sprite was found unconscious outside her home, having called for help.

Sprite's neighbor, Alhric, 40, had just returned from a trip when he heard her cries. He quickly transported her to the nearest hospital and notified the authorities, prompting an immediate investigation.

Upon entering the residence, police discovered the lifeless body of Ajee Arizin, with a fatal knife wound to the heart. The investigation revealed a disturbing scene inside the home, where dismembered body parts of other victims were found mutilated and cooked in the kitchen. The authorities have not yet disclosed the number of additional victims uncovered at the crime scene.

According to Sprite's testimony and ongoing police investigations, Ajee Arizin was killed during an attempted escape from captivity. While the investigation is still underway, officials suspect that Sprite may have acted in self-defense, as she faced a significant threat to her life.

The couple had been married for five years and did not have children. Neighbors reported that Ajee had shown signs of depression following his recent job loss, displaying increasingly erratic behavior. Authorities are currently exploring the possibility of mental health issues in the case.

As the community grapples with the aftermath of this tragic event, further updates from law enforcement are expected in the coming days.

Unraveling the Threads of the Brutal Murder of Ajee Arizin Linked to Serial Killings in BHS and Jimmi the Butcher

Mott Haven, NY — In a startling press release last Sunday (September 11), the Deputy Commissioner of Public Information (DCPI) revealed that Ajee Arizin, the perpetrator of a shocking murder and mutilation case, is also connected to a series of robbery and murder incidents that have plagued the Bronx Heritage Suites (BHS) over the past two months. Given the magnitude of this case, authorities are actively searching for the possibility of additional suspects still at large.

"This case is significant, and the perpetrator is highly skilled; it is too difficult to carry out alone. For this reason, we suspect there are unidentified accomplices. Unfortunately, the evidence we have gathered points to a single perpetrator, Ajee Arizin," stated DCPI Waelyn Kempton.

The police's inability to contain the escalation of this situation has faced criticism from both the public and media outlets. Ajee Arizin managed to evade law enforcement until he was ultimately killed by one of his victims—his own wife.

Crime expert Prof. Dodi Kump commented on the police's slow response to the situation, emphasizing the need for a better understanding of recurring criminal patterns in areas marked by significant social disparities, such as BHS and its surroundings.

"Longtime residents might recall from their elders that about thirty years ago, a similar series of events took place. At that time, there was a string of murders committed by a single perpetrator known as Jimmi the Butcher," Prof. Kump explained.

Jimmi Hadfield, infamously known as Jimmi the Butcher, was a robber and serial killer who terrorized the same area roughly thirty years ago. After falling victim to a business scam and being affected by the economic downturn, Jimmi resorted to a series of robberies and brutal murders, which captured the media's attention. He was ultimately shot dead by police a year later, alongside his girlfriend, in a hotel standoff.

Although the Jimmi the Butcher case occurred decades ago, it remains a topic of discussion as one of the most notorious criminal cases in the region. In addition to his heinous acts, Jimmi was remembered for his striking looks and flamboyant personality, which contributed to his notoriety among women. His relationship with his girlfriend has often been likened to infamous criminal couples like Bonnie and Clyde or Rosemary and Fred West.

As investigations into the connections between Ajee Arizin and the dark history of Jimmi the Butcher continue, the Mott Haven community remains on alert, hoping for justice and safety in their neighborhood.

Epilogue

She remembered how she used to walk this same stretch of road alone, every day, back when dreams were still a currency worth something. She'd look at these apartments and imagine herself living in one. Well, now that dream had come true—but the cost? A lifetime. Time had taken its toll, threading silver through her hair and turning cholesterol pills into part of her morning routine. The world had changed, too. The apartment complex had grown, looming like a concrete monster, while the open spaces where laughter once echoed were now just a graveyard of empty storefronts, waiting for life that might never come.

She watched the Saturday night bustle, the restaurants and cafés packed with newcomers, faces just as fresh as hers, all caught in the thrum of the neighborhood. The place had rebranded itself, tacking on *New* like a fresh coat of paint, but Bronx Heritage Suites still carried the scars. It had taken years to crawl back to something resembling safety. But the shadow of that serial killer case? That wasn't going anywhere. The gruesome details had soaked into the very bones of the place, turned into an urban legend that whispered from door to door, a ghost that refused to be buried.

The truth was, she wanted to bury her connection to that tragedy so deep only a handful of trusted souls would ever know. But the media? They were like spiders, spinning webs out of shadows, creeping into the corners of her life she thought were safe. At least the news cycle had shifted—political scandals, viral disasters—they'd taken the spotlight off her, let the whole mess sink into the public's forgetful haze, like a ghost fading back into the shadows where it belonged.

"There used to be a little alley right here," Sprite said, pointing to the spot where a slick two-story café now stood. "My apartment was tucked just behind it. Hard to believe it's all gone now."

The young woman beside her cast a quick, curious glance, eyes flickering with questions she didn't ask. Then, just as fast, she turned back to the road, her knuckles whitening on the steering wheel as the night pressed in, thick and heavy around them.

"Mama, you mean the apartment where... that thing happened?" she asked, her voice tinged with a mix of curiosity and something darker, like she wasn't sure she wanted to hear the answer.

"Yes, that incident, Winnie," she replied, her tone steady yet heavy with the weight of memory, as if each word carried the echoes of the past.

Windy, her daughter, was one of the few she could trust completely. But that didn't mean she laid bare every secret of her past. Some memories were better left locked away, buried deep like forgotten bones, concealed even from those she loved most.

Windy didn't say another word. She guided the car toward the second gate, the one that separated the residential area from the shopping district and park, just past the fountain where a statue of a man picking apples stood. The grand entrance loomed ahead, its imposing structure casting a shadow that felt almost sentient. In bold, inviting letters, it proclaimed, *Welcome to New Bronx Heritage Suites.* The words hung in the air like a promise, but beneath that warm façade, an unsettling whisper lingered, as if the very walls were steeped in secrets waiting to be unearthed.

Sprite watched from her car as two security guards crouched beneath, their detection devices glowing like ominous eyes in the twilight. She didn't know them, but she could sense their watchful gaze; they were keenly aware she was a newcomer, a resident for only a month, and that knowledge hung in the air between them, thick and palpable.

"Just a formality," one of them had said, but the weight of the moment said otherwise, heavy with unspoken tension.

With terrorism lurking like a specter during the holiday season, every protocol felt like a tightrope walk between safety and suspicion. When their car finally got the green light, they slipped into the parking area, gliding down a wide, spotless ramp that seemed almost inviting, as if it were trying to mask the tension that lay just beneath the surface.

"It's been over twenty years," Sprite murmured to herself, nostalgia lacing her voice like a bittersweet melody.

"So, Mama, you're coming to my graduation next week, right?" Windy asked, her voice light, clearly eager to steer the conversation toward something brighter.

Sprite smiled warmly. "God willing," she replied, her gaze drifting to her daughter, who was blossoming into a young woman right before her eyes.

At twenty-one, Windy radiated a maturity that seemed to eclipse her years, a wisdom that felt almost unsettling. The girl she once was faded into a distant memory, overshadowed by the woman she had become—as if time had taken her by the hand and led her through a labyrinth of unspoken trials and quiet resilience.

Sprite felt a profound sense of gratitude for that understanding. She knew that if she wanted this new chapter in her life to unfold better than the last, she couldn't let the bitterness in her heart fester for long. Yet, even with that realization, the shadows of her secrets lingered, tucked away in the corners of her mind, biding their time, waiting for the right moment to resurface.

"Are you sure about that proposal, Winnie?" Sprite asked as they crossed the threshold of their home.

Their apartment was one of the tiniest units in New Bronx Heritage Suites—a little jewel hidden within the sprawling complex. Yet, despite its size, the space radiated a surprising warmth, wrapping them in a cozy embrace that felt almost luxurious, as if the walls themselves had a story to tell—a tale of comfort nestled within the shadows of a bustling world beyond.

As a designer and boutique owner whose business had flourished like wildflowers in spring over the past decade, Sprite felt a deep sense of gratitude for this apartment. It was as if the universe had finally conspired to grant her the dream home she had always longed for—a sanctuary that whispered promises of comfort and possibility, enveloping her in the warmth of her hard-won success.

"Yeah, I'm sure. Why, Ma?" Windy replied, sitting cross-legged on the living room carpet, her eyes bright with curiosity.

"Don't you want to focus on your career first or something?" Sprite asked again, her tone laced with a blend of concern and curiosity.

"I'm sure. We've talked it over. I can still have a career after we get married, and he's going to support me," Windy replied. "Besides, why are you asking again? You already said you accepted, right?"

"No, it's nothing," Sprite replied, her voice casual, but a hint of something unspoken lingered just beneath the surface.

On the couch, mother and daughter embraced, their laughter mingling with the warm scent of cuchifritos that lingered in the air. Every so often, they reached for the crispy morsels, savoring each bite as if the simple act of sharing food could mend the frayed edges of their lives, weaving a tapestry of comfort in a world that often felt chaotic. After about half an hour huddled together in front of the TV, Windy's eyelids grew heavy, a telltale sign of fatigue creeping in.

She nestled into the couch, and before long, the rhythmic sound of her soft snoring filled the room—a gentle reminder of her exhaustion, as if the day had finally claimed her, wrapping her in a cocoon of peaceful slumber.

Sprite wasn't quite ready to surrender to sleep just yet. She left Windy sprawled on the couch and made her way to her bedroom, where shadows danced along the walls. In her wardrobe, a small locked drawer awaited—a hidden treasure chest that held her jewelry. Nestled within that drawer was a small metal box, also secured with a lock, its contents shrouded in mystery, as if it guarded secrets desperate to remain hidden from the light of day.

After turning the lock on her bedroom door, Sprite retrieved the metal box, her heart racing as she fished the key from her pants pocket. With a click, the lock gave way, and her breath caught in her throat, a rush of excitement and trepidation flooding over her. Inside the box, nestled against the soft lining, lay a diamond necklace, its brilliance glinting in the dim light like a forgotten memory yearning to be unearthed.

She weighed the decision like a heavy stone in her mind: Should she give the necklace to her daughter at her graduation or save it for her wedding? Or perhaps it was destined to remain locked away in the metal box, a future inheritance to be claimed only after she was gone.

Time and again, she had toyed with the idea of discarding or destroying it, yet the thought always made her hesitate. Not all the memories tied to the necklace were dark and terrifying; some shimmered with the light of her struggles, each a testament to her journey along life's winding path. The last time she had tried to part with it was after discovering she was pregnant—just a month after the tragedy that had shattered her world, leaving her still reeling, haunted by shadows that clung to her like a second skin.

In that dark chapter of her life, she fought to persuade the authorities that her actions had been nothing more than self-defense, a desperate struggle for survival. Meanwhile, like a slow, creeping fog, more evidence of the gruesome murders committed by Ajee began to surface, painting a chilling portrait of a man whose darkness seeped into every corner of her world. One morning, a wave of weakness and nausea washed over her, unsettling and unfamiliar, leaving her grappling with a sense of impending dread.

Convinced it was merely a physical manifestation of her troubled mind, she made her way to the doctor. When the news came—she was pregnant—a tempest of emotions swirled within her, each one battling for dominance. For a fleeting moment, the thought of abortion flickered in her mind, a desperate consideration born from the fear of raising a child alone. Yet, as quickly as it appeared, the idea slipped away, unable to take root. In the end, the tiny life growing inside her became a powerful beacon of hope, a fierce motivation lighting a path through the shadows of her existence, urging her to keep fighting for a future she had once thought lost.

Windy was her daughter, the product of a union with Ajee, though which Ajee was her father remained a haunting mystery that gnawed at her insides.

No, she couldn't unravel that tangled thread, nor did she dare to.

Ajee was Ajee, she told herself, a mantra forged to shield her from the truth. The murderous monster he had become was a different beast altogether—someone unworthy of fatherhood, someone who should have never been allowed near a child.

After years of wrestling with the ghosts of that event, she had started to carve out a fragile semblance of peace with the truth. Deep down, she still believed that marrying Ajee had been a colossal mistake, a truth no amount of rationalization could erase. Yet, surprisingly, she had found a way to forgive her late husband—a quiet act of release that felt both liberating and burdensome. But there was a secret that clung to her like a shadow: Ajee wasn't the real killer, and that was a truth she could never share with a soul. No one would buy that story; she knew it. Besides, if she appeared too eager to absolve him, suspicion would wrap around her like a noose. The media and history had already etched Ajee Arizin's name in blood—as a robber, a murderer, a cannibal who had come perilously close to sacrificing his own wife. His name was forever linked to the likes of Jayden Rivera, David Berkowitz, and Joel Rifkin—monsters of a different breed. This bitter residue clung to her memory, a stain that would likely haunt her for the rest of her days.

With deliberate slowness, she draped the necklace around her neck, the cool metal settling against her skin like a long-lost friend. "Still fits," she murmured, a bittersweet smile tugging at her lips. In that instant, she had made up her mind: she would wear it to her daughter's graduation and then pass it on as a wedding gift—a legacy wrapped in love and memory. In that moment, she felt whole, as if she had unfurled her own wings, strong enough to soar and land wherever her heart desired.

Don't miss out!

Visit the website below and you can sign up to receive emails whenever Frank Spreader publishes a new book. There's no charge and no obligation.

https://books2read.com/r/B-A-QABKB-PMNDF

BOOKS 2 READ

Connecting independent readers to independent writers.

Did you love *The Stranger at Home*? Then you should read *Shadows of Skull Valley*[1] by Frank Spreader!

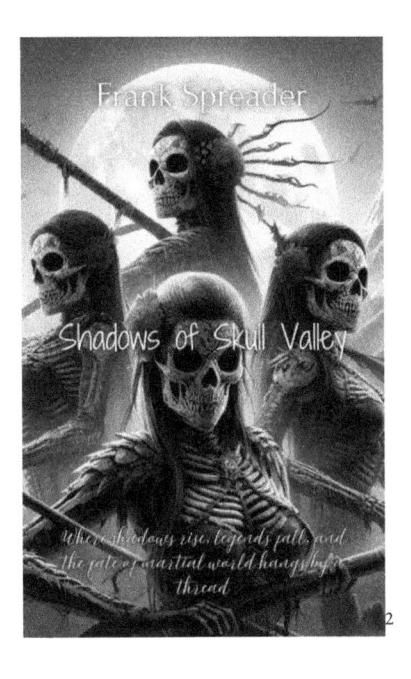

In the heart of Backbone Mountain, a deadly storm brews as four mysterious maidens in skull masks rise from a forgotten valley, heralding the birth of the sinister Skull Valley Clan. As they wreak havoc across the martial world, the legendary Sword Deity of Kentucke Country establishes the Sweet Lake Sect in a desperate bid for peace. But when the enigmatic Dragon Fire Axe Warrior, Wintie Rayado, crosses paths with the deadly Green Scorpion, the stage is set for a brutal clash of power, revenge, and forbidden passion. As the twelfth day of the twelfth month approaches, the martial world trembles, and the fates of heroes and villains alike hang in the balance. *Shadows of Skull Valley* is an epic tale of deadly ambition,

---

1. https://books2read.com/u/mK8aY5

2. https://books2read.com/u/mK8aY5

ruthless martial prowess, and a love that defies even the darkest of destinies.

Also by Frank Spreader

The Dragon Warrior
The Vengeance of the Mighty
Echoes of the Cuchillo
Shadows of Skull Valley
A Wedding to Die For

Standalone
Fond Memory in Indian Rocks Beach
Piece of Life: Undeserved Maid
Piece of Life: Adolescent Adventure
Piece of Life: Dramatic Karma
Piece of Life: Back to Hometown pt. 1
Piece of Life: Back to Hometown pt. 2
Piece of Life: Hillary, a Desperate Housewife
Lover's Smile pt. 1
Lover's Smile pt. 2
Lover's Smile pt. 3
Lover's Smile pt. 4
Dark Secrets
Dark Secrets II: A Long Sweet Night
Dark Secrets III: Too Fast to Die
Dark Secrets IV: Lost in the Echo

Dark Secrets V: One Step Closer
Dark Secrets VI: High Voltage
Revenge
Revenge II: Final Masquerade
Revenge: The Little Things You Give Me Away
Dark Lantern
Lily: The Story of a Call Girl, Part One
Lily: The Story of a Call Girl, Part Two
Lily: The Story of a Call Girl, Part Three
Lily Loves This Game
The Challenge for Lily
Lily Exceeds the Limit
The Bed Is Stained
Old Man & a Virgin
Jennifer's Nuptials
Dakota
Abused Billie: Part One
Abused Billie: Part Two
Rise of the Pervert
Jesslyn's Tragedy
Fall of the Pride
Home Alone
My Beloved Lecturer
Sex after Lunch
The Illicit Conspiracy
The Waiting Time
Quartet of Whiskers from the Abyss Within
Entangled Deceit: A Reflection on Second Chances
Echoes of Mortal Melodies in the New Realm of León
Echoes of Deceit: A Tapestry of Broken Hearts
The Stranger at Home

About the Author

Frank Spreader is a storyteller with a passion for exploring the complexities of human relationships and the psychological depths of suspense. Drawing inspiration from the everyday and the uncanny, Frank Spreader crafts narratives that blur the line between reality and illusion, pulling readers into gripping tales of intrigue and emotional tension. When not writing, he enjoys exploring historical sites, reading mystery or thriller novels, photography, people-watching, puzzle-solving or escape rooms, often finding new ideas in the quiet moments of life. "The Stranger at Home" is his latest exploration into the dark corners of domestic life and identity.

Frank Spreader lives in San Diego with family, always keeping a notebook nearby for when inspiration strikes.